BY EVELYN WAUGH

BLACK MISCHIEF

BLACK MISCHIEF

by

EVELYN WAUGH

LITTLE, BROWN AND COMPANY · BOSTON

LIBRARY OF CONGRESS CATALOG CARD NO. 77–88226

REPUBLISHED OCTOBER 1977

PRINTED IN THE UNITED STATES OF AMERICA

With love to

MARY and DOROTHY LYGON

BLACK MISCHIEF

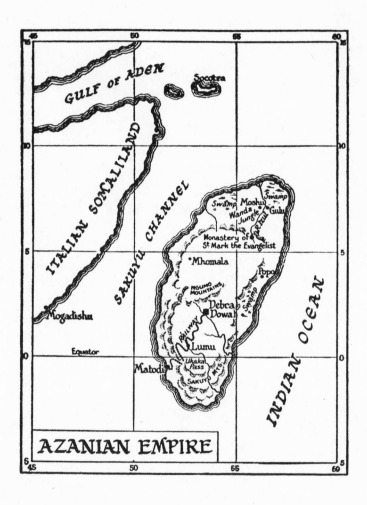

GULF OF ADEN

Socotra

ITALIAN SOMALILAND

SAKUYU CHANNEL

Swamp Moshu
Wanda
Jungle
Gulu

Monastery of
St Mark the Evangelist

•Mhomala

Popo•

NGUMO
MOUNTAINS

•Mogadishu

Debra
Dowa•

INDIAN OCEAN

Equator

Lumu

Matodi•

Ukaka
Pass

SAKUYU MTS.

AZANIAN EMPIRE

BLACK MISCHIEF

ONE

*W*E, *Seth, Emperor of Azania, Chief of the Chiefs of Sakuyu, Lord of Wanda and Tyrant of the Seas, Bachelor of the Arts of Oxford University, being in this the twenty-fourth year of our life, summoned by the wisdom of Almighty God and the unanimous voice of our people to the throne of our ancestors, do hereby proclaim . . ."* Seth paused in his dictation and gazed out across the harbour where in the fresh breeze of early morning the last dhow was setting sail for the open sea. "Rats," he said; "stinking curs. They are all running away."

The Indian secretary sat attentive, his fountain pen poised over the pad of writing paper, his eyes blinking gravely behind rimless pince-nez.

"Is there still no news from the hills?"

"None of unquestionable veracity, your majesty."

"I gave orders that the wireless was to be mended. Where is Marx? I told him to see to it."

"He evacuated the town late yesterday evening."

"He evacuated the town?"

9

"In your majesty's motor boat. There was a large company of them—the station master, the chief of police, the Armenian Archbishop, the Editor of the *Azanian Courier*, the American vice-consul. All the most distinguished gentlemen in Matodi."

"I wonder you weren't with them yourself, Ali."

"There was not room. I supposed that with so many distinguished gentlemen there was danger of submersion."

"Your loyalty shall be rewarded. Where had I got to?"

"The last eight words in reproof of the fugitives were an interpolation?"

"Yes, yes, of course."

"I will make the erasion. Your majesty's last words were '*do hereby proclaim.*'"

"*Do hereby proclaim amnesty and free pardon to all those of our subjects recently seduced from their loyalty, who shall during the eight days subsequent to this date return to their lawful allegiance. Furthermore . . .*"

They were in the upper story of the old fort at Matodi. Here, three hundred years before, a Portuguese garrison had withstood eight months' siege from the Omani Arabs; at this window they had watched for the sails of the relieving fleet, which came ten days too late.

Over the main door traces of an effaced escutcheon were still discernible, an idolatrous work repugnant to the prejudice of the conquerors.

For two centuries the Arabs remained masters of the coast. Behind them in the hills the native Sakuyu, black, naked, anthropophagous, had lived their own tribal life among their herds—emaciated, puny cattle with rickety shanks and elaborately branded hide. Further away still lay the territory of the Wanda—Galla immigrants from the mainland who, long before the coming of the Arabs, had settled in the North of the island and cultivated it in irregular communal holdings. The Arabs held aloof from the affairs of both these people; war-drums could often be heard inland and sometimes the whole hillside would be aflame with burning villages. On the coast a prosperous town arose; great houses of Arab merchants with intricate latticed windows and brass studded doors, courtyards planted with dense mango trees, streets heavy with the reek of cloves and pineapple, so narrow that two mules could not pass without altercation between their drivers; a bazaar where the money changers, squatting over their scales, weighed out the coinage of a world-wide trade, Austrian thalers, rough-stamped Mahratta gold, Spanish and Portuguese guineas. From Matodi the dhows sailed to the mainland, to Tanga, Dar-es-Salaam, Malindi and Kismayu, to meet the caravans coming down from the great lakes with ivory and slaves. Splendidly dressed Arab gentlemen paraded the water-front hand in hand and gossiped in the coffee houses. In early spring when the monsoon was blowing from the Northeast, fleets came down from the Persian Gulf bringing to market a people of fairer skin who spoke a pure Arabic barely intelligible to the islanders, for with the passage of years their language had become full of alien words—Bantu from the mainland, Sakuyu and Galla from the interior—and the slave markets had infused a richer and darker strain into their Semitic blood; instincts of swamp and forest mingled with the austere tradition of the desert.

In one of these Muscat trading fleets came Seth's grandfather, Amurath, a man wholly unlike his companions, a slave's son, sturdy, bow-legged, three-quarters negro. He had received education of a kind from Nestorian monks near Basra. At Matodi he sold his dhow and entered the Sultan's service.

It was a critical time in local history. The white men were returning. From Bombay they had fastened on Aden. They were in Zanzibar and the Sudan. They were pushing up round the Cape and down through the Canal. Their warships were cruising the Red Sea and the Indian Ocean intercepting slavers; the caravans from Tabora were finding difficulty in getting through to the coast. Trade in

Matodi was almost at a standstill and a new listlessness became apparent in the leisured life of the merchants; they spent their days in the town moodily chewing khat. They could no longer afford to keep up their villas round the bay. Gardens ran wild and roofs fell into disrepair. The grass huts of the Sakuyu began to appear on the more remote estates. Groups of Wanda and Sakuyu came into town and swaggered insolently about the bazaars; an Arab party returning from one of the country villas was ambushed and murdered within a mile of the walls. There were rumours of a general massacre, planned in the hills. The European powers watched their opportunity to proclaim a Protectorate.

In this uncertain decade there suddenly appeared the figure of Amurath; first as commander-in-chief of the Sultan's forces, then as general of an independent army; finally as Emperor Amurath the Great. He armed the Wanda and at their head inflicted defeat after defeat on the Sakuyu, driving off their cattle, devastating their villages and hunting them down in the remote valleys of the island. Then he turned his conquering army against his old allies on the coast. In three years he proclaimed the island a single territory and himself its ruler. He changed its name. Until now it had been scored on the maps as Sakuyu Island; Amurath renamed it the Empire of Azania. He founded a new capital at Debra-

Dowa, two hundred miles inland on the borders of the Wanda and Sakuyu territories. It was the site of his last camp, a small village, partially burnt out. There was no road to the coast, only a faltering bush path which an experienced scout could follow. Here he set up his standard.

Presently there was a railway from Matodi to Debra-Dowa. Three European companies held the concession in turn and failed; at the side of the line were the graves of two French engineers who went down with blackwater, and of numerous Indian coolies. The Sakuyu would wrench up the steel sleepers to forge spear heads and pull down lengths of copper telegraph wire to adorn their women. Lions came into the labour lines at night and carried off workmen; there were mosquitoes, snakes, tsetse fly, spirillum ticks; there were deep water courses to be bridged which for a few days in the year bore a great torrent down from the hills, bundling with it timber and boulders and an occasional corpse; there was a lava field to be crossed, a great waste of pumice five miles broad; in the hot season the metal blistered the hands of workmen; during the rains landslides and wash-outs would obliterate the work of months. Reluctantly, step by step, barbarism retreated; the seeds of progress took root and, after years of slow growth, burst finally into flower in the single, narrow gauge track of the Grand Chemin de

Fer Impérial d'Azanie. In the sixteenth year of his reign Amurath travelled in the first train from Matodi to Debra-Dowa. With him sat delegates from France, Great Britain, Italy, and the United States; his daughter and heir; her husband; while in a cattle truck behind, rode a dozen or so illegitimate children; in another coach sat the hierarchies of the various Churches of Azania; in another the Arab sheiks from the coast, the paramount chief of the Wanda, and a shrivelled, scared old negro, with one eye, who represented the Sakuyu. The train was decked with bunting, feathers and flowers; it whistled continuously from coast to capital; levies of irregular troops lined the way; a Jewish nihilist from Berlin threw a bomb which failed to explode; sparks from the engine started several serious bush fires; at Debra-Dowa Amurath received the congratulations of the civilized world and created the French contractor a Marquess in the Azanian peerage.

The first few trains caused numerous deaths among the inhabitants, who for some time did not appreciate the speed or strength of this new thing that had come to their country. Presently they became more cautious and the service less frequent. Amurath had drawn up an elaborate time-table of express trains, local trains, goods trains, boat trains, schemes for cheap return tickets and excursions; he

had printed a map showing the future developments
of the line in a close mesh all over the island. But
the railway was the last great achievement of his life;
soon after its opening he lapsed into a coma from
which he never recovered consciousness; he had a
wide reputation for immortality; it was three years
before his ministers, in response to insistent rumours, ventured to announce his death to the people. In the succeeding years the Grand Chemin de
Fer Impérial d'Azanie failed to develop on the lines
adumbrated by its founder. When Seth came down
from Oxford there was a weekly service; a goods
train at the back of which was hitched a single
shabby saloon car, upholstered in thread-bare plush.
It took two days to accomplish the journey, resting
the night at Lumo where a Greek hotel proprietor
had proposed a contract profitable to the president
of the line; the delay was officially attributed to the
erratic efficacy of the engine lights and the persist-
ence of the Sakuyu in their depredations of the permanent way.

Amurath instituted other changes, less sensational
than the railway, but nevertheless noteworthy. He
proclaimed the abolition of slavery and was warmly
applauded in the European Press; the law was
posted up prominently in the capital in English,
French and Italian where every foreigner might read
it; it was never promulgated in the provinces nor

translated into any of the native languages; the ancient system continued unhampered but European intervention had been anticipated. His Nestorian upbringing had strengthened his hand throughout in his dealings with the white men. Now he declared Christianity the official religion of the Empire, reserving complete freedom of conscience to his Mohammedan and pagan subjects. He allowed and encouraged an influx of missionaries. There were soon three Bishops in Debra-Dowa—Anglican, Catholic and Nestorian—and three substantial Cathedrals. There were also Quaker, Moravian, American-Baptist, Mormon and Swedish-Lutheran missions handsomely supported by foreign subscribers. All this brought money into the new capital and enhanced his reputation abroad. But his chief safeguard against European intrusion was a force of ten thousand soldiers, maintained under arms. These he had trained by Prussian officers. Their brass bands, goose-step and elaborate uniforms were at first the object of mild amusement. Then there was an international incident. A foreign commercial agent was knifed in a disorderly house on the coast. Amurath hanged the culprits publicly in the square before the Anglican Cathedral— (and with them two or three witnesses whose evidence was held to be unsatisfactory)—but there was a talk of indemnities. A punitive force was landed, composed half of European, half of mainland native troops. Amurath marched out against them with his new army and drove them in hopeless rout to the seashore where they were massacred under the guns of their own fleet. Six European officers of field rank surrendered and were hanged on the battlefield. On his triumphal return to the capital Amurath offered the White Fathers a silver altar to Our Lady of Victories.

Throughout the highlands his prestige became superhuman. 'I swear by Amurath' was a bond of inviolable sanctity. Only the Arabs remained unimpressed. He ennobled them, creating the heads of the chief families Earls, Viscounts and Marquesses, but these grave, impoverished men whose genealogies extended to the time of the Prophet, preferred their original names. He married his daughter into the house of the old Sultan—but the young man accepted the elevation and his compulsory baptism into the National Church, without enthusiasm. The marriage was considered a great disgrace by the Arabs. Their fathers would not have ridden a horse with so obscure a pedigree. Indians came in great numbers and slowly absorbed the business of the country. The large houses of Matodi were turned into tenements, hotels or offices. Soon the maze of mean streets behind the bazaar became designated as the 'Arab quarter.'

Very few of them migrated to the new capital, which was spreading out round the palace in a haphazard jumble of shops, missions, barracks, legations, bungalows and native huts. The palace itself, which occupied many acres enclosed by an irregular fortified stockade, was far from orderly or harmonious. Its nucleus was a large stucco villa of French design; all round this were scattered sheds of various sizes which served as kitchens, servants' quarters and stables, there was a wooden guard-house and a great thatched barn which was used for state banquets; a domed, octagonal chapel and the large rubble and timber residence of the Princess and her consort. The ground between and about the buildings was uneven and untidy; stacks of fuel, kitchen refuse, derelict carriages, cannon and ammunition lay in prominent places; sometimes there would be the flyblown carcase of a donkey or camel, and after the rains pools of stagnant water; gangs of prisoners. chained neck to neck, could often be seen shovelling as though some project were on hand of levelling or draining, but except for the planting of a circle of eucalyptus trees, nothing was done in the old Emperor's time to dignify his surroundings.

Many of Amurath's soldiers settled round him in the new capital; they in the first few years were reinforced by a trickle of detribalised natives, drawn from their traditional grounds by the glamour of city life; the main population, however, was always cosmopolitan, and as the country's reputation as a land of opportunity spread through the less successful classes of the outside world, Debra-Dowa gradually lost all evidence of national character. Indians and Armenians came first and continued to come in yearly increasing numbers. Goans, Jews, and Greeks followed, and later a race of partially respectable immigrants from the greater powers, mining engineers, prospectors, planters and contractors, on their world wide pilgrimage in quest of cheap concessions. A few were lucky and got out of the country with modest fortunes; most were disappointed and became permanent residents, hanging round the bars and bemoaning over their cups the futility of expecting justice in a land run by a pack of niggers.

When Amurath died, and the courtiers at last could devise no further explanation of his prolonged seclusion, his daughter reigned as Empress. The funeral was a great occasion in East African history. A Nestorian patriarch came from Iraq to say the mass; delegates from the European powers rode in the procession and as the bugles of the Imperial guard sounded the last post over the empty sarcophagus, vast crowds of Wanda and Sakuyu burst into wailing and lamentation, daubed their bodies with chalk and charcoal, stamped their feet, swayed and clapped in frantic, personal grief at the loss of their master.

Now the Empress was dead and Seth had returned from Europe to claim his Empire.

Noon in Matodi. The harbour lay still as a photograph, empty save for a few fishing boats moored motionless against the sea wall. No breeze stirred the royal standard that hung over the old fort. No traffic moved on the water-front. The offices were locked and shuttered. The tables had been cleared from the hotel terrace. In the shade of a mango the two sentries lay curled asleep, their rifles in the dust beside them.

"From Seth, Emperor of Azania, Chief of the Chiefs of Sakuyu, Lord of Wanda and Tyrant of the Seas, Bachelor of the Arts of Oxford University, to His Majesty of the King of England, Greeting. May this reach you. Peace be to your house . . ."

He had been dictating since dawn. Letters of greeting, Patents of Nobility, Pardons, Decrees of Attainder, Army Ordinances, police regulations, orders to European firms for motor cars, uniforms, furniture, electric plant, invitations to the Coronation; proclamations of a public holiday in honour of his victory, lay neatly clipped together on the secretary's table.

"Still no news from the hills. We should have

heard of the victory by now." The secretary recorded these words, considered them with his head cocked slightly to one side and then drew a line through them. "We should have heard, shouldn't we, Ali?"

"We should have heard."

"What has happened? Why don't you answer me? Why have we heard nothing?"

"Who am I? I know nothing. I only hear what the ignorant people are saying in the bazaar, since the public men evacuated the city. The ignorant people say that your majesty's army has not gained the victory you predict."

"Fools, what do they know? What can they understand? I am Seth, grandson of Amurath. Defeat is impossible. I have been to Europe. I know. We have the Tank. This is not a war of Seth against Seyid but of Progress against Barbarism. And Progress must prevail. I have seen the great tattoo of Aldershot, the Paris Exhibition, the Oxford Union. I have read modern books—Shaw, Arlen, Priestley. What do the gossips in the bazaars know of all this? The whole might of Evolution rides behind him; at my stirrups run woman's suffrage, vaccination, and vivisection. I am the New Age. I am the Future."

"I know nothing of these things," said Ali. "But the ignorant men in the bazaar say that your majesty's guards have joined Prince Seyid. You will remember my pointing out that they had received no wages for several months?"

"They shall be paid. I have said it. As soon as the war is over they shall be paid. Besides I raised them in rank. Every man in the brigade is now a full corporal. I issued the edict myself. Ungrateful curs. Old-fashioned fools. Soon we will have no more soldiers. Tanks and aeroplanes. That is modern. I have seen it. That reminds me. Have you sent off instructions for the medals?"

Ali turned over the file of correspondence.

"Your majesty has ordered five hundred Grand Cross of Azania, first class; five hundred second; and seven hundred third; also designs for the Star of Seth, silver gilt and enamel with parti-coloured ribbon . . ."

"No, no. I mean the Victory Medal."

"I received no instructions concerning the Victory Medal."

"Then take this down."

"The invitation to the King of England?"

"The King of England can wait. Take down the instructions for the Victory Medal. Obverse, the head of Seth—that is to be copied from the photograph taken in Oxford. You understand—it is to be modern, European—top hat, spectacles, evening dress collar and tie. Inscription SETH IMPERATOR IMMORTALIS. The whole to be simple and in good taste. Many of my grandfather's medals were florid. Reverse. The figure of Progress. She holds in one hand an aeroplane, in the other some small object symbolic of improved education. I will give you the detail of that later. The idea will come to me . . . a telephone might do . . . I will see. Meanwhile begin the letter:

"From Seth, Emperor of Azania, Chief of the Chiefs of Sakuyu, Lord of Wanda and Tyrant of the Seas, Bachelor of the Arts of Oxford University, to Messrs. Mappin and Webb of London. Greeting. May this reach you. Peace be to your house . . ."

Evening and a small stir of life. Muezzin in the minaret. Allah is great. There is no Allah but Allah and Mohammed is his prophet. Angelus from the mission church. Ecce ancilla Domini: fiat mihi secundum verbum tuum. Mr. Youkoumian behind the bar of the Amurath Café and Universal Stores mixed himself a sundowner of mastika and water.

"What I want to know is do I get paid for the petrol?"

"You know I am doing all I can for you, Mr. Youkoumian. I'm your friend. You know that. But the Emperor's busy to-day. I've only just got off. Been on all day. I'll try and get your money for you."

"I've done a lot for you, Ali."

"I know you have, Mr. Youkoumian, and I hope

I am not ungrateful. If I could get you your money just by asking for it you should have it this evening."

"But I must have it this evening. I'm going."

"Going?"

"I've made my arrangements. Well, I don't mind telling you, Ali, since you're a friend." Mr. Youkoumian glanced furtively round the empty bar—they were speaking in Sakuyu—"I've got a launch beached outside the harbour, behind the trees near the old sugar mill in the bay. What's more there's room in it for another passenger. I wouldn't tell this to any one but you. Matodi's not going to be a healthy place for the next week or two. Seth's beaten. We know that. I'm going to my brother on the mainland. Only I want my money for the petrol before I go."

"Yes, Mr. Youkoumian, I appreciate your offer. But you know it's very difficult. You can hardly expect the Emperor to pay for having his own motor-boat stolen."

"I don't know anything about that. All I know is that yesterday evening Mr. Marx came into my store and said he wanted the Emperor's motor-boat filled up with petrol. Eighty rupee's worth. I've served Mr. Marx with petrol before for the Emperor. How was I to know he wanted to steal the Emperor's motor-boat? Should I have given it to him if I did?"

Mr. Youkoumian spread his hands in the traditional gesture of his race. "I am a poor man. Is it right that I should suffer in this way? Is it fair? Now, Ali, I know you. You're a just man. I've done a lot for you in the past. Get me my eighty rupees and I will take you to stay with my brother in Malindi. Then when the troubles are over, we can come back or stay or go somewhere else, just as you like. You don't want your throat cut by the Arabs. I'll look after you."

"Well I appreciate your offer, Mr. Youkoumian, and I'll do what I can. I can't say more than that."

"I know you, Ali. I trust you as I'd trust my own father. Not a word to any one about the launch, eh?"

"Not a word, Mr. Youkoumian, and I'll see you later this evening."

"That's a good fellow. Au revoir and remember, not a word to any one about the launch."

When Ali had left the Amurath Café, Youkoumian's wife emerged from the curtain behind which she had been listening to the conversation.

"What's all this you've been arranging? We can't take that Indian to Malindi."

"I want my eighty rupees. My dear, you must leave these business matters to me."

"But there isn't room for any one else in the launch. We're overloaded already. You know that."

"I know that."

"Are you mad, Krikor. Do you want to drown us all?"

"You must leave these things to me, my flower. There is no need to worry. Ali is not coming with us. All I want is my eighty rupees for Mr. Marx's petrol. Have you finished your packing? We start as soon as Ali returns with the money."

"Krikor, you wouldn't . . . you aren't going to leave me behind, are you?"

"I should not hesitate to do so if I thought it necessary. Finish your packing, girl. Don't cry. Finish your packing. You are coming to Malindi. I have said it. Finish your packing. I am a just man and a peaceful man. You know that. But in time of war one must look after oneself and one's own family. Yes, one's family, do you hear me? Ali will bring us the money. We shall not take him to Malindi. Do you understand? If he is a trouble, I shall hit him with my stick. Don't stand there like a fool. Finish your packing."

The sun had now set. As Ali walked back to the fort through the dark lane he was aware of new excitement in the people around him. Groups were hurrying to the water-front, others stood in their doorways chattering eagerly. He heard the words 'Seyid,' 'Victory' and 'Army.' In the open space before the harbour he found a large crowd collected

27

with their backs to the water, gazing inland over the town. He joined them and in the brief twilight saw the whole dark face of the hills alight with little points of fire. Then he left the crowd and went to the old fort. Major Joab, the officer of the guard, stood in the court studying the hills through field glasses.

"You have seen the fires inland, secretary?"

"I have seen them."

"I think there is an army encamped there."

"It is the victorious army, major."

"Praise God. It is what we have waited to see."

"Certainly. We should praise God whether in prosperity or adversity," said Ali, piously; he had accepted Christianity on entering Seth's service. "But I bring orders from the Emperor. You are to take a picket and go with them to the Amurath Bar. There you will find the Armenian Youkoumian, a little fat man wearing a black skull cap. You know him? Very well. He is to be put under arrest and taken a little outside the town. It does not matter where, but take him some distance from the people. There you are to hang him. Those are the Emperor's orders. When it is done, report to me personally. There is no need to mention the matter directly to his majesty. You understand?"

"I understand, secretary."

Upstairs Seth was deep in a catalogue of wireless apparatus.

"Oh, Ali, I have decided on the Tudor model in fumed oak. Remind me to-morrow to write for it. Is there still no news?"

Ali busied himself in arranging the papers on the table and fitting the typewriter into its case.

"Is there no news?"

"There is news of a kind, Majesty. I opine that there is an army bivouacked in the hills. Their fires are visible. If your majesty will come outside, you will see them. No doubt they will march into the city to-morrow."

Seth sprang gaily from his chair and ran to the window.

"But this is magnificent news. The best you could have brought. Ali, I will make you a Viscount to-morrow. The army back again. It is what we have been longing for the last six weeks, eh, Viscount?"

"Your majesty is very kind. I said *an* army. There is no means of knowing which one it may be. If, as you surmise, it is General Connolly, is it not curious that no runner has come to salute your majesty with news of the victory?"

"Yes, he should have sent word."

"Majesty, you are defeated and betrayed. Every one in Matodi knows it except yourself."

For the first time since the beginning of the campaign, Ali saw that there was uncertainty in his master's mind. "If I am defeated," said Seth, "the barbarians will know where to find me."

"Majesty, it is not too late to escape. Only this evening I heard of a man in the town who has a launch hidden outside the harbour. He means to leave in it himself, for the mainland, but he would sell it at a price. There are ways for a small man to escape where a great man like your majesty would be trapped. For two thousand rupees he will sell this boat. He told me so, in so many words. He named the price. It is not much for the life of an Emperor. Give me the money, Majesty, and the boat shall be here before midnight. And in the morning Seyid's troops will march into the town and find it empty."

Ali looked hopefully across the table, but before he had finished speaking he realised that Seth's mood of uncertainty was past.

"Seyid's troops will not march into the town. You forget that I have the Tank. Ali, you are talking treasonable nonsense. To-morrow I shall be here to receive my victorious general."

"To-morrow will show, Majesty."

"To-morrow will show."

"Listen," said Ali, "my friend is very loyal to your majesty and a most devoted man. Perhaps if I were to use my influence he might reduce his price."

"I shall be here in the morning to receive my army."

"Suppose he would accept eighteen hundred rupees?"

"I have spoken."

Without further discussion Ali picked up his typewriter and left the room. As he opened the door his ears caught the inevitable shuffle of bare feet, as a spy slipped away down the dark passage. It was a sound to which they had grown accustomed during the past months.

In his own quarters Ali poured out a glass of whiskey and lit a cheroot. Then he drew out a fibre trunk from beneath the bed and began a methodical arrangement of his possessions preparatory to packing them. Presently there was a knock at the door and Major Joab came in.

"Good evening, secretary."

"Good evening, major. The Armenian is dead?"

"He is dead. Heaven, how he squealed. You have whiskey there."

"Will you help yourself?"

"Thank you, secretary . . . you seem to be preparing for a journey."

"It is well to be prepared—to have one's things in good order."

"I think there is an army in the hills."

"It is what they are saying."

"I think it is the army of Seyid."

"That, too, is being said."

"As you say, secretary, it is well to be prepared."

"Will you take a cheroot, major? I expect that there are many people in Matodi who would be glad to leave. The army will be here to-morrow."

"It is not far away. And yet there is no way of leaving the town. The boats are all gone. The railway is broken. The road leads straight to the encampment."

Ali folded a white drill suit and bent over the trunk, carefully arranging the sleeves. He did not look up as he said: "I heard of a man who had a boat. It was spoken of in the bazaar. I forget by whom. An ignorant fellow no doubt. But this man, whoever it was, spoke of a boat concealed outside the harbour. He was going to the mainland to-night. There was room for two others, so they said. Do you think a man would find passengers to the mainland at five hundred rupees each. That is what he asked."

"It is a great price for a journey to the mainland."

"It is not much for a man's life. Do you think such a man, supposing there is any truth in the tale, would find passengers?"

"Perhaps. Who can tell? A man of affairs who can take his wisdom with him—a foreigner with no stock but a typewriter and his clothes. I do not think a soldier would go."

"A soldier might pay three hundred?"

"It is not likely. What life would there be for him in a foreign country? And among his own people he would be dishonoured."

"But he would not hinder others from going. A man who would pay five hundred rupees for his passage money, would not grudge another hundred to the guard who allowed him to pass?"

"Who can say? Some soldiers might hold that a small price for their honour."

"But two hundred."

"I think soldiers are for the most part poor men. It is seldom they earn two hundred rupees. . . . Well, I must bid you good-night, secretary. I must return to my men."

"How late do you stay on guard, major?"

"Till after midnight. Perhaps I shall see you again."

"Who can say? . . . Oh, major, you have forgotten your papers."

"So I have. Thank you, secretary. And good night."

The major counted the little pile of notes which Ali had placed on the dressing table. Two hundred exactly. He buttoned them into his tunic pocket and returned to the guard house.

Here, in the inner room, sat Mr. Youkoumian talking to the captain. Half an hour before the little

33

Armenian had been very near death, and awe of the experience still overcast his normally open and loquacious manner. It was not until the rope was actually round his neck that he had been inspired to mention the existence of his launch. His face was damp and his voice jerky and subdued.

"What did the Indian dog say?"

"He wanted to sell me a place in the boat for five hundred rupees. Does he know where it is hidden?"

"Fool that I was, I told him."

"It is of little consequence. He gave me two hundred rupees to let him past the guard, also some whiskey and a cheroot. There is no need for us to worry about Ali. When do we start?"

"There is one point, officers . . . my wife. There is not room for her in the boat. She must not know of our departure. Where was she when you—when we left the café together?"

"She was making a noise. One of the corporals locked her in the loft."

"She will get out of there."

"You leave all that to us."

"Very well, major. I am a just man and a peaceable man. You know that. I only want to be sure that everything will be agreeable for every one."

Ali finished his packing and sat down to wait. "What's Major Joab up to?" he wondered. "It is

34

curious his refusing to leave the town. I suppose he thinks he will get a price for Seth in the morning."

Night and the fear of darkness. In his room at the top of the old fort Seth lay awake and alone, his eyes wild with the inherited terror of the jungle, desperate with the acquired loneliness of civilisation. Night was alive with beasts and devils and the spirits of dead enemies; before its power Seth's ancestors had receded, slid away from its attack, abandoning in retreat all the baggage of Individuality; they had lain six or seven in a hut; between them and night only a wall of mud and a ceiling of thatched grass; warm, naked bodies breathing in the darkness an arm's reach apart, indivisibly unified so that they ceased to be six or seven scared blacks and became one person of more than human stature, less vulnerable to the peril that walked near them. Seth could not expand to meet the onset of fear. He was alone, dwarfed by the magnitude of the darkness, insulated from his fellows, strapped down to mean dimensions.

The darkness pulsed with the drumming of the unknown conquerors. In the narrow streets of the city the people were awake—active and apprehensive. Dark figures sped to and fro on furtive errands, hiding from each other in doorways till the way was empty. In the houses they were packing away bundles in secret places, little hoards of coins and jewelry, pictures and books, ancestral sword hilts of fine workmanship, shoddy trinkets from Birmingham and Bombay, silk shawls, scent bottles, anything that might attract attention next morning when the city was given over to loot. Huddled groups of women and children were being herded to refuge in the cellars of the old houses or into the open country beyond the walls; goats, sheep, donkeys, livestock and poultry of all kinds jostled with them for precedence in the city gates. Mme. Youkoumian, trussed like a chicken on the floor of her own bedroom, dribbled through her gag and helplessly writhed her bruised limbs.

Ali, marching back to the fort under arrest between two soldiers, protested angrily to the captain of the guard.

"You are making a great mistake, captain. I have made all arrangements with the major for my departure."

"It is the Emperor's orders that no one leaves the city."

"When we see the major he will explain everything."

The captain made no reply. The little party marched on; in front between two other soldiers shambled Ali's servant, bearing his master's trunk on his head.

When they reached the guard-room, the captain reported: "Two prisoners, major, arrested at the South Gate attempting to leave the city."

"You know me, major; the captain has made a mistake. Tell him it is all right for me to go."

"I know you, secretary: captain, report the arrests to his majesty."

"But, major, only this evening I gave you two hundred rupees. Do you hear, captain, I gave him two hundred rupees. You can't treat me like this. I shall tell his majesty everything."

"We had better search his luggage."

The trunk was opened and the contents spread over the floor. The two officers turned them over with interest and appropriated the few articles of value it contained. The minor possessions were tossed to the corporals. At the bottom, wrapped in a grubby nightshirt, were two heavy objects which, on investigation, proved to be the massive gold crown of the Azanian Empire and an elegant ivory sceptre presented to Amurath by the President of the French Republic. Major Joab and the captain considered this discovery for some time in silence. Then the major answered the question that was in both their minds. "No," he said, "I think we had better show these to Seth."

"Both of them?"

"Well, at any rate, the sceptre. It would not be so

easy to dispose of. Two hundred rupees," said the major bitterly, turning on Ali, "two hundred rupees and you proposed to walk off with the Imperial regalia."

From the inner room Mr. Youkoumian listened to this conversation in a mood of sublime contentment; the sergeant had given him a cigarette out of a box lifted from the shop at the time of his arrest; the captain had given him brandy—similarly acquired—of his own distillation; a fiery, comforting spirit. The terrors of the gallows were far behind him. And now Ali had been caught red-handed with the crown jewels. Nothing was required to complete Mr. Youkoumian's happiness, except a calm sea for their crossing to the mainland; and the gentle night air gave promise that this, too, would be vouchsafed him.

It was only a matter of a few words for Major Joab to report the circumstances of Ali's arrest. The damning evidence of the sceptre and the soiled nightshirt was laid before Seth on the table. The prisoner stood between his captors without visible interest or emotion. When the charge had been made, Seth said, "Well, Ali."

Until now they had spoken in Sakuyu. Ali answered, as he always spoke to his master, in English. "It is regrettable that this should have happened.

These ignorant men have greatly disturbed the preparations for your majesty's departure."

"For *my* departure?"

"For whom else would I prepare a boat? What other reason could I have for supervising the safe conduct of your majesty's sceptre, and of the crown which the officers have omitted to bring from the guard-room."

"I don't believe you, Ali."

"Your majesty wrongs himself. You are a distinguished man, educated in Europe—not like these low soldiers. Would you have trusted me had I been unworthy? Could I, a poor Indian, hope to deceive a distinguished gentleman educated in Europe? Send these low men out and I will explain everything to you."

The officers of the guard had listened uneasily to these alien sentences; now at Seth's command they withdrew their men. "Shall I make preparations for the execution, Majesty?"

"Yes . . . no . . . I will tell you when. Stand by for further orders below, Major."

The two officers saluted and left the room. When they had gone Ali sat down opposite his master and proceeded at his ease. There was no accusation or reproach in the Emperor's countenance, no justice or decision, trust or forgiveness; one emotion only was apparent in the dark young face before him, blank terror. Ali saw this and knew that his case was won. "Majesty, I will tell you why the officers have arrested me. It is to prevent your escape. They are plotting to sell you to the enemy. I know it. I have heard it all from one of the corporals who is loyal to us. It was for this reason that I prepared the boat. When all was ready I would have come to you, told you of their treachery and brought you away safely."

"But, Ali, you say they would hand me over to the enemy. Am I then really beaten?"

"Majesty, all the world knows. The British General Connolly has joined Prince Seyid. They are there on the hills together now. To-morrow they will be in Matodi."

"But the Tank?"

"Majesty, Mr. Marx the distinguished mechanic who made the tank, fled last night, as you well know."

"Connolly too. Why should he betray me? I trusted him. Why does every one betray me? Connolly was my friend."

"Majesty, consider the distinguished general's position. What would he do? He might conquer Seyid and your majesty would reward him, or he might be defeated. If he joins Seyid, Seyid will reward him, and no one can defeat him. How would you expect a distinguished gentleman, educated in Europe, should choose?"

"They are all against me. All traitors. There is no one I can trust."

"Except me, Majesty."

"I do not trust you. You, least of all."

"But you must trust me. Don't you understand. If you do not trust me there will be no one. You will be alone, quite alone."

"I am alone. There is no one."

"Then since all are traitors, trust a traitor. Trust me. You must trust me. Listen. It is not too late to escape. No one but I knows of the boat. The Armenian Youkoumian is dead. Do you understand, Majesty? Give the order to the guards to let me pass. I will go to where the boat is hidden. In an hour I will have it here, under the sea wall. Then when the guard is changed you will join me. Don't you understand. It is the only chance. You must trust me. Otherwise you will be alone."

The Emperor stood up. "I do not know if I can trust you. I do not think there is any one I can trust. I am alone. But you shall go. Why should I hang you? What is one life more or less when all are traitors. Go in peace."

"Your majesty's faithful servant."

Seth opened the door; again the scamper of the retreating spy.

"Major."

"Majesty."

"Ali is to go free. He may leave the fort."

"The execution is cancelled?"

"Ali may leave the fort."

"As your majesty commands." Major Joab saluted. As Ali left the lighted room he turned back and addressed the Emperor.

"Your majesty does well to trust me."

"I trust no one . . . I am alone."

The Emperor was alone. Faintly on the night air he heard the throbbing of drums from the encamped army. Quarter past two. Darkness for nearly four hours more.

Suddenly the calm was splintered by a single, shrill cry—a jet of sound, spurting up from below, breaking in spray over the fort, then ceasing. Expressive of nothing; followed by nothing; no footste s; no voices; silence and the distant beat of the tomtoms.

Seth ran to the door. "Hullo! Who is there? What is that? Major! Officer of the guard." No answer. Only the inevitable scuffle of the retreating spy. He went to the window. "Who's there? What has happened? Is there no one on guard?"

A long silence.

Then a quiet voice from below. "Majesty?"

42

"Who is that?"

"Major Joab of the Imperial Infantry at your majesty's service."

"What was that?"

"Majesty?"

"What was that cry?"

"It was a mistake, your majesty. There is no cause for alarm."

"What has happened?"

"The sentry made a mistake. That is all."

"What has he done?"

"It is only the Indian, Majesty. The sentry did not understand his orders. I will see to it that he is punished."

"What has happened to Ali? Is he hurt?"

"He is dead, your majesty. It is a mistake of the sentry's. I am sorry your majesty was disturbed."

Presently Major Joab, the captain of the guard, and Mr. Youkoumian accompanied by three heavily burdened corporals, left the fort by a side door and made their way out of the town along the coast path towards the disused sugar mills.

And Seth was alone.

Another dawn. With slow feet Mr. Youkoumian trudged into Matodi. There was no one about in the streets. All who could, had left the city during the darkness; those who remained lurked behind barred doors and barricaded windows; from the cracks of shutters and through keyholes a few curious eyes observed the weary little figure dragging down the lane to the Amurath Café and Universal Stores.

Mme. Youkoumian lay across the bedroom doorstep. During the night she had bitten through her gag and rolled some yards across the floor; that far her strength had taken her. Then, too exhausted to cry out or wrestle any further with the ropes that bound her, she had lapsed into intermittent coma, disturbed by nightmares, acute spasms of cramp and the scampering of rats on the earthen floor. In the green and silver light of dawn, this bruised, swollen and dusty figure presented a spectacle radically repugnant to Mr. Youkoumian's most sensitive feelings.

"Krikor, Krikor. Oh, praise God you've come . . . I thought I should never see you again . . . Blessed Mary and Joseph . . . Where have you been? . . . What has happened to you? . . . Oh, Krikor, my own husband, praise God and his angels who have brought you back to me."

Mr. Youkoumian sat down heavily on the bed and pulled off his elastic-sided button boots. "I'm tired," he said. "God, how tired I am. I could sleep for a

44

week." He took a bottle from the shelf and poured out a drink. "I have had one of the most disagreeable nights of my life. First I am nearly hanged. Will you believe it. The noose was actually round my neck. Then I am made to walk out as far as the sugar mills, then the next thing I know I am alone, lying on the beach. My luggage is gone, my boat is gone, the damned soldiers are gone and I have a lump on the back of my head the size of an egg. Just you feel it."

"I'm tied up, Krikor. Cut the string and let me help you. Oh, my poor husband."

"How it aches. What a walk back. And my boat gone. I could have got fifteen hundred rupees for that boat yesterday. Oh, my head. Fifteen hundred rupees. My feet ache too. I must go to bed."

"Let me loose, Krikor, and I will attend to you, my poor husband."

"No, it doesn't matter, my flower. I'll go to bed. I could sleep for a week."

"Krikor, let me loose."

"Don't worry. I shall be all right when I have had a sleep. Why, I ache all over." He tossed off the drink and with a little grunt of relief drew his feet up onto the bed and rolled over with his face to the wall.

"Krikor, please . . . you must let me loose . . .

don't you see. I've been like this all night, I'm in
such pain . . ."

"You stay where you are. I can't attend to you
now. You're always thinking of yourself. What about
me? I'm tired. Don't you hear me?"

"But, Krikor—"

"Be quiet, you slut."

And in less than a minute Mr. Youkoumian found
consolation for the diverse fortunes of the night in
profound and prolonged sleep.

He was awakened some hours later by the entry
into Matodi of the victorious army. Drums banging,
pipes whistling, the soldiers of Progress and the New
Age passed under his window. Mr. Youkoumian
rolled off the bed, rubbing his eyes, and peeped
through the chink of the shutters.

"God save my soul," he remarked. "Seth's won
after all." Then with a chuckle. "What a pair of
fools Major Joab and the captain turn out to be."

Mme. Youkoumian looked up from the floor with
piteous appeal in her dark eyes. He gave her a
friendly little prod in the middle with his stockinged
foot. "Stay there, that's a good girl, and don't make
a noise. I'll come and see to you in a minute or two."
Then he lay down on the bed, nuzzled into the bolster, and after a few preliminary grunts and wrig-
gles, relapsed into slumber.

It was a remarkable procession. First in tattered,

field grey uniforms, came the brass band of the Imperial Guard, playing:

> *Mine eyes have seen the glory of the coming of the Lord;*
> *He is trampling out the vintage where the grapes of wrath are stor'd,*
> *He hath loos'd the fateful lightning of His terrible swift sword;*
> *His truth is marching on.*

Behind them came the infantry; hard, bare feet rhythmically kicking up the dust, threadbare uniforms, puttees wound up anyhow, caps at all angles, Lee-Enfield rifles with fixed bayonets slung on their shoulders; fuzzy heads, jolly nigger-minstrel faces, black chests shining through buttonless tunics, pockets bulging with loot. Dividing these guardsmen from the irregular troops rode General Connolly on a tall, grey mule, with his staff officers beside him. He was a stocky Irishman in early middle age who had seen varied service in the Black and Tans, the South African Police and the Kenya Game Reserves before enlisting under the Emperor's colours. But on this morning his appearance was rather that of a lost explorer than a conquering commander-in-chief. He had a week's growth of reddish beard below his cavalry moustaches; irregular slashes had converted his breeches into shorts; open shirt and weather-worn white topee took the place of tunic and cap. Field glasses, map case, sword and revolver holster hung incongruously round him. He was smoking a pipe of rank local tobacco.

On their heels came the hordes of Wanda and Sakuyu warriors. In the hills these had followed in a diffuse rabble. Little units of six or a dozen trotted round the stirrups of the headmen; before them they drove geese and goats pillaged from surrounding farms. Sometimes they squatted down to rest; sometimes they ran to catch up. The big chiefs had bands of their own—mounted drummers thumping great bowls of cowhide and wood, pipers blowing down six-foot chanters of bamboo. Here and there a camel swayed above the heads of the mob. They were armed with weapons of every kind; antiquated rifles, furnished with bandoliers of brass cartridges and empty cartridge cases; short hunting spears, swords and knives; the great, seven-foot-broad bladed spear of the Wanda; behind one chief a slave carried a machine gun under a velvet veil; a few had short bows and iron-wood maces of im-memorial design.

The Sakuyu wore their hair in a dense fuzz; their chests and arms were embossed with ornamental scars; the Wanda had their teeth filed into sharp points, their hair braided into dozens of mud-caked pig-tails. In accordance with their unseemly usage, any who could, wore strung round his neck the members of a slain enemy.

As this great host swept down on the city and surged through the gates, it broke into a dozen divergent streams, spurting and trickling on all sides like water from a rotten hose pipe, forcing out jets of men, mounts and livestock into the by-ways and back streets, eddying down the blind alleys and into enclosed courts. Solitary musicians, separated from their bands, drummed and piped among the straggling crowds; groups split away from the mêlée and began dancing in the alleys; the doors of the liquor shops were broken in and a new and nastier element appeared in the carnival, as drink-crazed warriors began to re-enact their deeds of heroism, bloodily laying about their former comrades-in-arms with knives and clubs.

"God," said Connolly, "I shall be glad when I've got this menagerie off my hands. I wonder if his nibs has really bolted. Anything is possible in this abandoned country."

No one appeared in the streets. Only rows of furtive eyes behind the shuttered windows watched the victors' slow progress through the city. In the main square the General halted the guards and such of the irregular troops as were still amenable to discipline; they squatted on the ground, chewing at bits of sugar cane, crunching nuts and polishing their teeth with little lengths of stick, while above the drone of confused revelling which rose from the side streets, Connolly from the saddle of his mule in classical form exhorted his legions.

"Guards," he said loudly, "Chiefs and tribesmen of the Azanian Empire. Hear me. You are good men. You have fought valiantly for your Emperor. The slaughter was very splendid. It is a thing for which your children and your children's children will hold you in honour. It was said in the camp that the Emperor had gone over the sea. I do not know if that is true. If he has, it is to prepare a reward for you in the great lands. But it is sufficient reward to a soldier to have slain his enemy.

"Guards, Chiefs and tribesmen of the Azanian Empire. The war is over. It is fitting that you should rest and rejoice. Two things only, I charge you, are forbidden. The white men, their houses, cattle, goods or women you must not take. Nor must you burn anything or any of the houses nor pour out the petrol in the streets. If any man do this he shall be killed. I have spoken. Long live the Emperor.

"Go on, you lucky bastards," he added in English. "Go and make whoopee. I must get a brush up and some food before I do anything else."

He rode across to the Grand Azanian Hotel. It was shut and barred. His two servants forced the door and he went in. At the best of times, even when the fortnightly Messageries liner was in and gay European sight-seers paraded every corner of the city, the Grand Azanian Hotel had a gloomy and unwelcoming air. On this morning a chill of utter desolation struck through General Connolly as he passed through its empty and darkened rooms. Every movable object had been stripped from walls and floor and stowed away subterraneously during the preceding night. But the single bath at least was a fixture. Connolly set his servants to work pumping water and unpacking his uniform cases. Eventually an hour later he emerged, profoundly low in spirits, but clean, shaved and very fairly dressed. Then he rode towards the fort where the Emperor's colours hung limp in the sultry air. No sign of life came from the houses; no welcome; no resistance. Marauding bands of his own people skulked from corner to corner; once a terrified Indian rocketed up from the gutter and shot across his path like a rabbit. It was not until he reached the White Fathers' mission that he heard news of the Emperor. Here he encountered a vast Canadian priest with white habit and sunhat and spreading crimson beard, who was at that moment occupied in shaking almost to death the brigade sergeant-major of the Imperial Guard. At the General's approach the reverend father released his victim with one hand—keeping a firm grip in his woollen hair with the other—removed the cheroot from his mouth and waved it cordially.

"Hullo, general, back from the wars, eh? They've been very anxious about you in the city. Is this creature part of the victorious army?"

"Looks like one of my chaps. What's he been up to?"

"Up to? I came in from mass and found him eating my breakfast." A tremendous buffet on the side of his head sent the sergeant-major dizzily across the road. "Don't you let me find any more of your fellows hanging round the mission to-day or there'll be trouble. It's always the same when you have troops in a town. I remember in Duke Japheth's rebellion, the wretched creatures were all over the place. They frightened the sisters terribly over at the fever hospital."

"Father, is it true that the Emperor's cut and run?"

"If he hasn't he's about the only person. I had that old fraud of an Armenian Archbishop in here the other night, trying to make me join him in a motor-boat. I told him I'd sooner have my throat cut on dry land than face that crossing in an open boat. I'll bet he was sick."

"But you don't know where the Emperor is?"

"He might be over in the fort. He was the other

day. Silly young ass, pasting up proclamations all over the town. I've got other things to bother about than young Seth. And mind you keep your miserable savages from my mission or they'll know the reason why. I've got a lot of our people camped in here so as to be out of harm's way, and I am not going to have them disturbed. Good morning to you, General."

General Connolly rode on. At the fort he found no sentry on guard. The courtyard was empty save for the body of Ali, which lay on its face in the dust, the cord which had strangled him still tightly twined round his neck. Connolly turned it over with his boot but failed to recognise the swollen and darkened face.

"So His Imperial Majesty *has* shot the moon."

He looked into the deserted guard house and the lower rooms of the fort; then he climbed the spiral stone staircase which led to Seth's room and here lying across the camp bed in spotted silk pyjamas recently purchased in the Place Vendôme, utterly exhausted by the horror and insecurity of the preceding night, lay the Emperor of Azania fast asleep.

From his bed Seth would only hear the first, rudimentary statement of his victory. Then he dismissed his commander-in-chief and with remarkable self-restraint insisted on performing a complete and fairly elaborate toilet before giving his mind to the details of the situation. When, eventually, he came down stairs dressed in the full and untarnished uniform of the Imperial Horse Guards, he was in a state of some elation. "You see, Connolly," he cried, clasping his general's hand with warm emotion, "I was right. I knew that it was impossible for us to fail."

"We came damned near it, once or twice," said Connolly.

"Nonsense, my dear fellow. We are Progress and the New Age. Nothing can stand in our way. *Don't you see?* The world is already ours; it is our world now, because we are of the Present. Seyid and his ramshackle band of brigands were the Past. Dark barbarism. A cobweb in a garret; dead wood; a whisper echoing in a sunless cave. We are Light and Speed and Strength, Steel and Steam, Youth, To-day and To-morrow. Don't you see? Our little war was won on other fields five centuries back." The young darky stood there transfigured; his eyes shining; his head thrown back; tipsy with words. The white man knocked out his pipe on the heel of his riding boot and felt for a pouch in his tunic pocket.

"All right, Seth, say it your own way. All I know is that *my* little war was won the day before yesterday and by two very ancient weapons—lies and the long spear."

"But my tank? Was it not that which gave us the victory?"

"Marx's tin can? A fat lot of use that was. I told you you were wasting money but you would have the thing. The best thing you can do is to present it to Debra-Dowa as a war memorial, only you couldn't get it so far. My dear boy, you can't take a machine like that over this country under this sun. The whole thing was red hot after five miles. The two poor devils of Greeks who had to drive it nearly went off their heads. It came in handy in the end, though. We used it as a punishment cell. It was the one thing these black bastards would really take notice of. It's all right getting on a high horse about progress now that everything's over. It doesn't hurt any one. But if you want to know, you were as near as nothing to losing the whole bag of tricks at the end of last week. Do you know what that clever devil Seyid had done. Got hold of a photograph of you taken at Oxford in cap and gown. He had several thousand printed and circulated among the guards. Told them you'd deserted the Church in England and that there you were in the robes of an English Mohammedan. All the mission boys fell for it. It was no good telling them. They were going over to the enemy in hundreds every night. I was all in. There didn't seem a damned thing to do. Then I got an idea. You know what the name of Amurath means

55

among the tribesmen? Well, I called a shari of all
the Wanda and Sakuyu chiefs and spun them the
yarn. Told them that Amurath never died—which
they believed already most of them—but that he had
crossed the sea to commune with the spirits of his
ancestors; that you were Amurath, himself, come
back in another form. It went down from the word
go. I wish you could have seen their faces. The moment they'd heard the news they were mad to be at
Seyid there and then. It was all I could do to keep
them back until I had him where I wanted him.
What's more the story got through to the other side
and in two days we had a couple of thousand of
Seyid's boys coming over to us. Double what we'd
lost on the Mohammedan story, and real fighters—
not dressed-up mission boys. Well, I kept them back
as best I could for three days. We were on the crest
of the hills all the time and Seyid was down in the
valley, kicking up the devil, burning villages, trying
to make us come down to him. He was getting worried about the desertions. Well, on the third day I
sent half a company of guards down with a band
and a whole lot of mules and told them to make
themselves as conspicuous as they could straight in
front of him in the Ukaka pass. Trust the guards to
do that. He did just what I expected; thought it was
the whole army and spread out on both sides trying
to surround them. Then I let the tribesmen in on

his rear. My word, I've never seen such a massacre. Didn't they enjoy themselves, bless them. Half of them haven't come back yet; they're still chasing the poor devils all over the hills."

"And the usurper Seyid, did he surrender?"

"Yes, he surrendered all right. But, look here, Seth, I hope you aren't going to mind about this, but you see how it was, well, you see Seyid surrendered and . . ."

"You don't mean you've let him escape?"

"Oh, no, nothing like that, but the fact is, he surrendered to a party of Wanda . . . and, well, you know what the Wanda are."

"You mean . . ."

"Yes, I'm afraid so. I wouldn't have had it happen for anything. I didn't hear about it until afterwards."

"They should not have eaten him—after all he was my father . . . It is so . . . so barbarous."

"I knew you'd feel that way about it, Seth, and I'm sorry. I gave the headmen twelve hours in the tank for it."

"I am afraid that as yet the Wanda are totally out of touch with modern thought. They need education. We must start some schools and a university for them when we get things straight."

"That's it, Seth, you can't blame them. It's want of education. That's all it is."

"We might start them on Montessori methods," said Seth dreamily. "You can't blame them." Then rousing himself: "Connolly, I shall make you a Duke."

"That's nice of you, Seth. I don't mind so much for myself but Black Bitch will be pleased as punch about it."

"And, Connolly."

"Yes."

"Don't you think that when she is a Duchess, it might be more suitable if you were to try and call your wife by another name. You see, there will probably be a great influx of distinguished Europeans for my coronation. We wish to break down colour barriers as far as possible. Your name for Mrs. Connolly, though suitable as a term of endearment in the home, seems to emphasise the racial distinction between you in a way which might prove disconcerting."

"I daresay you're right, Seth. I'll try and remember when we're in company. But I shall always think of her as Black Bitch, somehow. By the way, what has become of Ali?"

"Ali? Yes, I had forgotten. He was murdered by Major Joab yesterday evening. And that reminds me of something else. I must order a new crown."

TWO

"LOVEY dovey, cat's eyes."

"You got that out of a book."

"Well, yes. How did you know?"

"I read it too. It's been all round the compound."

"Anyway, I said it as a quotation. We have to find new things to say somehow sometimes, don't we?"

William and Prudence rolled apart and lay on their backs; sun hats tilted over their noses shading their eyes from the brilliant equatorial sun. They were on the crest of the little hills above Debra-Dowa; it was cool there, eight thousand feet up. Behind them in a stockade of euphorbia trees stood a thatched Nestorian shrine. At its door the priest's youngest child lay sunning his naked belly, gazing serenely into the heavens, indifferent to the flies which settled on the corners of his mouth and sauntered across his eye-balls. Below them the tin roofs of Debra-Dowa and a few thin columns of smoke were visible among the blue gums. At a distance the Legation syce sat in charge of the ponies.

"William darling, there's something so extraordinary on your neck. I believe it's two of them."

59

"Well, I think you might knock it off."

"I believe it's that kind which sting worst."

"Beast."

"Oh, it's gone now. It *was* two."

"I can feel it walking about."

"No, darling, that's me. I think you might *look* sometimes when I'm being sweet to you. I've invented a new way of kissing. You do it with your eye-lashes."

"I've known that for years. It's called a butterfly kiss."

"Well, you needn't be so high up about it. I only do these things for your benefit."

"It was very nice, darling. I only said it wasn't very new."

"I don't believe you liked it at all."

"It was so like the stinging thing."

"Oh, how maddening it is to have no one to make love with except you."

"Sophisticated voice."

"That's not sophisticated. It's my gramophone record voice. My sophisticated voice is quite different. It's like this."

"I call that American."

"Shall I do my vibrant-with-passion voice?"

"No."

"Oh, dear, men are hard to keep amused." Prudence sat up and lit a cigarette. "I think you're effeminate and undersexed," she said, "and I **hate** you."

"That's because you're too young to arouse serious emotion. You might give me a cigarette."

"I hoped you'd say that. It happens to be the last. Not only the last in my pocket but the last in Debra-Dowa. I got it out of the Envoy Extraordinary's bedroom this morning."

"Oh, Lord, when will this idiotic war be over? We haven't had a bag for six weeks. I've run out of hair wash and detective stories and now no cigarettes. I think you might give me some of that."

"I hope you go bald. Still, I'll let you have the cigarette."

"Pru, how sweet of you. I never thought **you** would."

"I'm that kind of girl."

"I think I'll give you a kiss."

"No, try the new way with eyelashes."

"Is that right?"

"Delicious. Do it some more."

Presently they remounted and rode back to the Legation. On the way William said:

"I hope it doesn't give one a twitch."

"What doesn't, darling?"

"That way with the eyelashes. I've seen people with twitches. I daresay that's how they got it. There was once a man who got run in for winking at girls

61

in the street. So he said it was a permanent affliction and he winked all through his trial and got off. But the sad thing is that now he can't stop and he's been winking ever since."

"I will say one thing for you," said Prudence. "You do know a lovely lot of stories. I daresay that's why I like you."

Three powers—Great Britain, France and the United States—maintained permanent diplomatic representatives at Debra-Dowa. It was not an important appointment. Mr. Schonbaum, the doyen, had adopted diplomacy late in life. Indeed the more formative years of his career had already passed before he made up his mind, in view of the uncertainty of Central European exchanges, to become a citizen of the republic he represented. From the age of ten until the age of forty he had lived an active life variously engaged in journalism, electrical engineering, real estate, cotton broking, hotel management, shipping and theatrical promotion. At the outbreak of the European war he had retired first to the United States, and then, on their entry into the war, to Mexico. Soon after the declaration of peace he became an American citizen and amused himself in politics. Having subscribed largely to a successful Presidential campaign, he was offered his choice of several public preferments, of which the ministry at Debra-Dowa was by far the least prominent or lucrative. His European upbringing, however, had invested diplomacy with a glamour which his later acquaintance with the great world had never completely dimmed; he had made all the money he needed; the climate at Debra-Dowa was reputed to be healthy and the environment romantic. Accordingly he had chosen that post and had not regretted it, enjoying during the last eight years a popularity and prestige which he would hardly have attained among his own people.

The French Minister, M. Ballon, was a Freemason.

His Britannic Majesty's minister, Sir Samson Courteney, was a man of singular personal charm and wide culture whose comparative ill success in diplomatic life was attributable rather to inattention than to incapacity. As a very young man he had had great things predicted of him. He had passed his examinations with a series of papers of outstanding brilliance; he had powerful family connexions in the Foreign Office; but almost from the outset of his career it became apparent that he would disappoint expectations. As third secretary at Peking he devoted himself, to the exclusion of all other interests, to the construction of a cardboard model of the Summer Palace; transferred to Washington he conceived a sudden enthusiasm for bicycling and would disappear for days at a time to return dusty but triumphant with reports of some broken record for speed or endurance; the scandal caused by this hobby culminated in the discovery that he had entered his name for an international long distance championship. His uncles at the Foreign Office hastily shifted him to Copenhagen, marrying him, on his way through London, to the highly suitable daughter of a Liberal cabinet minister. It was in Sweden that his career was finally doomed. For some time past he had been noticeably silent at the dinner table when foreign languages were being spoken; now the shocking truth became apparent that he was losing his mastery even of French; many ageing diplomats, at loss for a word, could twist the conversation and suit their opinions to their vocabulary; Sir Samson recklessly improvised or lapsed into a kind of pidgin English. The uncles were loyal. He was recalled to London and established in a department of the Foreign Office. Finally, at the age of fifty, when his daughter Prudence was thirteen years old, he was created a Knight of St. Michael and St. George and relegated to Azania. The appointment caused him the keenest delight. It would have astonished him to learn that any one considered him unsuccessful or that he was known throughout the service as the 'Envoy Extraordinary.'

The Legation lay seven miles out of the capital;

a miniature garden city in a stockaded compound, garrisoned by a troop of Indian cavalry. There was wireless communication with Aden and a telephone service of capricious activity, to the town. The road, however, was outrageous. For a great part of the year it was furrowed by watercourses, encumbered with boulders, landslides and fallen trees, and ambushed by cut-throats. On this matter Sir Samson's predecessor had addressed numerous remonstrances to the Azanian government with the result that several wayfarers were hanged under suspicion of brigandage; nothing, however, was done about the track; the correspondence continued and its conclusion was the most nearly successful achievement of Sir Samson's career. Stirred by his appointment and zealous for his personal comfort, the Envoy Extraordinary had, for the first time in his life, thrown himself wholeheartedly into a question of public policy. He had read through the entire file bearing on the subject and within a week of presenting his papers, reopened the question in a personal interview with the Prince Consort. Month after month he pressed forward the interchange of memoranda between Palace, Legation, Foreign Office and Office of Works (the posts of Lord Chamberlain, Foreign Secretary and Minister of Works were all, as it happened at that time, occupied by the Nestorian Metropolitan) until one memorable day, Prudence returned from her ride to say that a caravan of oxen, a load of stones and three chain-gangs of convicts had appeared on the road. Here, however, Sir Samson suffered a set back. The American commercial attaché acted in his ample spare time as agent for a manufacturer of tractors, agricultural machinery and steam-rollers. At his representation the convicts were withdrawn and the Empress and her circle settled down to the choice of a steam-roller. She had always had a weakness for illustrated catalogues and after several weeks' discussion had ordered a threshing machine, a lawn mower and a mechanical saw. About the steam-roller she could not make up her mind. The Metropolitan Archbishop (who was working with the American attaché on a half commission basis), supported a very magnificent engine named Pennsylvania Monarch; the Prince Consort, whose personal allowance was compromised by any public extravagance, headed a party in favour of the more modest Kentucky Midget. Meanwhile guests to the British Legation were still in most seasons of the year obliged to ride out to dinner on mule-back, preceded by armed askar and boy with a lantern. It was widely believed that a decision was imminent, when the Empress's death and the subsequent civil war postponed all immediate hope of improvement. The Envoy Extraordinary bore the reverse with composure but real pain.

He had taken the matter to heart and he felt hurt and disillusioned. The heap of stones at the roadside remained for him as a continual reproach, the monument to his single ineffective excursion into statesmanship.

In this isolation, life in the compound was placid and domestic. Lady Courteney devoted herself to gardening. The bags came out from London laden with bulbs and cuttings and soon there sprang up round the Legation a luxuriant English garden; lilac and lavender, privet and box, grass walks and cro-quet lawn, rockeries and wildernesses, herbaceous borders, bowers of rambler roses, puddles of water lilies and an immature maze.

William Bland, the honorary attaché, lived with the Courteneys. The rest of the staff were married. The Second Secretary had clock golf and the Consul two tennis courts. They called each other by their Christian names, pottered in and out of each other's bungalows and knew the details of each other's housekeeping. The Oriental Secretary, Captain Walsh, alone maintained certain reserves. He suf-fered from recurrent malaria and was known to ill-treat his wife. But since he was the only member of the Legation who understood Sakuyu, he was a man of importance, being in frequent demand as arbiter in disputes between the domestic servants.

The unofficial British population of Debra-Dowa

was small and rather shady. There was the manager of the bank and his wife (who was popularly believed to have an infection of Indian blood); two subordinate bank clerks; a shipper of hides who described himself as President of the Azanian Trading Association; a mechanic on the railway who was openly married to two Azanians; the Anglican Bishop of Debra-Dowa and a shifting community of canons and curates; the manager of the Eastern Exchange Telegraph Company; and General Connolly. Intercourse between them and the Legation was now limited to luncheon on Christmas Day to which all the more respectable were invited, and an annual garden party on the King's Birthday which was attended by every one in the town from the Georgian Prince who managed the Perroquet Night Club to the Mormon Missionary. This aloofness from the affairs of the town was traditional to the Legation, being dictated partly by the difficulties of the road and partly by their inherent disinclination to mix with social inferiors. On Lady Courteney's first arrival in Debra-Dowa she had attempted to break down these distinctions, saying that they were absurd in so small a community. General Connolly had dined twice at the Legation and a friendship seemed to be in bud when its flowering was abruptly averted by an informal call paid on him by Lady Courteney in his own quarters. She had been lunching with the Empress and turned aside on her way home to deliver an invitation to croquet. Sentries presented arms in the courtyard, a finely uniformed servant opened the door, but this dignified passage was interrupted by a resolute little negress in a magenta tea-gown who darted suddenly across the hall and barred her way to the drawing-room.

"I am Black Bitch," she had explained simply. "What do you want in my house?"

"I am Lady Courteney. I came to see General Connolly."

"The General is drunk to-day and he doesn't want any more ladies."

After that Connolly was not asked even to Christmas luncheon.

Other less dramatic incidents occurred with most of the English community until now, after six years, the Bishop was the only resident who ever came to play croquet on the Legation lawn. Even his Lordship's visits had become less welcome lately. His strength did not enable him to accomplish both journeys in the same day, so that an invitation to luncheon involved also an invitation for the night and, usually, to luncheon next day as well. More than this the Envoy Extraordinary found these incursions from the outside world increasingly disturbing and exhausting as his momentary interest in Azania began to subside. The Bishop would insist on talking about Problems and Policy, Welfare, Education and Finance. He knew all about native law and customs and the relative importance of the various factions at court. He had what Sir Samson considered an ostentatious habit of referring by name to members of the royal household and to provincial governors, whom Sir Samson was content to remember as 'the old black fellow who drank so much Kummel' or 'that what-do-you-call-him Prudence said was like Aunt Sarah' or 'the one with glasses and gold teeth.'

Besides the Bishop's croquet was not nearly up to Legation standards.

As it happened however they found him at table when, twenty minutes late for luncheon, Prudence and William returned from their ride.

"Do you know," said Lady Courteney, "I thought for once you *had* been massacred. It would have pleased Monsieur Ballon so much. He is always warning me of the danger of allowing you to go out alone during the crisis. He was on the telephone this morning asking what steps we had taken to fortify the Legation. Madame Ballon has made sandbags and put them all round the windows. He told me he was keeping his last cartridge for Madame Ballon."

"Every one is in a great state of alarm in the town," said the Bishop. "There are so many rumours. Tell me, Sir Samson, you do not think really, seriously, there is any danger of a massacre?"

The Envoy Extraordinary said: "We seem to have tinned asparagus for luncheon every day . . . I can't think why . . . I'm so sorry—you were talking about the massacre. Well, I hardly know. I haven't really thought about it . . . Yes, I suppose there might be one. I don't see what's to stop them, if the fellows take it into their heads. Still I daresay it'll all blow over, you know. Doesn't do to get worried . . . I should have thought we could have grown it ourselves. Much better than spending so much time on that Dutch garden. So like being on board ship, eating tinned asparagus."

For some minutes Lady Courteney and Sir Samson discussed the relative advantages of tulips and asparagus. Presently the Bishop said: "One of the things which brought me here this morning was to find out if there was any News. If I could take back something certain to the town . . . You cannot imagine the distress every one is in . . . It is silence for so many weeks and the rumours. Up here you must at least know what is going on."

"News," said the Envoy Extraordinary. "News. Well, we've generally got quite a lot going on. Let's see, when were you here last? You knew that the Anstruthers have decided to enter David for Uppingham? Very sensible of them, I think. And Percy

Legge's sister in England is going to be married—
the one who was out here staying with them last
year—you remember her? Betty Anstruther got run
away with and had a nasty fall the other morning.
I thought that pony was too strong for the child.
What else is there to tell the Bishop, my dear."

"The Legges' frigidaire is broken and they can't
get it mended until after the war. Poor Captain
Walsh has been laid up with fever again. Prudence
began another novel the other day . . . or wasn't I
to tell about that, darling?"

"You certainly were not to. And anyway it isn't
a novel. It's a Panorama of Life. Oh, I've got some
news for all of you. Percy scored twelve-hundred-
and-eighty at bagatelle this morning."

"No, I say," said Sir Samson, "did he really?"

"Oh, but that was on the chancery table," said
William. "I don't count that. We've all made colossal
scores there. The pins are bent. I still call my eleven-
hundred-and-sixty-five at the Anstruthers' a record."

For some minutes they discussed the demerits of
the chancery bagatelle table. Presently the Bishop
said:

"But is there no news about the *war*?"

"No, I don't think so. Can't remember anything
particularly. I leave all that to Walsh, you know,
and he's down with fever at the moment. I daresay
when he comes back we shall hear something. He

keeps in touch with all these local affairs . . . There were some cables the other day, now I come to think of it. Was there anything about the war in them, William, d'you know?"

"I can't really say, sir. The truth is we've lost the cypher book again."

"Awful fellow, William, he's always losing things. What would you say if you had a chaplain like that, Bishop? Well, as soon as it turns up, get them decyphered, will you. There might be something wanting an answer."

"Yes, sir."

"Oh, and, William—I think you ought to get those pins put straight on the chancery bagatelle board. It's an awful waste of time playing if it doesn't run true."

"Golly," said William to Prudence when they were alone. "Wasn't the Envoy on a high horse at luncheon. Telling me off right and left. First about the cypher book and then about the bagatelle. Too humiliating."

"Poor sweet, he was only showing off to the Bishop. He's probably frightfully ashamed of himself already."

"That's all very well, but why should I be made to look a fool just so as he can impress the Bishop?"

"Sweet, sweet William, please don't be in a rage.

73

It isn't my fault if I have a martinet for a father, is it, darling? Listen, I've got a whole lot of new ideas for us to try."

The Legges and the Anstruthers came across to tea: cucumber sandwiches, gentleman's relish, hot scones and seed-cake.

"How's Betty after her fall?"

"Rather shaken, poor mite. Arthur wants her to start riding again as soon as she can. He's afraid she may lose her nerve permanently."

"But not on Majesty."

"No, we hope Percy will lend her Jumbo for a bit. She can't really manage Majesty yet, you know."

"More tea, Bishop? How is every one at the Mission?"

"Oh, dear, how bare the garden is looking. It really is heart breaking. This is just the time it should be at its best. But all the antirrhinums are in the bag, heaven knows where."

"This war is too exasperating. I've been expecting the wool for baby's jacket for six weeks. I can't get on with it at all and there are only the sleeves to finish. Do you think it would look too absurd if I put in the sleeves in another colour?"

"It might look rather sweet."

"More tea, Bishop? I want to hear *all* about the infant school, sometime."

"I've found the cypher book, sir."

"Good boy; where was it?"

"In my collar drawer. I'd been decoding some telegrams in bed last week."

"Splendid. It doesn't matter as long as it's safe, but you know how particular the F.O. are about things like that."

"Poor Monsieur Ballon. He's been trying to get an aeroplane from Algiers."

"Mrs. Schonbaum told me that the reason we're all so short of supplies is that the French Legation have been buying up everything and storing it in their cellars."

"I wonder if they'd like to buy my marmalade. It's been rather a failure this year."

"More tea, Bishop. I want to talk to you sometime about David's confirmation. He's getting such an independent mind, I'm sometimes quite frightened what he'll say next."

"I wonder if you know anything about this cable. I can't make head or tail of it. It isn't in any of the usual codes. *Kt to QR₃ CH.*"

"Yes, they're all right. It's a move in the chess game. Percy's playing with Babbitt at the F.O. He was wondering what had become of it."

"Poor Mrs. Walsh. Looking quite done up. I'm sure the altitude isn't good for her."

"I'm sure Uppingham is just the place for David."

"More tea, Bishop. I'm sure you must be tired after your ride."

Sixty miles southward in the Ukaka pass bloody bands of Sakuyu warriors played hide and seek among the rocks, chivvying the last fugitives of the army of Seyid, while behind them down the gorge, from cave villages of incalculable antiquity, the women crept out to rob the dead.

After tea the Consul looked in and invited Prudence and William over to play tennis.

"I'm afraid the balls are pretty well worn out. We've had some on order for two months. Confound this war."

When it was too dark to play, they dropped in on the Legges for cocktails, overstayed their time and ran back to the Legation to change for dinner. They tossed for first bath. Prudence won but William took it. He finished her bath salts and they were both very late for dinner. The Bishop, as had been feared, stayed the night. After dinner a log fire was lit in the hall; the evenings were cold in the hills. Sir Samson settled down to his knitting. Anstruther and Legge came in to make up the bridge table with Lady Courteney and the Bishop.

Legation bridge was played in a friendly way.

"I'll go one small heart."

"One no trump and I hope you remember what that means, partner."

"How you two do cheat."

"No."

"I say, can't you do better than that."

"What did you call?"

"A heart."

"Oh, well, I'll go two hearts."

"That's better."

"Damn. I've forgotten what a no-trump call means. I shall have to pass."

"No. I'm thinking of riding Vizier with a gag. He's getting heavy in the mouth."

"No. Then it's you to play, Bishop. It's hopeless using a steel bit out here."

"I say what a rotten dummy: is that the best you can do, partner?"

"Well, you wanted me to put you up. If you can make the syces water the bit before bridling it's all right."

Prudence played the gramophone to William, who lay on his back in front of the hearth smoking one of the very few remaining cigars. "Oh, dear," he said, "when will the new records come?"

"I say, Prudence, do come and look at the jumper. I'm starting on the sleeves."

"Envoy, you *are* clever."

"Well, it's very exciting. . . ."

"Pretty tune that. I say, is it my turn?"

"Percy, *do* attend to the game."

"Sorry, anyway I've taken the trick."

"It was ours already."

"No, I say was it? Put on the other side, Prudence —the one about Sex Appeal Sarah."

"*Percy*, it's you to play again. Now trump it this time."

"Sorry, no trumps left. Good that about '*start off with cocktails and end up with Eno's.*"

A few miles away at the French Legation, the minister and the first secretary were discussing the report of the British movements which was brought to them every evening by Sir Samson's butler.

"Bishop Goodchild is there again."

"*Clericalism.*"

"That is how they keep in touch with the town. He is an old fox, Sir Courteney."

"It is quite true that they have made no attempt to fortify the Legation. I have confirmed it."

"No doubt they have made their preparations in another quarter. Sir Courteney had been financing Seth."

"Without doubt."

"I think he is behind the fluctuations of the currency."

"They are using a new code. Here is a copy of

to-day's telegram. It means nothing to me. Yesterday there was one the same."

"*Kt to QR, CH*. No, that is not one of the ordinary codes. You must work on that all night. Pierre will help."

"I should not be surprised if Sir Samson were in the pay of the Italians."

"It is more than likely. The guard has been set?"

"They have orders to shoot at sight."

"Have the alarms been tested?"

"All are in order."

"Excellent. Then I will wish you good-night."

M. Ballon ascended the stairs to bed. In his room he first tested the steel shutters, then the lock of the door. Then he went across to the bed where his wife was already asleep, and examined the mosquito curtains. He squirted a little Flit round the windows and door, sprayed his throat with antiseptic and rapidly divested himself of all except his woollen cummerbund. He slipped on his pyjamas, examined the magazine of his revolver and laid it on the chair at his bedside; next to it he placed his watch, electric torch and a bottle of Vittel. He slipped another revolver under his pillow. He tiptoed to the window and called down softly: "Sergeant."

There was a click of heels in the darkness. "Excellence."

"Is all well?"

"All well, Excellence."

M. Ballon moved softly across to the electric switches and before extinguishing the main lamp switched on a small electric night-light which shed a faint blue radiance throughout the room. Then he cautiously lifted the mosquito curtain; flashed his torch round to make sure that there were no insects there and finally with a little grunt lay down to sleep. Before losing consciousness his hand felt, found and grasped a small carved nut which he kept under his bolster in the belief that it would bring him good luck.

Next morning by eleven o'clock the Bishop had been seen off the premises and the British Legation had settled down to its normal routine. Lady Courteney was in the potting shed; Sir Samson was in the bath; William, Legge and Anstruther were throwing poker dice in the chancery; Prudence was at work on the third chapter of the *Panorama of Life*. *Sex*, she wrote in round, irregular characters, *is the crying out of the Soul for Completion*. Presently she crossed out 'Soul' and substituted 'Spirit'; then she inserted 'of man'; changed it to 'manhood' and substituted 'humanity.' Then she took a new sheet of paper and copied out the whole sentence. Then she wrote a letter. *Sweet William. You looked so lovely at breakfast you know all half awake and I wanted to pinch you only didn't. Why did you go away at once. Saying 'decode.' You know you hadn't got to. I suppose it was the Bishop. Darling, he's gone now so come back and I will show you something lovely. The Panorama of Life, is rather a trial to-day. Very literary and abstruse but it won't get any LONGER. Oh, dear. Prudence. xxxx.* She folded this letter very carefully into a three-cornered hat, addressed it *The Honble. William Trench, Attaché Honoraire, près La Legation de Grande Bretagne* and sent it down to the chancery, with instructions to the boy to wait for an answer. William scribbled *So sorry darling desperately busy to-day see you at luncheon. Longing to read Panorama. W.* and threw four kings in two.

Prudence disconsolately abandoned her fountain pen and went out to watch her mother thinning the Michaelmas daisies.

Prudence and William had left an inflated indiarubber sea-serpent behind them in the bath-room. Sir Samson sat in the warm water engrossed with it. He switched it down the water and caught it in his toes; he made waves for it; he blew it along; he sat on it and let it shoot up suddenly to the surface between his thighs; he squeezed some of the air out of it and made bubbles. Chance treats of this kind made or marred the happiness of the Envoy's day. Soon he was rapt in daydream about the Pleistocene age, where among mists and vast, unpeopled crags, schools of deep-sea monsters splashed and sported; oh, happy fifth day of creation, thought the Envoy Extraordinary, oh, radiant infant sun, newly weaned from the breasts of darkness, oh, rich steam of the soggy continents, oh, jolly whales and sea-serpents frisking in new brine . . . Knocks at the door. William's voice outside.

"Walker's just ridden over, sir. Can you see him?"

Crude disillusionment.

Sir Samson returned abruptly to the twentieth century, to a stale and crowded world; to a bath grown tepid and an india-rubber toy. "Walker? Never heard of him."

"Yes, sir, you know him. The American secretary."

"Oh, yes, to be sure. Extraordinary time to call. What on earth does the fellow want? If he tries to borrow the tennis marker again, tell him it's broken."

"He's just got information about the war. Apparently there's been a decisive battle at last."

"Oh, well, I'm glad to hear that. Which side won, do you know?"

"He did tell me, but I've forgotten."

"Doesn't matter. I'll hear all about it from him. Tell him I'll be down directly. Give him a putter and let him play clock golf. And you'd better let them know he'll be staying to luncheon."

Half an hour later Sir Samson came downstairs and greeted Mr. Walker.

"My dear fellow, how good of you to come. I couldn't get out before; the morning is always rather busy here. I hope they've been looking after you properly. I think it's about time for a cocktail, William."

"The Minister thought that you'd like to have news of the battle. We got it on the wireless from Matodi. We tried to ring you up yesterday evening but couldn't get through."

"No, I always have the telephone disconnected after dinner. Must keep some part of the day for oneself, you know."

"Of course we haven't got any full details yet."

"Of course not. Still the war's over, William tells me, and I, for one, am glad. It's been on too long. Very upsetting to everything. Let me see, which of them won it?"

"Seth."

"Ah, yes, to be sure. Seth. I'm very glad. He was . . . now let me see . . . which was he?"

"He's the old Empress's son."

"Yes, yes, now I've got him. And the Empress, what's become of her."

"She died last year."

"I'm glad. It's very disagreeable for an old lady of her age to get involved in all these disturbances. And What's-his-name, you know the chap she was married to? He dead, too?"

"Seyid? There's no news of him. I think we may take it that we've seen the last of him."

"Pity. Nice fellow. Always liked him. By the bye, hadn't one of the fellows been to school in England?"

"Yes, that's Seth."

"Is it, by Jove? Then he speaks English?"

"Perfectly."

"That'll be one in the eye for Ballon, after all the trouble he took to learn Sakuyu. Here's William with the cocktails."

"I'm afraid they won't be up to much this morning, sir. We've run out of Peach Brandy."

"Well, never mind. It won't be long now before we get everything straight again. You must tell us all your news at luncheon. I hear Mrs. Schonbaum's mare is in foal. I'll be interested to see how she does We've never had any luck breeding. I don't believe the native syces understand bloodstock."

At the French Legation, also, news of Seth's victory had arrived. "Ah," said M. Ballon, "so the English and the Italians have triumphed. But the game is not over yet. Old Ballon is not outwitted yet.

There is a trick or two still to be won. Sir Samson must look to his laurels."

While at that moment the Envoy was saying: "Of course, it's all a question of the altitude. I've not heard of any one growing asparagus up here but I can't see why it shouldn't do. We get the most delicious green peas."

THREE

TWO days later news of the battle of Ukaka was published in Europe. It made very little impression on the million or so Londoners who glanced down the columns of their papers that evening.

"Any news in the paper to-night, dear?"

"No, dear, nothing of interest."

"Azania? That's part of Africa, ain't it?"

"Ask Lil, she was at school last."

"Lil, where's Azania?"

"I don't know, father."

"What do they teach you at school, I'd like to know."

"Only niggers."

"It came in a cross-word quite lately. *Independent native principality*. You would have it was Turkey."

"Azania? It sounds like a Cunarder to me."

"But, my dear, surely you remember that *madly* attractive blackamoor at Balliol."

"Run up and see if you can find the atlas, deary.

. . . Yes, where it always is, behind the stand in father's study."

"Things look quieter in East Africa. That Azanian business cleared up at last."

"Care to see the evening paper? There's nothing in it."

In Fleet Street, in the offices of the daily papers; "Randall, there might be a story in the Azanian cable. The new bloke was at Oxford. See what there is to it."

Mr. Randall typed: *His Majesty B.A. . . . ex-undergrad among the cannibals . . . scholar emperor's desperate bid for throne . . . barbaric splendour . . . conquering hordes . . . ivory . . . elephants . . . east meets west . . .*

"Sanders. Kill that Azanian story in the London edition."

"Anything in the paper this morning?"
"No, dear, nothing of interest."

Late in the afternoon Basil Seal read the news on the Imperial and Foreign page of *The Times* as he stopped at his club on the way to Lady Metroland's to cash a bad cheque.

For the last four days Basil had been on a racket. He had woken up an hour ago on the sofa of a totally strange flat. There was a gramophone playing. A lady in a dressing jacket sat in an armchair by the gas fire, eating sardines from the tin with a shoe horn. An unknown man in shirtsleeves was shaving, the glass propped on the chimney-piece.

The man had said: "Now you're awake you'd better go."

The woman: "Quite thought you were dead."

Basil: "I can't think why I'm here."

"I can't think why you don't go."

"Isn't London hell?"

"Did I have a hat?"

"That's what caused half the trouble."

"What trouble?"

"Oh, why don't you go?"

So Basil had gone down the stairs, which were covered in worn linoleum, and emerged through the side door of a shop into a busy street which proved to be the King's Road, Chelsea.

Incidents of this kind constantly occurred when Basil was on a racket.

At the club he found a very old member sitting before the fire with tea and hot muffins. He opened *The Times* and sat on the leather topped fender.

"You see the news from Azania?"

The elderly member was startled by the suddenness of his address. "No . . . no . . . I am afraid I can't really say that I have."

"Seth has won the war."

"Indeed . . . well, to tell you the truth I haven't been following the affair very closely."

"Very interesting."

"No doubt."

"I never thought things would turn out quite in this way, did you?"

"I can't say I've given the matter any thought."

"Well, fundamentally it is an issue between the Arabs and the christianised Sakuyu."

"I see."

"I think the mistake we made was to under-estimate the prestige of the dynasty."

"Oh."

"As a matter of fact, I've never been satisfied in my mind about the legitimacy of the old Empress."

"My dear young man, no doubt you have some particular interest in the affairs of this place. Pray understand that I know nothing at all about it and that I feel it is too late in the day for me to start improving my knowledge."

The old man shifted himself in his chair away from Basil's scrutiny and began reading his book.

A page came in with the message: "No reply from either of those numbers, sir."

"Don't you hate London?"

"Eh?"

"Don't you hate London?"

"No, I do not. Lived here all my life. Never get tired of it. Fellow who's tired of London is tired of life."

"Don't you believe it," said Basil.

"I'm going away for some time," he told the hall-porter as he left the club.

"Very good, sir. What shall I do about correspondence."

"Destroy it."

"Very good, sir." Mr. Seal was a puzzle to him. He never could forget Mr. Seal's father. He had been a member of the club. Such a different gentleman. So spick and span, never without silk hat and an orchid in his buttonhole. Chief Conservative Whip for twenty-five years. Who would have thought of him having a son like Mr. Seal? *Out of town until further notice. No letters forwarded* he entered against Basil's name in his ledger. Presently the old gentleman emerged from the smoking room.

"Arthur, is that young man a member here?"

"Mr. Seal, sir? Oh, yes, sir."

"What d'you say his name is?"

"Mr. Basil Seal."

"Basil Seal, eh. Basil Seal. Not Christopher Seal's son?"

"Yes, sir."

"Is he now? Poor old Seal. 'Pon my soul, what a sad thing. Who'd have thought of that? Seal of all people . . ." and he shuffled back into the smoking room, to the fire and his muffins, full of the comfort that glows in the hearts of old men when they contemplate the misfortunes of their contemporaries.

Basil walked across Piccadilly and up to Curzon Street. Lady Metroland was giving a cocktail party.

"Basil," she said, "you had no business to come. I particularly didn't ask you."

"I know. I only heard you had a party quite indirectly. What I've really come for is to see if my sister is here."

"Barbara? She may be. She said she was coming. How horrible you look."

"Dirty?"

"Yes."

"Not shaven?"

"No."

"Well, I've only just woken up. I haven't been home yet." He looked round the room. "All the same people. You don't make many new friends, Margot."

"I hear you've given up your constituency?"

"Yes, in a way. It wasn't worth while. I told the

P.M. I wasn't prepared to fight on the tariff issue. He had a chance to hold over the bill but the Outrage section were too strong so I threw in my hand. Besides I want to go abroad. I've been in England too long."

"Cocktail, sir?"

"No, bring me a Pernod and water, will you . . . there isn't any? Oh, well, whiskey. Bring it into the study. I want to go and telephone. I'll be back soon, Margot."

"God, what I feel about that young man," said Lady Metroland.

Two girls were talking about him.

"Such a lovely person."

"Where?"

"Just gone out."

"You don't mean Basil Seal?"

"Do I?"

"Horrible clothes, black hair over his face."

"Yes, tell me about him."

"My dear, he's enchanting . . . Barbara Sothill's brother, you know. He's been in hot water lately. He'd been adopted as candidate somewhere in the North. Father says he was bound to get in at the next election. Angela Lyne was paying his expenses. But they had trouble over something. You know how careful Angela is. I never thought Basil was really her tea. They never quite made sense I mean, did they? So that's all over."

"It's nice his being so dirty."

Other people discussed him.

"No, the truth about Basil is just that he's a *bore*. No one minds him being rude, but he's so *teaching*. I had him next to me at dinner once and he would talk all the time about Indian dialects. Well, what *was* one to say? And I asked afterwards and apparently he doesn't know anything about them either."

"He's done all kinds of odd things."

"Well, yes, and I think that's so boring too. Always in revolutions and murders and things I mean what is one to *say?* Poor Angela is *literally* off her head with him. I was there yesterday and she could talk of nothing else but the row he's had with his committee in his constituency. He does seem to have behaved rather oddly at the Conservative ball and then he and Alastair Trumpington and Peter Pastmaster and some others had a five day party up there and left a lot of bad cheques behind and had a motor accident and one of them got run in—you know what Basil's parties are. I mean that sort of thing is all right in London, but you know what provincial towns are. So what with one thing and another they've asked him to stand down. The trouble is that poor Angela still fancies him rather."

"What's going to happen to him?"

"I *know*. That's the *point*. Barbara says she won't do another thing for him."

Some one else was saying, "I've given up trying to be nice to Basil. He either cuts me or corners me with an interminable lecture about Asiatic politics. It's odd Margot having him here—particularly after the way he's always getting Peter involved."

Presently Basil came back from telephoning. He stood in the doorway, a glass of whiskey in one hand, looking insolently round the room, his head back, chin forward, shoulders rounded, dark hair over his forehead, contemptuous grey eyes over grey pouches, a proud rather childish mouth, a scar on one cheek.

"My word, he is a corker," remarked one of the girls.

His glance travelled round the room. "I'll tell you who I want to see, Margot. Is Rex Monomark here?"

"He's over there somewhere. But, Basil, I absolutely forbid you to tease him."

"I won't tease him."

Lord Monomark, owner of many newspapers, stood at the far end of the drawing room discussing diet. Round him in a haze of cigar smoke were ranged his ladies and gentlemen in attendance; three almost freakish beauties, austerely smart, their exquisite, irregular features eloquent of respect; two gross men of the world, wheezing appreciation; a dapper elderly secretary, with pink, bald pate and in his eyes that glazed, gin-fogged look that is common to sailors and the secretaries of the great, and comes from too short sleep.

"Two raw onions and a plate of oatmeal porridge," said Lord Monomark. "That's all I've taken for luncheon in the last eight months. And I feel two hundred per cent. better—physically, intellectually and ethically."

The group was slightly isolated from the rest of the party. It was very rarely that Lord Monomark consented to leave his own houses and appear as a guest. The few close friends whom he honoured in this way observed certain strict conventions in the matter; new people were not to be introduced to him except at his own command; politicians were to be kept at a distance; his cronies of the moment were to be invited with him; provision had to be made for whatever health system he happened to be following. In these conditions he liked now and then to appear in society—an undisguised Haroun al-Raschid among his townspeople—to survey the shadow-play of fashion, and occasionally to indulge the caprice of singling out one of these bodiless phantoms and translating her or him into the robust reality of his own world. His fellow guests, meanwhile, flitted in and out as though unconscious of his presence, avoiding any appearance of impinging on the integrity of this glittering circle.

"If I had my way," said Lord Monomark, "I'd make it compulsory throughout the country. I've had a notice drafted and sent round the office recommending the system. Half the fellows think nothing of spending one and six or two shillings on lunch every day—that's out of eight or nine pounds a week."

"Rex, you're wonderful."

"Read it out to Lady Everyman, Sanders."

"Lord Monomark wishes forcibly to bring to the attention of his staff the advantages to be derived from a carefully chosen diet . . ." Basil genially intruded himself into the party.

"Well, Rex, I thought I'd find you here. It's all stuff about that onion and porridge diet, you know. Griffenbach exploded that when I was in Vienna three years ago. But that's not really what I came to talk about."

"Oh, Seal, isn't it? I've not seen you for a long time. I remember now you wrote to me some time ago. What was it about, Sanders?"

"Afghanistan."

"Yes, of course. I turned it over to one of my editors to answer. I hope he explained."

Once, when Basil had been a young man of promise, Lord Monomark had considered taking him up and invited him for a cruise in the Mediterranean. Basil at first refused and then, after they had sailed, announced by wireless his intention of joining the yacht at Barcelona; Lord Monomark's party had waited there for two sultry days without hearing news and then sailed without him. When they next met in London Basil explained rather inadequately that he had found at the last minute he couldn't manage it after all. Countless incidents of this kind had contributed to Basil's present depreciated popularity.

"Look here, Rex," he said, "what I want to know is what you're going to do about Seth."

"Seth?" Lord Monomark turned an inquiring glance at Sanders. "What am I doing about Seth?"

"Seth?"

"It seems to me there's an extremely tricky political situation developing there. You've seen the news from Ukaka. It doesn't tell one a thing. I want to get some first-hand information. I'm probably sailing almost at once. It occurred to me that I might cover it for you in the *Excess*."

Towards the end of this speech, Lord Monomark's bewilderment was suddenly illumined. This was nothing unusual after all. It was simply some one after a job. "Oh," he said, "I'm afraid I don't interfere with the minor personnel of the paper. You'd better go and see one of the editors about it.

But I don't think you'll find him anxious to take on new staff at the moment."

"I'll tell them you sent me."

"No, no, I never interfere. You must just approach them through the normal channels."

"All right. I'll come up and see you after I've fixed it up. Oh, and I'll send you Griffenbach's report on the onion and porridge diet if I can find it. There's my sister. I've got to go and talk to her now, I'm afraid. See you before I sail."

Barbara Sothill no longer regarded her brother with the hero-worship which had coloured the first twenty years of her life.

"Basil," she said, "what on earth have you been doing? I was lunching at mother's to-day and she was wild about you. She's got one of her dinner parties and you promised to be in. She said you hadn't been home all night and she didn't know whether to get another man or not."

"I was on a racket. We began at Lottie Crump's. I rather forget what happened except that Allan got beaten up by some chaps."

"And she's just heard about the committee."

"Oh, *that*. I meant to give up the constituency anyhow. It's no catch being in the Commons now. I'm thinking of going to Azania."

"Oh, were you—and what'll you do there?"

"Well, Rex Monomark wants me to represent the

Excess but I think as a matter of fact I shall be better off if I keep a perfectly free hand. The only thing is I shall need some money. D'you think our mother will fork out five hundred pounds?"

"I'm sure she won't."

"Well, some one'll have to. To tell you the truth I can't very well stay on in England at the moment. Things have got into rather a crisis. I suppose you wouldn't like to give me some money?"

"Oh, Basil, what's the good? You know I can't do it except by getting it from Freddy and he was furious last time."

"I can't think why. He's got packets."

"Yes, but you might try and be a little polite to him sometimes—just in public, I mean."

"Oh, of course if he thinks that by lending me a few pounds he's setting himself up for life as a good fellow . . ."

In the days when Sir Christopher was Chief Whip, Lady Seal had entertained frequently and with relish. Now, in her widowhood, with Barbara successfully married and her sons dispersed, she limited herself to four or five dinner parties every year. There was nothing elastic or informal about these occasions. Lady Metroland was a comparatively rich woman and it was her habit when she was tired to say casually to her butler at cocktail time, "I am not going out to-night. There will be about twenty to dinner," and then to sit down to the telephone and invite her guests, saying to each, "Oh, but you *must* chuck them to-night. I'm all alone and feeling like death." Not so Lady Seal, who despatched engraved cards of invitation a month in advance, supplied defections from a secondary. list one week later, fidgeted with place cards and a leather board as soon as the acceptances began to arrive, borrowed her sister's chef and her daughter's footmen, and on the morning of the party exhausted herself utterly by trotting all over her house in Lowndes Square arranging flowers. Then at half past five when she was satisfied that all was ready she would retire to bed and doze for two hours in her darkened room; her maid would call her with cachet Farine and clear China tea; a touch of ammonia in the bath; a touch of rouge on the cheeks; lavender water behind the ears; half an hour before the glass, fiddling with her jewel case while her hair was being done; final conference with the butler; then a happy smile in the drawing room for all who were less than twenty minutes late. The menu always included lobster cream, saddle of mutton and brown-bread ice and there were silver gilt dishes ranged down the table holding a special kind of bon-bon supplied to Lady Seal for twenty years by a little French shop whose name she would sometimes coyly disclose.

Basil arrived among the first guests. There was carpet on the steps; the doors opened with unusual promptness; the hall seemed full of chrysanthemums and footmen.

"Hullo, her ladyship got a party? I forgot all about it. I'd better change."

"Frank couldn't find your evening clothes, Mr. Basil. I don't think you can have brought them back last time you went away. I don't think her Ladyship is expecting you to dinner."

"Any one asked for me?"

"There *were* two persons, sir."

"Duns?"

"I couldn't say, sir. I told them that we had no information about your whereabouts."

"Quite right."

"Mrs. Lyne rang up fifteen times, sir. She left no message."

"If any one else wants me, tell them I've gone to Azania."

"Sir?"

"Azania."

"Abroad?"

"Yes, if you like."

"Excuse me, Mr. Basil . . ."

The Duke and Duchess of Stayle had arrived. The Duchess said, "So you are not dining with us to-night. You young men are all so busy nowadays.

No time for going out. I hear things are going very well up in your constituency." She was often behind-hand with her news. As they went up the Duke said, "Clever young fellow that. Wonder if he'll ever come to anything though."

Basil went into the dark little study next to the front door and rang up the Trumpingtons.

"Sonia, are you and Alastair doing anything to-night?"

"We're at home. Basil, what have you been doing to Alastair. I'm furious with you. I think he's going to die."

"We had rather a racket. Shall I come to dinner?"

"Yes, do. We're in bed."

He drove to Montagu Square and was shown up to their room. They lay in a vast, low bed, with a backgammon board between them. Each had a separate telephone, on the tables at the side, and by the telephone a goblet of 'black velvet.' A bull terrier and a chow flirted on their feet. There were other people in the room, one playing the gramophone, one reading, one trying Sonia's face things at the dressing table. Sonia said, "It's such a waste not going out after dark. We have to stay in all day because of duns."

Alastair said, "We can't have dinner with these infernal dogs all over the place."

Sonia: "You're a cheerful chap to be in bed with,

aren't you?" and to the dog, "Was oo called infernal woggie by owid man? Oh, God, he's made a mess again."

Alastair: "Are those chaps staying to dinner?"

"We asked one."

"Which?"

"Basil."

"Don't mind him, but all those others."

"I do hope not."

They said: "Afraid we'll have to. It's so late to go anywhere else."

Basil: "How dirty the bed is, Sonia."

"I know. It's Alastair's dog. Anyway you're a nice one to talk about dirt."

"Isn't London hell."

Alastair: "I don't anyway see why those chaps shouldn't have dinner downstairs."

They said: "It *would* be more comfortable."

"What are their names?"

"One we picked up last night. The other has been staying here for days."

"It's not only the expense I mind. They're boring."

They said: "We wouldn't stay a moment if we had anywhere else to go."

"Ring for dinner, sweet. I forget what there is, but I know it's rather good. I ordered it myself."

There was whitebait, grilled kidneys and toasted

cheese. Basil sat between them on the bed and they ate from their knees. Sonia threw a kidney to the dogs and they began a fight.

Alastair: "It's no good. I can't eat anything."

Sonia's maid brought in the trays. She asked her: "How are the gentlemen getting on downstairs?"

"They asked for champagne."

"I suppose they'd better have it. It's very bad."

Alastair: "It's very good."

"Well, it tasted awful to me. Basil, sweety, what's your news."

"I'm going to Azania."

"Can't say I know much about that. Is it far?"

"Yes."

"Fun?"

"Yes."

"Oh, Alastair, why not us too?"

"Hell, now those dogs have upset everything again."

"How pompous you're being."

After dinner they all played happy families. "Have you got Miss Chipps, the Carpenter's daughter."

"*Not at home* but have *you* got Mr. Chipps the Carpenter? *Thank you and* Mrs. Chipps the Carpenter's wife. *Thank you* and Basil have *you* got Miss Chipps? *Thank you.* That's the Chipps family."

Basil left early so as to see his mother before she went to bed.

Sonia said, "Good-bye, darling. Write to me from where ever it is. Only I don't expect we'll be living here much longer."

One of the young men said: "Could you lend me a fiver. I've a date at the Café de Paris."

"No, you'd better ask Sonia."

"But it's so boring. I'm *always* borrowing money from *her*."

In the course of the evening Lady Seal had found time to touch her old friend Sir Joseph Mannering on the sleeve and say, "Don't go at once, Jo. I'd like to talk to you afterwards." As the last guests left he came across to the fireplace, hands behind his coat tails and on his face an expression of wisdom, discretion, sympathy, experience and contentment. He was a self-assured old booby who in the easy and dignified rôle of family friend was invoked to aggravate most of the awkward situations that occurred in the lives of his circle.

"A delightful evening, Cynthia, typically delightful. I sometimes think that yours is the only house in London nowadays where I can be sure both of the claret and the company. But you wanted to consult me. Not, I hope, that little trouble of Barbara's?"

"No, it's nothing about Barbara. What's the child been doing?"

"Nothing, nothing. It was just some idle bit of gossip I heard. I'm glad it isn't worrying you. I suppose Basil's been up to some mischief again."

"Exactly, Jo. I'm at my wits' end with the boy. But what was it about Barbara?"

"Come, come, we can't fuss about too many things. I *did* hear Basil had been up to something. Of course there's plenty of good in the boy. It only wants bringing out."

"I sometimes doubt it."

"Now, Cynthia, you're overwrought. Tell me exactly what has been happening."

It took Lady Seal some time to deliver herself of the tale of Basil's misdemeanours. ". . . if his father were alive . . . spent all the money his Aunt left him on that idiotic expedition to Afghanistan . . . give him a very handsome allowance . . . all and more than all that I can afford . . . paid his debts again and again . . . no gratitude . . . no self-control . . . no longer a child, twenty-eight this year . . . his father . . . the post kind Sir William secured him in the bank in Brazil . . . great opening and such interesting work . . . never went to the office once . . . never know where or whom he is with . . . most undesirable friends, Sonia Trumpington, Peter Pastmaster, all sorts of people whose names I've never even heard . . . **of course** I couldn't **really** *approve* of his going about so much with Mrs. Lyne—though I daresay there was nothing *wrong* in it—but at least I hoped she might steady him a little . . . stand for Parliament . . . his father . . . behaved in the most irresponsible way in the heart of his constituency . . . Prime Minister . . . Central Office . . . Sonia Trumpington threw it at the mayor . . . Conservative ball . . . one of them actually arrested . . . come to the end, Jo . . . I've made up my mind. I won't do another thing for him—it's not fair on Tony that I should spend all the money on Basil that should go to them equally . . . marry and settle down . . . if his father were alive . . . it isn't even as though he were the kind of man who would do in Kenya," she concluded hopelessly.

Throughout the narration Sir Joseph maintained his air of wisdom, discretion, sympathy, experience and contentment; at suitable moments he nodded and uttered little grunts of comprehension. At length he said: "My dear Cynthia. I had no idea it was as bad as that. What a terrible time you have have had and how brave you have been. But you mustn't let yourself worry. I daresay even this disagreeable incident may turn to good. It may very likely be the turning point in the boy's life . . .

Learned his lesson. I shouldn't wonder if the reason he hasn't come home is that he's ashamed to face you. I tell you what, I think I'd better have a talk to him. Send him round as soon as you get into touch with him. I'll take him to lunch at the club. He'll probably take advice from a man he might resent from a woman. Didn't he begin reading for the bar once? Well, let's set him going at that. Keep him at home. Don't give him enough money to go about. Let him bring his friends here. Then he'll only be able to have friends he's willing to introduce to you. We'll try and get him into a different set. He didn't go to any dances all last summer I remember you telling me. Heaps of jolly girls coming out he hasn't had the chance of meeting yet. Keep him to his work. The boy's got brains, bound to find it interesting. Then when you're convinced he's steadied up a bit, let him have chambers of his own in one of the Inns of Court. Let him feel you trust him. I'm sure he'll respond . . ."

For nearly half an hour they planned Basil's future, punctually rewarding each stage of his moral recuperation. Presently Lady Seal said: "Oh, Jo, what a help you are. I don't know what I should do without you."

"Dear Cynthia, it is one of the privileges of maturity to bring new strength and beauty to old friendships."

"I shan't forget how wonderful you've been to-night, Jo."

The old boy bounced back in his taxicab to St. James and Lady Seal slowly ascended the stairs to her room; both warm at heart and aglow from their fire-lit nursery game of "let's pretend." She sat before her bedroom fire, slipped off her dress and rang the bell beside the chimney-piece.

"I'll have my milk now, Bradshawe, and then go straight to bed."

The maid lifted the jug from the fender where it had been keeping warm and deftly held back the skin with a silver apostle-spoon as she poured the hot milk into a glass. Then she brought the jewel case and held it while wearily, one by one, the rings, bracelet, necklace and ear-rings were slipped off and tumbled in. Then she began taking the pins from her mistress' hair. Lady Seal held the glass in both hands and sipped.

"Don't trouble to brush it very long to-night, I'm tired."

"I hope the party was a success, my lady."

"I suppose so. Yes, I'm sure it was. Captain Cruttwell is very silly, but it was kind of him to come at all at such short notice."

"It's the first time Her Grace's youngest daughter has been to dinner?"

"Yes, I think it is. The child looked very well, I thought, and talked all the time."

Lady Seal sipped the hot milk, her thoughts still wandering innocently in the soft places where Sir Joseph had set them. She saw Basil hurrying to work in the morning, by bus at first, later—when he had proved his sincerity—he should have a two-seater car; he would be soberly but smartly dressed and carry some kind of business-like attaché case or leather satchel with him. He would generally have papers to go through before changing for dinner. They would dine together and afterwards often go out to the theatre or cinema. He would eat with good appetite, having lunched quickly and economically at some place near his work. Quite often she would entertain for him, small young peoples' parties of six or eight—intelligent, presentable men of his own age, pretty, well-bred girls. During the season he would go to two dances a week, and leave them early . . . "Bradshawe, where is the spoon? It's forming a skin again" . . . Later she went to tea with him in his rooms in Lincolns Inn. He lifted a pile of books from the armchair before she sat down. 'I've brought you a looking glass.' 'Oh, Mother, how sweet of you.' 'I saw it in Helena's shop this morning and thought it just the thing to go over your fire. It will lighten the room. It's got a piece chipped off in one place but it is a good one.' 'I *must* try it at once.' 'It's down in the car, dear. Tell Andrews to bring it up' . . .

A knock at the door.

"What can they want at this time? See who it is, Bradshawe."

"Mr. Basil, my lady."

"Oh, dear."

Basil came in, so unlike the barrister of her dream that it required an effort to recognise him.

"I'll ring for you in a few minutes, Bradshawe . . . Basil, I really can't talk to you now. I have a great deal to say and I am very tired. Where have you been?"

"Different places."

"You might have let me know. I expected you at dinner."

"Had to go and dine with Alastair and Sonia. Was the party a success?"

"Yes, I think so, so far as can be expected. I had to ask poor Toby Cruttwell. Who else *was* there I *could* ask at the last moment. I do wish you wouldn't fiddle with things. Shut the jewel case like a good boy."

"By the way, I've given up politics; did you know."

"Yes, I am most distressed about the whole business—vexed and distressed, but I can't discuss it now.

I'm so tired: It's all arranged. You are to lunch with
Sir Joseph Mannering at his club and he will explain everything. You are to meet some new girls
and later have tea—I mean rooms—in Lincoln's Inn.
You'll like that, won't you, dear? Only you mustn't
ask about it now."

"What I came to say is that I'm just off to Azania."

"No, no, dear boy. You are to lunch with Jo at
The Travellers."

"And I shall need some money."

"It's all decided."

"You see I'm fed up with London and English
politics. I want to get away. Azania is the obvious
place. I had the Emperor to lunch once at Oxford.
Amusing chap. The thing is this," said Basil, scratching in his pipe with a delicate pair of gold manicure
scissors from the dressing table. "Every year or so
there's *one* place on the globe worth going to where
things are happening. The secret is to find out where
and be on the spot in time."

"Basil, dear, *not* with the scissors."

"History doesn't happen everywhere at once.
Azania is going to be terrific. Anyway I'm off there
to-morrow. Flying to Marseilles and catching the
Messageries ship. Only I must raise at least five
hundred before I start. Barbara wanted to give it to
me but I thought the simplest thing was to compound for my year's allowance. There may be a few

debts that'll want settling while I'm away. I thought of giving you a power of attorney . . ."

"Dear boy, you are talking nonsense. When you've had luncheon with Sir Joseph you'll understand. We'll get into touch with him first thing in the morning. Meanwhile run along and get a good night's sleep. You aren't looking at all well, you know."

"I must have at least three hundred."

"There. I've rung for Bradshawe. You'll forget all about this place in the morning. Good-night, darling boy. The servants have gone up. Don't leave the lights burning downstairs, will you?"

So Lady Seal undressed and sank at last luxuriously into bed. Bradshawe softly paddled round the room performing the last offices; she picked up the evening gown, the underclothes, and the stockings, and carried them outside to her workroom; she straightened the things on the dressing table, shut the drawers, wiped the points of the nail scissors with a wad of cotton; she opened the windows four inches at the top, banked up the fire with a shovelful of small coal, hitched on the wire guard, set a bottle of Vichy water and a glass on the chamber cupboard beside the bed and stood at the door one hand holding the milk tray, the other on the electric switch.

"Is that everything for the night, my lady?"

"That's all, Bradshawe. I'll ring in the morning. Good-night."

"Good-night, my lady."

Basil went back to the telephone and called Mrs. Lyne. A soft, slightly impatient voice answered him. "Yes, who is it?"

"Basil."

A pause.

"Hullo, are you there, Angela? Basil speaking."

"Yes, darling, I heard. Only I didn't quite know what to say . . . I've just got in . . . such a dull evening . . . I rang you up to-day . . . couldn't get on to you."

"How odd you sound."

"Well, yes . . . why did you ring up? It's late."

"I'm coming round to see you."

"My dear, you can't possibly."

"I was going to say good-bye—I'm going away for some time."

"Yes, I suppose that's a good thing."

"Well, don't you want me to come?"

"You'll have to be sweet to me. You see I've been in rather a muddle lately. You will be sweet, darling, won't you? I don't think I could bear it if you weren't."

And later, as they lay on their backs smoking, her foot just touching his under the sheets, Angela interrupted him to say: "How would it be if, just for a little, we didn't talk about this island? . . . I'm going to find things different when you've gone."

"I'm mad for it."

"I know," said Angela. "I'm not kidding myself."

"You're a grand girl."

"It's time you went away . . . shall I tell you something?"

"What?"

"I'm going to give you some money."

"Well, that is nice."

"You see, when you rang up I knew that was what you wanted. And you've been sweet to-night really though you were boring about that island. So I thought that just for to-night I'd like to have you not asking for money. Before I've enjoyed making it awkward for you. Did you know? Well, I had to have *some* fun, hadn't I, and I think I used to embarrass even you sometimes. And I used to watch you steering the conversation round. I knew that anxious look in your eye so well . . . I had to have something to cheer me up all these weeks, hadn't I. You don't do much for a girl. But to-night I thought it would be a treat just to let you be nice and no bother and I've enjoyed myself. I made out a cheque before you came . . . on the dressing table. It's for rather a lot."

"You're a grand girl."

"When d'you start?"

"To-morrow."

"I'll miss you. Have a good time."

Next morning at twenty to ten Lady Seal rang her bell. Bradshawe drew the curtains and shut the windows, brought in the orange juice, the letters and the daily papers.

"Thank you, Bradshawe. I had a very good night. I only woke up once and then was asleep again almost directly. Is it raining?"

"I'm afraid so, my lady."

"I shall want to see Mr. Basil before he goes out."

"Mr. Basil has gone already."

"So early. Did he say where?"

"He did say, my lady, but I am not sure of the name. Somewhere in Africa."

"How very provoking. I know there was something I wanted him to do to-day."

At eleven o'clock a box of flowers arrived from Sir Joseph Mannering and at twelve Lady Seal attended a committee meeting; it was four days before she discovered the loss of her emerald bracelet and by that time Basil was on the sea.

Croydon, le Bourget, Lyons, Marseilles; colourless, gusty weather, cloud-spray dripping and trickling on the windows; late in the afternoon, stillness from the roar of the propellers; sodden turf; the road from the aerodrome to the harbour heavily scented with damp shrub; wind-swept sheds on the quay; an Annamite boy swabbing the decks; a surly steward, the ship does not sail until to-morrow, the commissaire knows of the allotment of the cabins, he is on shore, it is not known when he will return, there is nowhere to leave the baggage, the baggage room is shut and the commissaire has the key, any one might take it if it were left on deck—twenty francs—the luggage could go in one of the cabins, it will be safe there, the steward has the key, he will see to it. Dinner at the restaurant de Verdun. Basil alone with a bottle of fine Burgundy.

Next afternoon they sailed. She was an ugly old ship snatched from Germany after the war as part of the reparation; at most hours of the day two little men in alpaca coats played a fiddle and piano in the deck bar; luncheon at twelve, dinner at seven; red Algerian wine; shrivelled, blotchy dessert; a small saloon full of children; a smoking-room full of French officials and planters playing cards. The big ships do not stop at Matodi. Basil at table talking excellent French ceaselessly, in the evenings paying attention to a woman of mixed blood from Madagascar, getting bored with her and with the ship, sitting sulkily at meals with a book, complaining to the captain about the inadequacy of the wireless bulletins, lying alone in his bunk for hours at a time.

smoking cheroots and gazing blankly at the pipes on the ceiling.

At Port Said he sent lewd postcards to Sonia, disposed of his mother's bracelet at a fifth of its value to an Indian jeweller, made friends with a Welsh engineer in the bar of the Eastern Exchange, got drunk with him, fought him, to the embarrassment of the Egyptian policeman, and returned to the ship next morning a few minutes before the companion way was raised, much refreshed by his racket.

A breathless day in the canal; the woman from Madagascar exhausted with invitation. The Red Sea, the third class passengers limp as corpses on the lower deck; fiddle and piano indefatigable; dirty ice swimming in the dregs of lemon juice; Basil in his bunk sullenly consuming cheroots undeterred by the distress of his cabin-companion. Djibouti; port holes closed to keep out the dust, coolies jogging up the planks with baskets of coal; contemptuous savages in the streets scraping their teeth with twigs; an Abyssinian noblewoman in a green veil shopping at the French Emporium; an ill-intentioned black monkey in an acacia tree near the post office. Basil took up with a Dutch South African; they dined on the pavement of the hotel and drove later in a horse-cab to the Somali quarter where in a lamplit mud hut Basil began to talk of the monetary systems of the world until the Boer fell asleep on a couch of plaited hide and the four dancing girls huddled together in the corner like chimpanzees and chattered resentfully among themselves.

The ship was sailing for Azania at midnight. She lay far out in the bay, three lines of lights reflected in the still water; the sound of fiddle and piano was borne through the darkness, harshly broken by her siren intermittently warning passengers to embark. Basil sat in the stern of the little boat, one hand trailing in the sea; half way to the ship the boatman shipped their oars and tried to sell him a basket of limes; they argued for a little in broken French, then splashed on irregularly towards the liner; an oil lantern bobbed in the bows. Basil climbed up the companion way and went below; his companion was asleep and turned over angrily as the light went up; the port hole had been shut all day and the air was gross; Basil lit a cheroot and lay for some time reading. Presently the old ship began to vibrate and later, as she drew clear of the bay, to pitch very slightly in the Indian Ocean. Basil turned out the light and lay happily smoking in the darkness.

In London Lady Metroland was giving a party. Sonia said: "No one asks us to parties now except Margot. Perhaps there aren't any others."

"The boring thing about parties is that it's far too much effort to meet new people, and if it's just all the ordinary people one knows already one might just as well stay at home and ring them up instead of having all the business of remembering the right day."

"I wonder why Basil isn't here? I thought he was bound to be."

"Didn't he go abroad?"

"I don't think so. Don't you remember, he had dinner with us the other evening."

"Did he? When?"

"Darling, how *can* I remember that? . . . there's Angela—she'll know."

"Angela, has Basil gone away?"

"Yes, somewhere quite extraordinary."

"My dear, is that rather heaven for you?"

"Well, in a way . . ."

Basil was awakened by the clank and rattle of steel cable as the anchor was lowered. He went up on deck in pyjamas. The whole sky was aflame with green and silver dawn. Half covered figures of other passengers sprawled asleep on benches and chairs. The sailors paddled between them on bare feet, clearing the hatches; a junior officer on the bridge shouting orders to the men at the winch. Two lighters were already alongside preparing to take off cargo. A dozen small boats clustered round them, loaded with fruit.

Quarter of a mile distant lay the low sea front of Matodi; the minaret, the Portuguese ramparts, the mission church, a few warehouses taller than the rest, the Grand Hotel de l'Empereur Amurath stood out from the white and dun cluster of roofs; behind and on either side stretched the meadowland and green plantations of the Azanian coast line, groves of tufted palm at the water's edge. Beyond and still obscured by mist rose the great crests of the Sakuyu mountains, the Ukaka pass and the road to Debra-Dowa.

The purser joined Basil at the rail.

"You disembark here, Mr. Seal, do you not?"

"Yes."

"You are the only passenger. We sail again at noon."

"I shall be ready to go ashore as soon as I am dressed."

"You are making a long stay in Azania?"

"Possibly."

"On business? I have heard it is an interesting country."

But for once Basil was disinclined to be instructive. "Purely for pleasure," he said. Then he went below, dressed and fastened his bags. His cabin companion looked at his watch, scowled and turned his face to the wall; later he missed his shaving soap, bedroom slippers and the fine topee he had bought a few days earlier at Port Said.

FOUR

THE Matodi terminus of the Grand Chemin de Fer d'Azanie lay half a mile inland from the town. A broad avenue led to it, red earth scarred by deep ruts and pot holes; on either side grew irregular lines of acacia trees. Between the trees were strings of different coloured flags. A gang of convicts, chained neck to neck, were struggling to shift a rusty motor car which lay on its side blocking the road. It had come to grief there six months previously, having been driven recklessly into some cattle by an Arab driver. He was now doing time in prison in default of damages. White ants had devoured the tyres; various pieces of mechanism had been removed from time to time to repair other engines. A Sakuyu family had set up house in the back, enclosing the space between the wheels with an intricate structure of rags, tin, mud and grass.

That was in the good times when the Emperor was in the hills. Now he was back again and the town was overrun with soldiers and government officials. It was by his orders that this motor car was being removed. Everything had been like that for three weeks, bustle everywhere, proclamations posted up on every wall, troops drilling, buglings, hangings, the whole town kept awake all day; in the Arab **Club** feeling ran high against the new régime.

Mahmud el Khali bin Sai'ud, frail descendant **of** the oldest family in Matodi, sat among his kinsmen, moodily browsing over his lapful of khat. The sunlight streamed in through the lattice shutters, throwing a diaper of light over the worn carpets and divans; two of the amber mouthpieces of the hubble-bubble were missing; the rocking chair in the corner was no longer safe, the veneer was splitting and peeling off the rosewood table. These poor remnants were all that remained of the decent people of Matodi; the fine cavaliers had been scattered and cut down in battle. Here were six old men and two dissipated youngsters, one of whom was liable to fits of epilepsy. There was no room for a gentleman in Matodi nowadays, they remarked. You could not recount an anecdote in the streets or pause on the water front to discuss with full propriety the sale of land or the pedigree of a stallion, but you were jostled against the wall by black men or Indians, dirty fellows with foreskins; unbelievers, descendants of slaves; judges from up country, upstarts, jacks-in-office giving decisions against you in the courts . . . Jews foreclosing on mortgages . . . taxation . . . vulgar display . . . no respect of leisure, hanging up wretched little flags everywhere, clearing up the streets, moving derelict motor **cars** while their owners were not in a position to defend them. To-day there was an ordinance forbidding the use of Arab dress. Were they, at their time of life, to start decking themselves out in coat and trousers and topee like a lot of half-caste bank clerks? . . . besides, the prices tailors charged . . . it was a put-up job . . . you might as well be in a British colony.

Meanwhile with much overseeing and shouting, and banging of behinds, preparations were in progress on the route to the railway station; the first train since the troubles was due to leave that afternoon.

It had taken a long time to get a train together. On the eve of the battle of Ukaka the station master and all the more responsible members of his staff had left for the mainland. In the week that followed Seth's victory they had returned one by one with various explanations of their absence. Then there had been the tedious business of repairing the line which both armies had ruined at several places; They had had to collect wood fuel for the engine and wire for the telegraph lines. This had been the longest delay, for no sooner was it procured from the mainland than it was stolen by General Connolly's disbanded soldiers to decorate the arms and legs of their women. Finally when everything had been prepared it was decided to delay the train a few days until the arrival of the mail ship from Europe. It thus happened that Basil Seal's arrival in Matodi coincided with the date fixed for Seth's triumphal return to Debra-Dowa.

Arrangements for his departure had been made with great care by the Emperor himself, and the chief features embodied in a proclamation in Sakuyu, Arabic and French, which was posted prominently among the many pronouncements which heralded the advent of Progress and the New Age.

ORDER FOR THE DAY OF THE EMPEROR'S DEPARTURE

(1) *The Emperor will proceed to Matodi railway station at 14.30 here (8.30 Mohammedan time). He will be attended by his personal suite, the Commander-in-Chief and the General Staff. The guard of honour will be composed of the first battalion of the Imperial Life Guards. Full dress uniform (boots for officers), will be worn by all ranks. Civilian gentlemen will wear jacket and orders. Ball ammunition will not be issued to the troops.*

(2) *The Emperor will be received at the foot of the station steps by the station master who will conduct him to his carriage. The public will not be admitted to the platforms, or to any of the station buildings with the exception of the following, in the following order of precedence: Consular repre-*

sentatives of foreign powers, the Nestorian Metro-
politan of Matodi, the Vicar Apostolic, the Mor-
mon elder, officers of H.I.M. forces, directors of the
Grand Chemin de Fer d'Azanie; peers of the Azan-
ian Empire, representatives of the Press. No person,
irrespective of rank, will be admitted to the platform
improperly dressed or under the influence of al-
cohol.

(3) The public will be permitted to line the
route to the station. The police will prevent the dis-
charge of firearms by the public.

(4) The sale of alcoholic liquor is forbidden
from midnight until the departure of the Imperial
train.

(5) One coach will be available for the use of the
unofficial travellers to Debra-Dowa. Applications
should be made to the station master. No passenger
will be admitted to the platform after 14.0.

(6) Any infringement of the foregoing regula-
tions renders the offender liable to a penalty not
exceeding ten years imprisonment, or confiscation
of property and loss of rights, or both.

Basil read this at the railway station, where he
drove in a horse cab as soon as he landed. He went
to the booking office and bought a first-class ticket
to Debra-Dowa. It cost two hundred rupees.

"Will you please reserve me a seat on this afternoon's train?"

"That is impossible. There is only one carriage. The places have been booked many days."

"When is the next train?"

"Who can say? Perhaps next week. The engine must come back from Debra-Dowa. The others are broken and the mechanic is busy on the tank."

"I must speak to the station master."

"I am the station master."

"Well, listen, it is very urgent that I go to Debra-Dowa to-day."

"You should have made your arrangements sooner. You must understand, monsieur, that you are no longer in Europe."

As Basil turned to go, a small man who had been sitting fanning himself on a heap of packing cases, scrambled down and came across the booking hall towards him. He was dressed in alpaca and skull cap; he had a cheerful, round, greasy, yellowish face and 'Charlie Chaplin' moustache.

" 'Ullo, Englishmans, you want something?"

"I want to go to Debra-Dowa."

"O.K. I fix it."

"That's very nice of you."

"Honour to fix it. You know who I am? Look here." He handed Basil a card on which was printed: *M. Krikor Youkoumian, Grande Hotel et Bar*

Amurath Matodi, grande Hotel Café Epicerie, et Bibliothèque Empereur Seyid Debra-Dowa. Touts les renseignements. The name Seyid had been obliterated in purple ink and *Seth* substituted for it.

"You keep that," said Mr. Youkoumian. "You come to Debra-Dowa. You come to me. I fix everything. What's your name, sir?"

"Seal."

"Well, look, Mr. Seal. You want to come Debra-Dowa. I got two seats. You pay me two hundred rupees, I put Mme. Youkoumian in the mule truck. Ows that, eh?"

"I'm not going to pay anything like that, I'm afraid."

"Now, listen, Mr. Seal. I fix it for you. You don't know this country. Stinking place. You miss this train, you stay in Matodi one, two, three, perhaps six weeks. How much you pay then? I like Englishmens. They are my favourite gentlemen. Look, you give me hundred and fifty rupees I put Mme. Youkoumian with the mules. You don't understand what that will be like. They are the General's mules. Very savage stinking animals. All day they will stamp at her. No air in the truck. 'Orrible, unhealthy place. Very like she die or is kicked. She is good wife, work hard, very loving. If you are not Englishmans I would not put Mme. Youkoumian with the mules for less than five hundred. I fix it for you O.K.?"

"O.K." said Basil. "You know, you seem to me a good chap."

"Look, how about you give me money now. Then I take you to my café. Dirty little place, not like London. But you see. I got fine brandy. Very fresh, I make him myself Sunday."

Basil and Mr. Youkoumian took their seats in the train at two o'clock and settled down to wait for the arrival of the Imperial party. There were six other occupants of the carriage—a Greek who offered them oranges and soon fell asleep, four Indians who discussed their racial grievances in an eager undertone, and an Azanian nobleman with his wife who shared a large pie of spiced mutton, lifting the slices between pieces of newspaper and eating silently and almost continuously throughout the afternoon. Mr. Youkoumian's personal luggage was very small but he had several crates of merchandise for his Debra-Dowa establishment: by a distribution of minute tips he had managed to get these into the mail van. Mme. Youkoumian squatted disconsolately in a corner of the van clutching a little jar of preserved cherries which her husband had given her to compensate for the change of accommodation; a few feet from her in the darkness came occasional nervous brays and whinnies and a continuous fretful stamping of the straw.

In spite of Seth's proclamation the police were

129

at some difficulty in keeping the platform clear of
the public; twenty or thirty of them prosecuted a
vigorous defence with long bamboo staves, whack-
ing the woolly heads as they appeared above the corrugated iron fence. Even so, large numbers of un-
authorised spectators were established out of reach
on the station roof. The Indian who supplied pictures of local colour to an International Press
Agency was busily taking snapshots of the notables.
These had not observed the Emperor's instructions
to the letter. The Nestorian Metropolitan swayed
on the arm of his chaplain, unquestionably drunk;
the representative of the *Courier d'Azanie* wore an
open shirt, a battered topee, crumpled white trousers and canvas shoes; the Levantine shipping agent
who acted as vice-consul for Great Britain, the
Netherlands, Sweden, Portugal and Latvia had put
on a light waterproof over his pyjamas and come
to the function straight from bed; the Eurasian bank
manager who acted as vice-consul for Soviet Russia,
France, and Italy, was still asleep; the general merchant of inscrutable ancestry who represented the
other great powers, was at the moment employed on
the mainland making final arrangements for the
trans-shipment from Alexandria of a long-awaited
consignment of hashish. Some Azanian dignitaries
in national costume, sat in a row on the carpets their
slaves had spread for them, placidly scratching the

soles of their bare feet and conversing intermittently on questions of sex. The station master's livestock—two goats and a few small turkeys—had been expelled in honour of the occasion from their normal quarters in the ladies' waiting room, and wandered at will about the platform gobbling at fragments of refuse.

It was more than an hour after the appointed time when the drums and fifes of the Imperial guard announced the Emperor's arrival. They had been held up by the derelict motor car which had all the morning resisted the efforts of the convicts to move it. The Civil Governor on whom rested the ultimate responsibility for this mishap, was soundly thrashed and degraded from the rank of Viscount to that of Baronet before the procession could be resumed. It was necessary for the Emperor to leave his car and complete the journey on mule back, his luggage bobbing behind him on the heads of a dozen suddenly conscripted spectators.

He arrived in a bad temper, scowled at the station master and the two vice-consuls, ignored the native nobility and the tipsy Bishop, and bestowed only the most sour of smiles on the press photographer. The guards presented arms, the interlopers on the roof set up an uncertain cheer and he strode across to the carriage prepared for him. General Connolly and the rest of the royal entourage bun-

dled into their places. The station master stood hat
in hand waiting for orders.

"His Majesty is now ready to start."

The station master waved his hat to the engine
driver; the guards once more presented their arms.
The drums and fifes struck up the national anthem.
The two daughters of the director of the line scattered rose petals round the steps of the carriage. The
engine whistled, Seth continued to smile . . . nothing happened. At the end of the verse the band
music died away; the soldiers stood irresolutely at
the present; the Nestorian Metropolitan continued
to beat the time of some interior melody; the goats
and turkeys wandered in and out among the embarrassed spectators. Then, when all seemed frozen in
silence, the engine gave a great wrench, shaking the
train coach by coach from the tender to the mule
boxes, and suddenly, to the immense delight of the
darkies on the roof, shot off by itself into the country.

"The Emperor has given no orders for a delay."

"It is a thing I did not foresee," said the station
master, "our only engine has gone away alone. I
think I shall be disgraced for this affair."

But Seth made no comment. The other passengers came out onto the platform, smoking and making jokes. He did not look out at them. This gross
incident had bruised his most vulnerable feelings.

He had been made ridiculous at a moment of dignity and triumph; he had been disappointed in plans he had made eagerly; his own superiority was compromised by contact with such service. Basil passed his window and caught a glimpse of a gloomy but very purposeful black face under a white sun helmet. And at that moment the Emperor was resolving. "My people are a worthless people. I give orders; there is none to obey me. I am like a great musician without an instrument. A wrecked car broadside across the line of my procession . . . a royal train without an engine . . . goats on the platform . . . I can do nothing with these people. The Metropolitan is drunk. Those old landowners giggled when the engine broke away; I must find a man of culture, a modern man . . . a representative of Progress and the New Age." And Basil again passed the window; this time in conversation with General Connolly.

Presently, amid cheers, the runaway engine puffed backwards into the station.

Mechanics ran out to repair the coupling.

At last they started.

Basil began the journey in a cheerful temper. He had got on very well with the general and had accepted an invitation to "Pop in for a spot any time" when they reached the capital.

The train which brought the Emperor to Debra-Dowa, also brought the mail. It was a great day at the British Legation. The bags were brought into the dining-room and they all sat round dealing out the letters and parcels, identifying the hand-writings and reading over each other's shoulders . . . "Peter's heard from Flora." "Do let me read Anthony's letter after you, Mabel." "Here's a page to go on with." "Does any one want Jack's letter from Sybil?" "Yes, I do, but I haven't finished Mabel's from Agnes yet." "What a lot of money William owes. Here's a bill for eighty-two pounds from his tailor." "And twelve from his book-shop." "Who's this from, Prudence, I don't know the writing . . . ?"

"Awful lot of official stuff," complained Sir Samson. "Can't bother about that now. You might take charge of it, Peter, and have a look through it when you get time."

"It won't be for a day or two I'm afraid, sir. We're simply snowed under with work in the Chancery over this gymkhana."

"Yes, yes, my boy, of course, all in good time. Always stick to the job in hand. I dare say there's nothing that needs an answer, and anyway there's no knowing when the next mail will go . . . I say, though, here's something interesting, my word it is. Can't make head or tail of the thing. It says, '*Good luck. Copy this letter out nine times and send it to nine different friends'* . . . What an extraordinary idea."

"Envoy, dear, do be quiet; I want to try the new records."

"No, but, Prudence, do listen. It was started by an American officer in France. If one breaks the chain one gets bad luck, and if one sends it on, good luck. There was one woman lost her husband and another one who made a fortune at roulette—all through doing it and not doing it . . . you know I should never have believed that possible . . ."

Prudence played the new records. It was a solemn thought to the circle that they would hear these eight tunes daily, week after week, without release, until that unpredictable day when another mail should arrive from Europe. In their bungalows, in their compound, in their rare, brief excursions into the outer world, these words would run in their heads. . . . Meanwhile they opened their letters and unrolled their newspapers.

"Envoy, what *have* you got there?"

"My dear, another most extraordinary thing. Look here. It's all about the Great Pyramid. You see it's all a 'cosmic allegory.' It depends on the 'Displacement factor.' Listen, *'The combined lengths of the two tribulation passages is precisely 153 Pyramid inches—153 being the number symbolic*

*of 'the Elect' in Our Lord's mystical enactment of
the draught of 153 great fishes.'* I say, I must go into
this. It sounds frightfully interesting! I can't think
who sends me these things. Jolly decent of them
whoever it is."

Eleven *Punches*, eleven *Graphics*, fifty-nine copies
of *The Times*, two *Vogues* and a mixed collection
of *New Yorkers, Week End Reviews, St. James's
Gazettes, Horses and Hounds, Journals of Oriental
Studies*, were unrolled and distributed. Then came
novels from Mudies, cigars, soda-water sparklets.

"We ought to have a Christmas tree next time
the bag comes in."

Several Foreign Office despatches were swept up
and incinerated among the litter of envelopes and
wrappings.

"Apparently inside the Pyramid there is a chamber of the Triple Veil of Ancient Egyptian Prophecy
. . . the east wall of the Antichamber symbolises
Truce in Chaos . . ."

"There is a card announcing a gala night at the
Perroquet to-morrow, Envoy, don't you think we
might go?"

". . . *Four limestone blocks representing the
Final Tribulation in 1936* . . ."

"*Envoy.*"

"Eh . . . I'm so sorry. Yes, we'll certainly go.
Haven't been out for weeks."

"By the way," said William, "we had a caller in to-day."

"Not the Bishop?"

"No, some one new. He wrote his name in the book. Basil Seal."

"What does *he* want, I wonder. Know anything about him?"

"I seem to have heard his name. I don't quite know where."

"Ought we to ask him to stay? He didn't bring any letters?"

"No."

"Thank God. Well, we'll ask him to luncheon one day. I expect he'll find it too hot to come out often."

"Oh," said Prudence, "somebody *new*. That's more than one could have hoped for. Perhaps he'll be able to teach us backgammon."

That evening M. Ballon received a disquieting report.

"Mr. Basil Seal, British politican travelling under private title, has arrived in Debra-Dowa, and is staying in M. Youkoumian's house. He is avoiding all open association with the Legation. This evening he called, but presented no credentials. He is obviously expected. He has been seen in conversation with General Connolly, the new Duke of Ukaka."

"I do not like the look of this Mr. Seal. The old fox, Sir Courteney, is playing a deep game—but old Ballon will outwit him yet."

The Victory Ball at the Perroquet exceeded all its promoters' highest expectations in splendour and gaiety. Every side of Azanian life was liberally represented. The court circle and diplomatic corps, the army and government services, the church, commerce, the native nobility and the cosmopolitan set.

A gross of assorted novelties—false noses, paper caps, trumpets and dolls—had arrived by the mail from Europe, but demands exceeded the supply. Turbans and tarbooshes bobbed round the dancing floor; there were men in Azanian state robes, white jackets, uniforms, and reach-me-down tail coats; women of all complexions in recently fashionable gowns, immense imitation jewels and lumpy ornaments of solid gold. There was Mme. 'Fifi' Fatim Bey, the town courtesan, and her present protector, Viscount Boaz, the Minister of the Interior; there was the Nestorian Patriarch and his favourite deacon; there was the Duke and Duchess of Ukaka; there was the manager, Prince Fyodor Krononin, elegant and saturnine, reviewing the late arrivals at the door; there was Basil Seal and Mr. Youkoumian, who had been hard at work all that day, making

champagne for the party. At a long table near the
back were the British Legation in full force.

"Envoy, you *can't* wear a false nose."

"I don't at all see why not. I think it's very amusing."

"I don't think that you ought really to be here at
all."

"Why? M. Ballon is."

"Yes, but *he* doesn't look as if he were enjoying
himself."

"I say, shall I send him one of those chain letters?"

"Yes, I don't see why you shouldn't do that."

"It will puzzle him terribly."

"Envoy, who's that young man? I'm sure he's
English."

Basil had gone across to Connolly's table.

"Hullo, old boy. Take a pew. This is Black
Bitch."

"How do you do." The little negress put down
her trumpet, bowed with grave dignity and held
out her hand. "Not Black Bitch any more. Duchess
of Ukaka now."

"My word, hasn't she got an ugly mug," said the
Duke. "But she's a good little thing."

Black Bitch flashed a great, white grin of pleasure
at the compliment. It was a glorious night for her;
it would have been rapture enough to have her man

back from the wars; but to be made a Duchess and taken to supper among all the white ladies . . . all in the same day. . . .

"You see," said M. Ballon to his first secretary, "*That* is the man, over there with Connolly. You are having him watched?"

"Ceaselessly."

"You have instructed the waiter to attend carefully to the conversation at the English table?"

"He reported to me just now in the cloak-room. It is impossible to understand. Sir Samson speaks all the time of the dimensions of the Great Pyramid."

"A trap, doubtless."

The Emperor had signified his intention of making an appearance some time during the evening. At the end of the ball-room a box had been improvised for him with bunting, pots of palm, and gilt cardboard. Soon after midnight he came. At a sign from Prince Fyodor the band stopped in the middle of the tune and struck up the national anthem. The dancing couples scuttled to the side of the ball-room; the guests at supper rose awkwardly to their feet, pushing their tables forward with a rattle of knives and glasses; there was a furtive self-conscious straightening of ties and removing of paper caps. Sir Samson Courteney alone absentmindedly retained his false nose. The royal entourage in frogged uniforms advanced down the polished floor; in their centre, half a pace ahead, looking neither to right nor left, strode the Emperor in evening dress, white kid gloves, heavily starched linen, neat pearl studs and jet-black face.

"Got up just as though he were going to sing Spirituals at a party," said Lady Courteney.

Prince Fyodor glided in front and ushered him to his table. He sat down alone. The suite ranged themselves behind his chair. He gave a slight nod to Prince Fyodor. The band resumed the dance music. The Emperor watched impassively as the company began to settle down to a state of enjoyment.

Presently by means of an agency, he invited the wife of the American minister to dance with him. The other couples fell back. With gravity and grace he led Mrs. Schonbaum into the centre, danced with her twice round the room, led her back to her table, bowed and returned to his box.

"Why, he dances beautifully," reported Mrs. Schonbaum. "I often wonder what they would say back home to see me dancing with a man of colour."

"I do pray he comes and dances with Mum," said Prudence. "Do you think it's any use me trying to vamp him, or does he only go for wives?"

The evening went on.

The maître d'hotel approached Prince Fyodor in some distress.

"Highness, they are complaining about the champagne."

"Who are?"

"The French Legation."

"Tell them we will make a special price for them."

" . . . Highness, more complaints of the champagne."

"Who this time?"

"The Duke of Ukaka."

"Take away the bottle, pour in a tumbler of brandy and bring it back."

". . . Highness, is it proper to serve the Minister of the Interior with more wine? He is pouring it in his lady's lap."

"It is proper. You ask questions like an idiot."

The English party began to play consequences on the menu cards. They were of the simplest sort: *The amorous Duke of Ukaka met the intoxicated Mme. Ballon in the Palace w.c. He said to her 'Floreat Azania'* . . .

"Envoy, if you laugh so much we'll have to stop playing."

"Upon my soul, though, that's funny."

"Mum, do you think that young man with the Connollys is the one who called?"

"I daresay. We must ask him to something sometime. Perhaps he'll be here for the Christmas luncheon . . . but he seems to have plenty of friends already."

"Mum, don't be snobbish—particularly now Connolly's a Duke. Do let's have him to everything always . . ."

Basil said, "I've been trying to catch the Emperor's eye. I don't believe he remembers me."

"The old boy's on rather a high horse now the war's over. He'll come down a peg when the bills start coming in. They've brought us a better bottle of fizz this time. Like Fyodor's impudence trying to palm off that other stuff on us."

"I wonder if it would be possible to arrange an audience."

"Look here, old boy, have you come here to enjoy yourself or have you not? I've been in camp with that Emperor off and on for the last six months and I want to forget him. Give Black Bitch some bubbly and help yourself and for the love of Mike talk smut."

"Monsieur Jean, something terrible has come to my knowledge," said the French second secretary.

"Tell me," said the first secretary.

"I can scarcely bring myself to do so. It affects the honour of the Minister's wife."

"Incredible. Tell me at once. It is your duty to France."

"For France, then . . . when affected by wine she made an assignation with the Duke of Ukaka. He loves her."

"Who would have thought it possible? Where?"

"In the toilette at the Palace."

"But there is no toilette at the Palace."

"Sir Samson Courteney has written evidence to that effect. The paper has been folded into a narrow strip. No doubt it was conveyed to him by one of his spies. Perhaps in a roll of bread."

"Extraordinary. We will keep this from the Minister. We will watch, ourselves. It is a secret between us. No good can come of it. Alas, poor Monsieur Ballon. He trusted her. We must prevent this thing."

"For France."

"For France and Monsieur Ballon."

". . . I have never observed Madame Ballon the worse for drink . . ."

Paper caps were resumed; bonnets of liberty, conical dunces' hats, jockey caps, Napoleonic casques, hats for pierrots and harlequins, postmen, highlanders, old Mothers Hubbard and little Misses Muffet over faces of every complexion, brown as boots, chalk white, dun and the fresh boiled pink of Northern Europe. False noses again; brilliant sheaths of pigmented cardboard attached to noses of every anthropological type, the high arch of the Semite, freckled Nordic snouts, broad black nostrils from swamp villages of the mainland, the pulpy inflamed flesh of the alcoholic, and unlovely syphilitic voids. Ribbons of coloured paper tangled and snapped about the dancers' feet; coloured balls volleyed from table to table. One, erratically thrown by Madame Fifi, bounced close to the royal box; the Minister of the Interior facetiously applauded her aim. Prince Fyodor glanced anxiously about him. His patrons were beginning to enjoy themselves. If only the Emperor would soon leave; an *incident* might occur at any moment.

But Seth sat alone among the palms and garlands, apparently deep in thought; his fingers fidgeted with the stem of his wine glass; sometimes, without raising his head, he half furtively surveyed the room. The equerries behind his chair despaired of permission to dance. If only His Majesty would go home, then they could slip back before the fun was all over . . .

"Old boy, your pal the Great Panjandrum is something of a damper on this happy throng. Why can't the silly mutt go off home and leave us to have a jolly up."

"Can't conceive why young Seth doesn't move. Can't be enjoying himself."

But the Emperor sat tight. This was the celebration of his Victory. This was the society of Debra-Dowa. There was the British Minister happy as a parent at a children's party. There was the Minister of the Interior, behaving hideously. There was the Commander-in-Chief of the Azanian army. And with him was Basil Seal. Seth recognised him in his first grave survey of the restaurant and suddenly, on this triumphal night in his own capital, he was overcome by shyness. It was nearly three years since they last met, and Seth recalled the light drizzle of rain in the Oxford quadrangle, a scout carrying a tray of dirty plates, a group of undergraduates in tweeds lounging about among bicycles in the porch. He had been an undergraduate of no account in his College, amiably classed among Bengali babus, Siamese and grammar school scholars as one of the remote and praiseworthy people who had come a long way to the University. Basil had enjoyed a reputation of peculiar brilliance among his contemporaries. On the rare occasions when evangelically-minded under-

graduates asked Seth to tea or coffee, his name occurred in the conversation with awed disapproval.
He played poker for high stakes. His luncheon parties lasted until dusk, his dinner parties dispersed in
riot. Lovely young women visited him from London
in high-powered cars. He went away for week-ends
without leave and climbed into College over the tiles
at night. He had travelled all over Europe, spoke
six languages, called dons by their Christian names
and discussed their books with them.

Seth had met him at breakfast with the Master
of the College. Basil had talked to him about Azanian topography, the Nestorian Church, Sakuyu dialects, the idosyncrasies of the chief diplomats in
Debra-Dowa. Two days later he invited him to
luncheon. There had been two peers present and
the President of the Union, the editor of a new undergraduate paper and a young don. Seth had sat
silent and entranced throughout the afternoon.
Later after long consultation with his scout, he had
returned the invitation. Basil accepted and at the
last moment made his excuses for not coming. There
the acquaintance had ended. Three years had inter-
vened during which Seth had become Emperor, but
Basil still stood for him as the personification of all
that glittering, intangible Western culture to which
he aspired. And there he was, unaccountably, at the
Connollys' table. What must he be thinking? If only

the Minister for the Interior were more sober . . .

The maître d'hotel again approached Prince Fyodor.

"Highness, there is some one at the door who I do not think should be admitted."

"I will see him."

But as he turned to the door, the newcomer appeared. He was a towering negro in full gala dress; on his head a lion's mane busby; on his shoulders a shapeless fur mantle; a red satin skirt; brass bangles and a necklace of lion's teeth; a long, ornamental sword hung at his side; two bandoliers of brass cartridges circled his great girth; he had small bloodshot eyes and a touzle of black wool over his cheeks and chin. Behind him stood six unsteady slaves carrying antiquated riffles.

It was one of the backwoods peers, the Earl of Ngumo, feudal overlord of some five hundred square miles of impenetrable highland territory. He had occupied himself throughout the civil war in an attempt to mobilise his tribesmen. The battle of Ukaka occurring before the levy was complete, saved him the embarrassment of declaring himself for either combatant. He had therefore left his men in the hills and marched down with a few hundred personal attendants to pay his respects to the victorious side. His celebrations had lasted for some days already and had left some mark upon even his rugged constitution.

Prince Fyodor hurried forward. "The tables are all engaged. I regret very much that there is no room. We are full up."

The Earl blinked dully and said, "I will have a table, some gin and some women and some raw camels' meat for my men outside."

"But there is no table free."

"Do not be put out. That is a simple matter. I have some soldiers with me who will quickly find room."

The band had stopped playing and a hush fell on the crowded restaurant. Scared faces under the paper hats and false noses.

"Under the table, Black Bitch," said Connolly. "There's going to be a rough house."

Mr. Youkoumian's plump back disappeared through the service door.

"*Now* what's happening?" said the British Minister. "Some one's up to something I'll be bound."

But at that moment the Earl's bovine gaze moving up the rows of scared faces to its natural focus among the palms and bunting, reached the Emperor. His hand fell to the jewelled hilt of his sword —and twenty hands in various parts of the room felt for pistols and bottle necks—a yard of tarnished damascene flashed into the light and with a roar of homage he sank to his knees in the centre of the polished floor.

Seth rose and folded his hands in the traditional gesture of welcome.

"Peace be upon your house, Earl."

The vassal rose and Prince Fyodor's perplexities were solved by the departure of the royal party.

"I will have that table," said the Earl, pointing to the vacated box.

And soon, quite unconscious of the alarm he had caused, with a bottle of M. Youkoumian's gin before him, and a vast black cheroot between his teeth, the magnate was pacifically winking at the ladies as they danced past him.

Outside the royal chauffeur was asleep and only with difficulty could be awakened. The sky was ablaze with stars; dust hung in the cool air, fragrant as crushed herbs; from the Ngumo camp, out of sight below the eucalyptus trees, came the thin smoke of burning dung and the pulse and throb of the hand drummers. Seth drove back alone to the black litter of palace buildings.

"Insupportable barbarians," he thought. "I am sure that the English lords do not behave in that way before their King. Even my loyalest officers are ruffians and buffoons. If I had *one* man by me whom I could trust . . . a man of progress and culture . . ."

SIX WEEKS PASSED

SIX weeks passed. The victorious army slowly demobolised and dispersed over the hills in a hundred ragged companies; livestock and women in front, warriors behind laden with alarm clocks and nondescript hardware looted in the bazaars; soldiers of Progress and the New Age homeward bound to the villages.

The bustle subsided and the streets of Matodi resumed their accustomed calm; copra, cloves, mangoes and khat; azan and angelus; old women with obdurate donkeys; trays of pastry black with flies, shrill voices in the mission school reciting the catechism; lepers and pedlars, and Arab gentlemen with shabby gamps decently parading the water front at the close of day. In the derelict van outside the railway station, a patient black family repaired the ravages of invasion with a careful architecture of mud, twigs, rag and flattened petrol tins.

Two mail ships outward bound from Marseilles, three on the home journey from Madagascar and Indo-China paused for their normal six hours in the little bay. Four times the train puffed up from Matodi to Debra-Dowa; palm belt, lava fields, bush and upland; thin cattle scattered over the sparse fields;

shallow furrows in the brittle earth; white-gowned Azanian ploughboys scratching up furrows with wooden ploughs; conical grass roofs in stockades of euphorbia and cactus; columns of smoke from the tukal fires, pencil-drawn against the clear sky.

Vernacular hymns in the tin-roofed missions, ancient liturgy in the murky Nestorian sanctuaries; tonsure and turban, hand drums and innumerable jingling bells of debased silver. And beyond the hills on the low Wanda coast where no liners called, and the jungle stretched unbroken to the sea, other more ancient rites and another knowledge furtively encompassed; green, sunless paths; forbidden ways unguarded save for a wisp of grass plaited between two stumps, ways of death and initiation, the forbidden places of juju and the masked dancers; the drums of the Wanda throbbing in sunless, forbidden places.

Fanfare and sennet; tattoo of kettle drums; tricolour bunting strung from window to window across the Boulevard Amurath, from Levantine café to Hindu drug store; Seth in his Citroën drove to lay the foundation stone of the Imperial Institute of Hygiene; brass band of the Imperial army raised the dust of main street. Floreat Azania.

FIVE

ON the south side of the Palace Compound, between the kitchen and the stockade, lay a large irregular space where the oxen were slaughtered for the public banquets. A minor gallows stood there which was used for such trivial, domestic executions as now and then became necessary within the royal household. The place was now deserted except for the small cluster of puzzled blacks who were usually congregated round the headquarters of the One Year Plan and a single dog who gnawed her hindquarters in the patch of shadow cast by two corpses, which rotated slowly face to face, half circle East, a half circle West, ten foot high in the limpid morning sunlight.

The Ministry of Modernisation occupied what had formerly been the old Empress' oratory; a circular building of concrete and corrugated iron, its outer wall enriched with posters from all parts of Europe and the United States advertising machinery, fashion and foreign travel. The display was rarely without attendance and to-day the customary loafers were reinforced by five or six gentlemen in the blue cotton cloaks which the official class of Debra-Dowa assumed in times of bereavement.

These were mourners for the two criminals—peculators and perjurers both—who had come to give a dutiful tug at their relatives' heels in case life might not yet be extinct, and had stayed to gape, entranced by the manifestations of Progress and the New Age.

On the door was a board painted in Arabic, Sakuyu and French with the inscription:—

MINISTRY OF MODERNISATION
HIGH COMMISSIONER & COMPTROLLER GENERAL:
MR. BASIL SEAL.
FINANCIAL SECRETARY: MR. KRIKOR
YOUKOUMIAN.

A vague smell of incense and candle-grease still possessed the interior; in all other ways it had been completely transformed. Two partitions divided it into unequal portions. The largest was Basil's office, which contained nothing except some chairs, a table littered with maps and memoranda and a telephone. Next door Mr. Youkoumian had induced a more homely note; his work was economically confined to two or three penny exercise books filled with figures and indecipherable jottings, but his personality extended itself and pervaded the room, finding concrete expression in the seedy red plush sofa that he had scavenged from one of the state apartments, the scraps of clothing hitched negligently about the furniture, the Parisian photographs pinned to the walls, the vestiges of food on enamelled tin plates, the scent spray, cigarette ends, spittoon, and the little spirit-stove over which perpetually simmered a brass pan of coffee. It was his idiosyncrasy to prefer working in stockinged feet, so that when he was at his post a pair of patent leather, elastic-sided boots proclaimed his presence from the window ledge.

In the vestibule sat a row of native runners with whose services the modernising party were as yet unable to dispense.

At nine in the morning both Basil and Mr. Youkoumian were at their desks. Instituted a month previously by royal proclamation, the Ministry of Modernisation was already a going concern. Just how far it was going, indeed, was appreciated by very few outside its circular, placarded walls. Its function as defined in Seth's decree was *"to promote the adoption of modern organisation and habits of life throughout the Azanian Empire"* which, liberally interpreted, comprised the right of interference in most of the public and private affairs of the nation. As Basil glanced through the correspondence that awaited him and the rough agenda for the day he felt ready to admit that any one but himself and Mr. Youkoumian would have bitten off more than he could chew. Reports from eight provincial viceroys on a questionnaire concerning the economic resources and population of their territory—documents full of ponderous expressions of politeness and the minimum of trustworthy information; detailed recommendations from the railway authorities at Matodi; applications for concessions from European prospectors; inquiries from tourist bureaux about the possibilities of big game hunting, surf bathing and mountaineering; applications for public appointments; protests from missions and legations; estimates for building; details of court etiquette and precedence—everything seemed to find its way to Basil's table. The other ministers of the crown had not yet begun to feel uneasy about their own positions. They regarded Basil's arrival as a direct intervention of heaven on their behalf. Here was an Englishman who was willing to leave them their titles and emoluments and take all the work off their hands. Each was issued with the rubber stamp, *REFER TO BUREAU OF MODERNISATION*, and in a very few days the Minister of the Interior, the Lord Chamberlain, the Justiciar, the City Governor and even Seth himself, acquired the habit of relegating all decisions to Basil, with one firm stab of indelible ink. Two officials alone, the Nestorian patriarch and the Commander-in-Chief of the army, failed to avail themselves of the convenient new institution, but continued to muddle through the routine of their departments in the same capricious, dilatory, but independent manner as before the establishment of the new régime.

Basil had been up very late the night before working with the Emperor on a codification of the criminal law, but the volume of business before him left him undismayed.

"Youkoumian."

" 'Ullo. Mr. Seal?"

The financial secretary padded in from the next room.

"Connolly won't have boots."

"Won't ave boots? But, Mr. Seal, he got to ave boots. I bought them from Cape Town. They come next ship. I bought them, you understand, as a personal enterprise, out of my own pocket. What in ell can I do with a thousand pair boots if Connolly won't take them?"

"You ought to have waited."

"Waited? and then when the order is out and every one knows Guards to ave boots, what'll appen then? Some pig wanting to make money will go to the Emperor and say I get you boots damned cheaper than Youkoumian. Where am I then? They might as well go barefoot all same as they do now like the dirty niggers they are. No, Mr. Seal, that is not business. I fix it so that one morning the Army Order says Guards must have boots. Every one say but where are boots? No one got enough boots in this stinking hole. Some one say I get you boots in three weeks, month, five weeks, so long. I come up and say *I* got boots. How many pairs you want? Thousand? O.K. I fix it. That is business. What does the General say?"

Basil handed him the letter. It was emphatic and almost ungenerously terse, coming as it did in answer to a carefully drafted recommendation beginning: *The Minister of Modernisation presents his compliments to the Commander-in-Chief of the Imperial Army and in pursuance of the powers granted him by royal decree begs to advise . . .*

It consisted of a single scrap of lined paper torn from a note-book across which Connolly had scrawled in pencil: *The Minister of Damn All can go to blazes. My men couldn't move a yard in boots. Try and sell Seth top hats next time. Ukaka C. in C.*

"Well," said Mr. Youkoumian doubtfully, "I *could* get top ats."

"That is one of Connolly's jokes, I'm afraid."

"Jokes is it? And ere am I with a thousand pair black boots on my ands. Ha. Ha. Like ell it's a joke. There isn't a thousand people in the whole country that wears boots. Besides these aren't the kind of boots people buys for themselves. Government stuff. Damn rotten. See what I mean?"

"Don't you worry," Basil said. "We'll find a use for them. We might have them served out to the

clergy." He took back the General's note, glanced
through it frowning and clipped it into the file of
correspondence; when he raised his head his eyes
were clouded in an expression characteristic to him,
insolent, sulky and curiously childish. "But as a matter of fact," he added, "I shouldn't mind a show-
down with Connolly. It's nearly time for one."

"They are saying that the General is in love with
Madame Ballon."

"I don't believe it."

"I am convinced," said Mr. Youkoumian. "It was
told me on very igh authority by the barber who
visits the French Legation. Every one in the town
is speaking of it. Even Madame Youkoumian has
heard. I tell you ow it is," he added complacently.
"Madame Ballon drinks. That is ow Connolly first
ad er."

Quarter of an hour later both Basil and Mr. Youkoumian were engaged in what seemed more important business.

A morning's routine at the Ministry of Modernisation.

"Now, look, Mister, I tell you exactly how we are
fixed. We have His Majesty's interests to safeguard.
See what I mean. You think there is tin in the
Ngumo mountains in workable quantities. So do we.
So do other companies. They want concession too.

Only to-day two gentlemen come to ask me to fix it for them. What do I do? I say, we can only give concession to company we have confidence in. Look. How about if on your board of directors you had a man of financial status in the country; some one who His Majesty trusts . . . see what I mean . . . some one with a fair little block of share allocated to him. He would protect His Majesty's interests and interests of company too . . . see?"

"That's all very well, Mr. Youkoumian, but it isn't so easy to find any one like that. I can't think of any one at the moment."

"No, can't you? Can't you think?"

"Unless, of course, you yourself? But I can hardly suggest that. You are far too busy?"

"Mister, I have learned how to be busy and still have time for things that please me . . ."

Next door: Basil and the American commercial attaché: "The situation is this, Walker. I'm—the Emperor is spending quarter of a million sterling on road construction this year. It can't come out of the ordinary revenue. I'm floating a loan to raise the money. You're acting over here for Cosmopolitan Oil Trust and for Stetson cars. Every mile of road we make is worth five hundred cars a year and God knows how many gallons of oil. If your companies like to take up the loan I'm prepared to give them a ten years monopoly . . ."

Later, the editor of the *Courier d'Azanie*.

M. Bertrand did not look a man of any importance—nor, in fact, was he. The *Courier* consisted of a single sheet, folded quarto, which was issued weekly to rather less than a thousand subscribers in Debra-Dowa and Matodi. It retailed in French the chief local events of the week—the diplomatic entertainments, official appointments, court circular, the programmes of the cinemas, and such few items of foreign news as came through on the wireless. It occupied one day a week of M. Bertrand's time, the remainder of which was employed in printing menus, invitation cards, funeral and wedding announcements, in acting as local correspondent for a European news-agency, and in selling stationery over the counter of his little office. It was in the hope of a fat order for crested note-paper that he presented himself in answer to Basil's invitation at the offices of the new Ministry.

"Good-morning, Monsieur Bertrand. It's good of you to come. We may as well get to business at once. I want to buy your paper."

"Why, certainly, Monsieur Seal. I have a very nice cream laid line suitable for office use or a slightly more expensive quality azure tinted with a linen surface. I suppose you would want the name of the Ministry embossed at the head?"

"I don't think you understand me. I mean the *Courier d'Azanie.*"

M. Bertrand's face showed disappointment and some vexation. It was really unpardonably high-handed of this young man to demand a personal call from the proprietor and editor-in-chief whenever he bought a copy of his journal.

"I will tell my clerk. You wish to subscribe regularly?"

"No, no, you don't understand. I wish to become the proprietor—to own the entire concern. What is your price?"

Slowly the idea took root, budded and blossomed; then M. Bertrand said: "Oh, no, that would be quite impossible. I don't want to sell."

"Come, come. It can't be worth much to you and I am willing to pay a generous price."

"It is not that, sir, it is a question of prestige, you understand," he spoke very earnestly. "You see as the proprietor and editor of the *Courier* I am *some one.* Twice a year Madame Bertrand and I dine at the French Legation; once we go to the garden party, we go to the Court and the polo club. That is something. But if I become Bertrand, job-printer, who will regard me then? Madame Bertrand would not forgive it."

"I see," said Basil. To be some one in Debra-Dowa . . . it seemed a modest ambition; it would be a shame to deprive M. Bertrand. "I see. Well, suppose that you retained the position of editor and were nominally proprietor. That would fulfil my purpose. You see I am anxious to enlarge the scope of your paper. I wish it to publish leading articles explaining the political changes. Listen . . ." and for a quarter of an hour Basil outlined his intentions for the *Courier's* development . . . three sheets, advertisements of European firms and government services to meet increased cost of production; enlarged circulation; features in Sakuyu and Arabic; intelligent support of government policy . . . At the end of the interview M. Bertrand left, slightly bewildered, carrying with him a fair-sized cheque and the notes for a leading article forecasting possible changes in the penal code . . . convict settlements to replace local prisons . . . What extraordinary subjects to mention in the *Courier!*

At eleven the Anglican Bishop came to protest against the introduction of State Lotteries.

At quarter past, William came from Sir Samson Courteney to discuss the possibility of making a road out to the Legation. William and Basil did not like each other.

At half past, the Lord Chamberlain came to consult about cookery. A banquet was due to some

Wanda notables next week. Seth had forbidden raw beef. What was he to give them? "Raw beef," said Basil. "Call it steak tartare."

"That is in accordance with modern thought?"

"Perfectly."

At noon Basil went to see the Emperor.

The heat, rarely intolerable in the hills, was at this time of day penetrating and devitalising. The palace roofs glared and shimmered. A hot breeze lifted the dust and powdered the bodies of the dangling courtiers and carried across the yard a few waste shreds of paper, baked crisp and brittle as dead leaves. Basil sauntered with half-shut eyes to the main entrance.

Soldiers stood up and saluted clumsily; the captain of the guard trotted after him and plucked at his sleeve.

"Good-morning, captain."

"Good-morning, Excellency. You are on your way to the Emperor?"

"As usual."

"There is a small matter. If I could interest your Excellency . . . It is about the two gentlemen who were hanged. One was my cousin."

"Yes?"

"His post has not yet been filled. It has always been held by my family. My uncle has made a petition to His Majesty . . ."

"Yes, yes. I will speak on his behalf."

"But that is exactly what you must not do. My uncle is a wicked man, Excellency. It was he who poisoned my father. I am sure of it. He wanted my mother. It would be most unjust for him to have the post. There is my little brother—a man of supreme ability and devotion . . ."

"Very well, captain, I'll do what I can."

"The angels preserve your Excellency."

The Emperor's study was strewn with European papers and catalogues; his immediate concern was a large plan of Debra-Dowa on which he was working with ruler and pencil.

"Come in, Seal, I'm just rebuilding the city. The Anglican Cathedral will have to go, I think, and all the South quarter. Look, here is Seth Square with the avenues radiating from it. I'm calling this Boulevard Basil Seal."

"Good of you, Seth."

"And this Avenue Connolly."

"Ah, I wanted to talk about him." Basil sat down and approached his subject discreetly. "I wouldn't say anything against him. I know you like him and in his rough and tumble way he's a decent soldier. But d'you ever feel that he's *not quite modern?*"

"He never made full use of our tank."

"Exactly. He's opposed to progress throughout. He wants to keep the army under *his* control. Now there's the question of boots. I don't think we told you, but the matter came before the Ministry and we sent in a recommendation that the guards should be issued with boots. It would increase their efficiency a hundred per cent. Half the sick list is due to hookworm, which as you know comes from going about barefooted. Besides, you know, there's the question of prestige. There's not a single guards' regiment in Europe without boots. You've seen them for yourself at Buckingham Palace. You'll never get the full respect of the powers until you give your troops boots."

"Yes, yes, by all means. They shall have boots at once."

"I was sure you'd see it that way. But the trouble is that Connolly's standing out against it. Now we've no power at present to issue an army ordnance. That has to come through him—or through you as commander-in-chief of the army."

"I'll make out an order to-day. Of course they must have boots. I'll hang any man I see barefooted."

"Fine. I thought you'd stand by us, Seth. You know," he added reflectively, "we've got a much easier job now than we should have had fifty years ago. If we'd had to modernise a country then it would have meant constitutional monarchy, bi-cameral legislature, proportional representation, women's suffrage, independent judicature, freedom of the press, referendums . . ."

"What is all that?" asked the Emperor.

"Just a few ideas that have ceased to be modern."

Then they settled down to the business of the day.

"The British Legation are complaining again about their road."

"That is an old question. I am tired of it. Besides you will see from the plan I have orientated all the roads leading out of the capital; they go by the points of the compass. I cannot upset my arrangements."

"The Minister feels very strongly about it."

"Well, another time . . . no, I tell you what I will do. Look, we will name this street after him. Then he will be satisfied."

The Emperor took up his indiarubber and erased Connolly's name from the new metropolis. *Avenue Sir Samson Courteney* he wrote in its place.

"I wish we had a tube railway," he said. "Do you think it would pay?"

"No."

"So I feared. But one day we will have one. Listen. You can tell Sir Samson that. When there is a tube railway he shall have a private station in the Legation compound. Now listen; I have had a letter from the Society for the Prevention of Cruelty to

Animals. They want to send out a Commission to investigate Wanda methods of hunting. Is it cruel to spear lions, do you think?"

"No."

"No. However, here is the letter. From Dame Mildred Porch. Do you know her?"

"I've heard of her. An intolerable old gas-bag."

"What is gas-bag? An orator?"

"Yes in a way."

"Well, she is returning from South Africa and wishes to spend a week here. I will say yes?"

"I shouldn't."

"I will say yes . . . And another thing. I have been reading in my papers about something very modern called birth control. What is it?"

Basil explained.

"I must have a lot of that. You will see to it. Perhaps it is not a matter for an ordnance, what do you think? We must popularise it by propaganda—educate the people in sterility. We might have a little pageant in its honour . . ."

Sir Samson accepted the rebuff to his plans with characteristic calm. "Well, well, I don't suppose young Seth will keep his job long. There's bound to be another revolution soon. The boy's head over heels in debt they tell me. I daresay the next government, whoever they are, will be able to afford something. And anyway, you may laugh at me, Prudence, but I think it's uncommonly decent of the young fellow to name that avenue after me. I've always liked him. You never know. Debra-Dowa may become a big city one day. I like to think of all the black johnnies in a hundred years' time driving up and down in their motor cars and going to the shops and saying, 'Number a hundred Samson Courteney' and wondering who I was. Like, like . . ."

"Like the Avenue Victor Hugo, Envoy."

"*Exactly*, or St. James's Square."

But the question of the boots was less easily settled.

On the afternoon of the day when the new ordnance was issued, Basil and Mr. Youkoumian were in conference. A major difficulty had arisen with regard to the plans for the new guest house at the Palace. The Emperor had been captivated by some photographs he had discovered in a German architectural magazine and had decided to have the new building constructed of steel and vita-glass. Basil had spent half the morning in a vain attempt to persuade the royal mind that this was not a style at all suitable to his tropical climate and he was now at work with his financial secretary on a memorandum of the prohibitive extravagance of the new plans, when the door was pushed noisily open and the Duke of Ukaka strode into the room.

"Clear out, Youkoumian," he said. "I want to talk to your boss."

"O.K., General. I'll op off. No offence."

"Nonsense. Mr. Youkoumian is financial secretary of the Ministry. I should like him to be present at our interview."

"What me, Mr. Seal? I got nothing to say to the General."

"I wish you to stay."

"Quick," said the Duke, making a menacing motion towards him.

"Very sorry, gentlemen," said Mr. Youkoumian and shot through the door into his own office.

First trick to Connolly.

"I notice even that little dago has the sense to take off his boots."

Second trick to Connolly.

But in the subsequent interview Basil held his own. The General began: "Sorry to have to sling that fellow out. Can't stand his smell. Now let's talk. What's all this infernal nonsense about boots?"

"His Majesty's ordnance seemed perfectly explicit to me."

"*His Majesty's trousers.* For the Lord's sake come off the high horse, old boy, and listen to me. I don't give a hoot in hell about your modernisation. It's none of my business. You can set every damn coon in the place doing cross-word puzzles for all I care.

But I'm not going to have any monkeying about with my men. You'll lame the whole army in a day if you try to make 'em wear boots. Now look here, there's no reason why we should scrap over this. I've been in the country long enough to see through Youkoumian's game. Selling junk to the government has been the staple industry of Debra-Dowa as long as I can remember it. I'd as soon you got the boodle as any one else. Listen. If I tip the wink to the people on the line I can have the whole consignment of boots carried off by Sakuyu. You'll get compensation, the ordnance will be forgotten and no one will be any the worse off. What do you say? Is it a deal?"

For an appreciable time Basil hesitated in a decision of greater importance than either of them realised. The General sat jauntily on the edge of the table bending his rising cane over his knee; his expression was one of cordiality and of persuasive good sense. Basil hesitated. Was it some atavistic sense of a caste, an instinct of superiority, that held him aloof? Or was it vexed megalomania because Mr. Youkoumian had trotted so obediently from the room in his stockinged feet?

"You should have made your representations before," he said. "The tone of your first note made discussion impossible. The boots will be issued to the war department next week."

"Bloody young fool," said Connolly and took his leave.

As the door opened Mr. Youkoumian hastily stepped back from the keyhole. The General pushed past him and left the Ministry.

"Oh, Mr. Seal, why the ell do you want a bust up with im for? Look, how about I go after im and fix it, eh, Mr. Seal?"

"You won't do anything of the sort. We'll carry right on with the plans for the pageant of contraception."

"Oh dear, oh dear, Mr. Seal, there ain't no sense at all in aving bust ups."

News of the rupture spread like plague through the town. It was first-class gossip. The twenty or so spies permanently maintained by various interests in the Imperial Household carried tidings of the split through the legations and commercial houses; runners informed the Earl of Ngumo; Black Bitch told her hairdresser; an Eurasian bank clerk told his manager and the bank manager told the Bishop; Mr. Youkoumian recounted the whole incident in graphic gesture over the bar of the Empereur Seth; Connolly swore hideously about it at the Perroquet to Prince Fyodor; the Minister of the Interior roared out a fantastically distorted version to the assembled young ladies of the leading maison de société. That evening there was no dinner table of any importance in Debra-Dowa where the subject was not discussed in detail.

"Pity," remarked Sir Samson Courteney. "I suppose this'll mean that young Seal will be coming up here more than ever. Sorry, Prudence, I daresay he's all right, but the truth is I can never find much to say to the chap . . . interested in different things . . . always going on about local politics. . . . Damn fool thing to quarrel about anyway. Why shouldn't he wear boots if he wants to?"

"That wasn't quite the point, Envoy."

"Well, it was something of the kind, I know."

"Ha! Ha!" said Monsieur Ballon. "Here is a thing Sir Samson did *not* foresee. Where is his fine web now, eh? Gossamer in the wind. Connolly is our man."

"Alas, blind, trusting husband, if he only knew," murmured the first to the second secretary.

"The Seal-Courteney faction and their puppet emperor have lost the allegiance of the army. We must consolidate our party."

It was in this way it happened that next morning there occurred an event unique in Black Bitch's experience. She was in the yard in front of her house laundering some of the General's socks (for she could not bear another woman to touch her man's clothes), chewing nut and meditatively spitting the dark juice into the soap-suds, when a lancer dismounted before her in the crimson and green uniform of the French Legation.

"Her Grace, the Duchess of Ukaka."

She lifted her dress, so as not to soil it, and wiped her hands on her knickers. "Me," she said.

The man saluted, handed her a large envelope; saluted again, mounted and rode away.

The Duchess was left alone with her large envelope; she squatted on her heels and examined it, turning it this way and that, holding it up to her ear and shaking it, her head sagely cocked on one side. Then she rose, padded into the house and across the hall to her bedroom; there, after circumspection, she raised a loose corner of the fibre matting and slipped the letter beneath it.

Two or three times during the next hour she left her wash-tub to see if her treasure was safe. At noon the General returned to luncheon and she handed it over to him, to await his verdict.

"Hullo, Black Bitch, what do you suppose this is? Madame Ballon wants us to dine at the French Legation to-morrow."

"You go?"

"But it's for both of us, old girl. The invitation is addressed to you. What d'you think of that?"

"Oh, my! Me dine with Madame Ballon! Oh, my, that's good!"

The Duchess could not contain her excitement; she threw back her head, lolled her eyes, and emitting deep gurgles of pleasure began spinning about the room like a teetotum.

"Good for the old geyser," said the Duke, and later when the acceptance was written and despatched by the hand of the Imperial Guard's most inspiring sergeant-major, and Connolly had answered numerous questions about the proper conduct of knife, fork, glass and gloves, and the Duchess had gone bustling off to Mr. Youkoumian's store for ribbon and gold braid and artificial peonies to embellish her party frock, he went back to barracks with unusual warmth at heart towards the French Legation, remarking again, "Good for the old geyser. He's the first person who's troubled to ask Black Bitch to anything in eight years. And wasn't she pleased as Punch about it too, bless her black heart?"

As the time approached Black Bitch's excitement became almost alarming and her questions on etiquette so searching that the General was obliged to thump her soundly on the head and lock her in a cupboard for some hours before she could be reduced to a condition sufficiently subdued for diplomatic society. The dinner party, however, was a great success. The French Legation were there in full force, the director of the railway with his wife and daughters, and Lord Boaz, the Minister for the Interior. Black Bitch as Duchess of Ukaka took precedence and sat beside M. Ballon who spoke to her in English in praise of her husband's military skill, influence and discretion. Any small errors in deportment which she may have committed were completely eclipsed by the Minister for the Interior who complained of the food, drank far too much, pinched the ladies on either side of him, pocketed a dozen cigars and a silver pepper mill which happened to take his fancy, and later in the drawing-room insisted on dancing by himself to the gramophone until his slaves appeared to hoist him into his car and carry him back to Mme. 'Fifi,' of whose charms he had been loudly boasting throughout the evening with a splendour of anatomical detail which was, fortunately, unintelligible to many of the people present.

In the dining room when the succession of wines finally ended with the few ceremonial spoonfuls of sweet champagne and the men were left alone—the Minister for the Interior being restrained with difficulty from too precipitately following the ladies— M. Ballon signalled for a bottle of eau de vie and moving round to the General's side, filled his glass and prompted him to some frank criticism of the Emperor and the present régime.

In the drawing-room the French ladies crowded

about their new friend and before the evening was out several of them, including Madame Ballon, had dropped the 'Duchess' and were on terms of calling her 'Black Bitch.' They asked her to come and see their gardens and children, they offered to teach her tennis and picquet, they advised her about an Armenian dressmaker in the town and a Hindu fortune teller; they were eager to lend her the patterns of their pyjamas; they spoke seriously of pills; best of all they invited her to sit on the committee which was being organised in the French colony to decorate a car for the forthcoming Birth-Control Gala. There was no doubt about it; the Connollys had made the French set.

Ten days later the boots arrived at Debra-Dowa; there were some formalities to be observed but these were rendered simple by the fact that the departments involved were now under the control of the Ministry of Modernisation. Mr. Youkoumian drew up an application to himself from the Ministry of War for the delivery of the boots; he made out a chit from the War Office to Ministry of Supplies; passed it on to the treasury, examined and countersigned it, drew himself a cheque and in the name of the Customs and Excise Department allowed his own claim to rebate of duty on the importation of articles of 'national necessity.' The whole thing took ten minutes. A few hours later a thousand pairs of

black boots had been dumped in the square of the
Guards barracks where a crowd of soldiers rapidly
collected and studied them throughout the entire
afternoon with vivid but nervous interest.

That evening there was a special feast in honour
of the boots. Cook-pots steaming over the wood
fires; hand drums beating; bare feet shuffling un-
forgotten tribal rhythms; a thousand darkies croon-
ing and swaying on their haunches, white teeth
flashing in the fire light.

They were still at it when Connolly returned
from dinner at the French consulate.

"What in hell are the boys making whoopee for
to-night? It's not one of their days, is it?"

"Yes General, very big day," said the sentry.
"Boots day."

The singing reached Basil as he sat at his writing
table at the Ministry, working long after midnight
at the penal code.

"What's going on at the barracks?" he asked his
servant.

"Boots."

"They like em, eh?"

"They like em fine."

"That's one in the eye for Connolly," he said,
and next day, meeting the General in the Palace
Yard he could not forbear to mention it. "So the

boots went down all right with your men after all, Connolly."

"They went down."

"No cases of lameness yet I hope?"

The General leant over in his saddle and smiled pleasantly. "No cases of lameness," he replied. "One or two of belly ache though. I'm just writing a report on the matter to the Commissioner of Supplies —that's our friend Youkoumian, isn't it? You see my adjutant made rather a silly mistake. He hadn't had much truck with boots before and the silly fellow thought they were extra rations. My men ate the whole bag of tricks last night."

Dust in the air; a light wind rattling the leaves in the eucalyptus trees. Prudence sat over the *Panorama of Life* gazing through the window across the arid legation croquet lawn; dun grass rubbed bare between the hoops, a few sapless stalks in the beds beyond. She drew little arabesques in the corners of the page and thought about love.

It was the dry season before the rains when the cattle on the hills strayed miles from their accustomed pastures and herdsmen came to blows over the brackish dregs of the drinking holes; when, preceded by a scutter of children, lions would sometimes appear, parading the streets of the town in search of water; when Lady Courteney remarked that her herbaceous borders were a positive eyesore.

How out of tune with nature is the spirit of man! wrote Prudence in her sprawling, schoolroom characters. *When the earth proclaims its fertility, in running brooks, bursting seed, mating of birds and frisking of lambs then the thoughts of man turn to athletics and horticulture, water colour painting and amateur theatricals. Now in the arid season when nature seems all dead under the cold earth, there is nothing to think about except sex.* She bit her pen and read it through, substituting *hot soil* for *cold earth.* 'I am sure I've got something wrong in the first part,' she thought and called to Lady Courteney who, watering-can in hand, was gloomily surveying a withered rose tree. "Mum, how soon after the birds mate are the lambs born?"

"Eggs, dear, not lambs," said her mother and pottered off towards some azalea roots which were desperately in need of water.

"Damn the panorama of life," said Prudence, and she began drawing a series of highly-stylised profiles which by an emphasis of the chin and disordering of the hair had ceased during the last six weeks to be portraits of William and had come to represent Basil Seal. "To think that I wanted to be in love so much," she thought, "that I even practised on William."

"Luncheon," said her mother, repassing the window. "And I shall be late again. Do go in and be bright to your father."

But when Lady Courteney joined them in the dining-room she found father, daughter and William sitting in moody silence.

"Tinned asparagus," said Sir Samson. "And a letter from the Bishop."

"He's not coming out to dinner again?"

"No, no, it isn't as bad as that. But apparently Seth wants to pull down his Cathedral for some reason. What does he expect *me* to do about it I should like to know? Shocking ugly building anyhow. I wish, Prudence and William, you'd take the ponies out this afternoon. They haven't had any proper exercise for days."

"Too hot," said Prudence.

"Too busy," said William.

"Oh, well," said Sir Samson Courteney. And later he remarked to his wife: "I say, there isn't any trouble between those two, is there? They used to be such pals."

"I've been meaning to mention it for some time, Sam, only I was so worried about the antirrhinums. I don't think Prudence is at all herself. D'you think it's good for a girl of her age living at this height all the year round? It might be an idea to send her back to England for a few months. Harriet could put her up in Belgrave Place. I'm not sure it wouldn't be a good thing for her to go out in London for a season and meet some people of her own age. What d'you think?"

"I daresay you're right. All that What-d'you-call-it of Life she keeps working away at . . . Only you must write to Harriet. I'm far too busy at the moment. Got to think of something to say to the Bishop."

But next day Prudence and William went out with the ponies. She had an assignation with Basil.

"Listen, William, you're to go out of the city by the lane behind the Baptist school and the Jewish abattoirs, then past the Parsee death house and the fever hospital."

"Not exactly the prettiest ride."

"Darling. Don't be troublesome. You might get seen the other way. Once you're clear of the Arab cemetery you can go where you like. And you're to fetch me at Youkoumian's at five."

"Jolly afternoon for me, leading Mischief all the time."

"Now, William, you know you manage him perfectly. You're the only person I'd trust to take him. I can't leave him outside Youkoumian's, can I, because of *discretion*."

"What you don't seem to see is that it's pretty dim for me, floundering about half the day, I mean, in a dust heap with two ponies while you neck with the chap who's cut me out."

"*William,* don't be *coarse.* And anyway 'cut you out' nothing. You had me all to yourself for six months and weren't you just bored blue with it?"

"Well, I daresay he'll be bored soon."

"Cad."

Basil still lived in the large room over Mr. Youkoumian's Store. There was a verandah, facing onto a yard littered with scrap iron and general junk, accessible by an outside staircase. Prudence passed through the shop, out and up. The atmosphere of the room was rank with tobacco smoke. Basil, in shirt sleeves, rose from the deck chair to greet her. He threw the butt of his Burma cheroot into the tin hip bath which stood unemptied at the side of the bed; it sizzled and went out and floated throughout the afternoon, slowly unfurling in the soapy water. He bolted the door. It was half dark in the room. Dusty parallels of light struck through the shutters onto the floor boards and the few, shabby mats. Prudence stood isolated, waiting for him, her hat in her hand. At first neither spoke. Presently she said, "You might have shaved," and then, "Please help with my boots."

Below, in the yard, Madame Youkoumian up-braided a goat. Strips of sunlight traversed the floor as an hour passed. In the bath water, the soggy stub of tobacco emanated a brown blot of juice.

Banging on the door.

"Heavens," said Prudence, "that can't be William already."

"Mr. Seal, Mr. Seal."

"Well, what is it? I'm resting."

"Well you got to stop," said Mr. Youkoumian. "They're looking for you all over the town. Damn fine rest I've had this afternoon, like ell I aven't."

"What is it?"

"Emperor must see you at once. E's got a new idea. Very modern and important. Some damn fool nonsense about Swedish drill."

Basil hurried to the Palace to find his master in a state of high excitement.

"I have been reading a German book. We must draft a decree at once . . . communal physical exercises. The whole population, every morning, you understand. And we must get instructors from Europe. Cable for them. Quarter of an hour's exercise a morning. And community singing. That is very important. The health of the nation depends on it. I have been thinking it over. Why is there no cholera in Europe? Because of community singing and physical jerks . . . and bubonic plague . . . and leprosy."

Back in her room Prudence reopened the *Pano-*

rama of Life and began writing: *a woman in love* . . .

"A woman," said Mr. Youkoumian. "That's what Seth needs to keep im quiet. Always sticking is nose in too much everywhere. You listen to me, Mr. Seal—if we can fix Seth with a woman our modernisation will get along damn fine."

"There's always Fifi."

"Oh, Mr. Seal, e ad er when e was a little boy. Don't you worry. I'll fix it O.K."

Royal interruptions of the routine of the Ministry were becoming distressingly frequent in the last few days as the Emperor assimilated the various books that had arrived for him by the last mail. Worst of all the Pageant of Birth Control was proving altogether more trouble than it was worth; in spite of repeated remonstrances, however, it continued to occupy the mind of the Emperor in precedence of all other interests. He had already re-named the site of the Angelican Cathedral, Place Marie Stopes.

"Heaven knows what will happen if he ever discovers psycho-analysis," remarked Basil, gloomily foreseeing a Boulevard Kraft-Ebbing, an Avenue Œdipus and a pageant of coprophagists.

"He'll discover every damn modern thing," said Mr. Youkoumian, "if we don't find him a woman damn quick . . . ere's another letter from the Vicar

Apostolic. If I adn't ordered all that stuff from Cairo I'd drop the whole pageant. But you can't use it for nothing else but what it's for—so far as I can see, not like boots what they can eat."

The opposition to the pageant was firm and widespread. The conservative party rallied under the leadership of the Earl of Ngumo. This nobleman, himself one of a family of forty-eight (most of whom he had been obliged to assassinate on his succession to the title) was the father of over sixty sons and uncounted daughters. This progeny was a favourite boast of his; in fact he maintained a concert party of seven minstrels for no other purpose than to sing at table about this topic when he entertained friends. Now in ripe age, with his triumphs behind him, he found himself like some scarred war veteran surrounded by pacifists, his prestige assailed and his proudest achievements held up to vile detraction. The new proposals struck at the very roots of sport and decency and he expressed the general feeling of the landed gentry when he threatened amid loud grunts of approval to dismember any man on his estates whom he found using the new-fangled and impious appliances.

The smart set, composed (under the leadership of Lord Boaz) of cosmopolitan blacks, courtiers, younger sons and a few of the decayed Arab intelligentsia, though not actively antagonistic, were tepid in their support; they discussed the question languidly in Fifi's salon and, for the most part, adopted a sophisticated attitude maintaining that of course *they* had always known about these things, but why invite trouble by all this publicity; at best it would only make contraception middle class. In any case this circle was always suspect to the popular mind and their allegiance was unlikely to influence public opinion in the Emperor's favour.

The Churches came out strong on the subject. No one could reasonably accuse the Nestorian Patriarch of fanatical moral inflexibility—indeed there had been incidents in his Beatitude's career when all but grave scandal had been caused to the faithful—but whatever his personal indulgence, his theology had always been unimpeachable. Whenever a firm lead was wanted on a question of opinion, the Patriarch had been willing to forsake his pleasures and pronounce freely and intransigently for the tradition he had inherited. There had been the ugly affair of the Metropolitan of Matodi who had proclaimed himself fourth member of the Trinity; there was the parish priest who was unsound about the Dual Will; there was the ridiculous heresy that sprang up in the province of Mhomala that the prophet Esias had wings and lived in a tree; there was the painful case of the human sacrifices at the Bishop of Popo's consecration—on all these and other uncertain topics the Patriarch had given proof of a sturdy orthodoxy.

Now, on the question of birth control, his Beatitude left the faithful in no doubt as to where their duty lay. As head of the established Church he called a conference which was attended by the Chief Rabbi, the Mormon Elder and the chief representatives of all the creeds of the Empire; only the Anglican Bishop excused himself, remarking in a courteous letter of refusal, that his work lay exclusively among the British community who, since they were already fully informed and equipped in the matter, could scarcely be injured in any way by the Emperor's new policy; he wished his Beatitude every success in the gallant stand he was making for the decencies of family life, solicited his prayers and remarked that he was himself too deeply embroiled with the progressive party, who were threatening the demolition of his Cathedral, to confuse the issue with any other cause, however laudable it might be in itself.

As a result of the conference, the Patriarch composed an encyclical in rich, oratorical style and despatched copies of it by runners to all parts of the island. Had the influence of the established Church on the popular mind been more weighty, the gala should have been doomed, but as has already been mentioned the Christianising of the country was still so far incomplete that the greater part of the Empire retained with a minimum of disguise their older and grosser beliefs and it was, in fact, from the least expected quarter, the tribesmen and villagers, that the real support of Seth's policy suddenly appeared.

This development was due directly and solely to the power of advertisement. In the dark days when the prejudice of his people compassed him on every side and even Basil spoke unsympathetically of the wisdom of postponing the gala, the Emperor found among the books that were mailed to him monthly from Europe, a collection of highly inspiring Soviet posters. At first the difficulties of imitation appeared to be insuperable. The *Courier* office had no machinery for reproducing pictures. Seth was contemplating the wild expedient of employing slave labour to copy his design when Mr. Youkoumian discovered that some years ago an enterprising philanthropist had by bequest introduced lithography into the curriculum of the American Baptist school. The apparatus survived the failure of the attempt. Mr. Youkoumian purchased it from the pastor and resold it at a fine profit to the Department of Fine Arts in the Ministry of Modernisation. An artist was next found in the Armenian colony who, on Mr. Youkoumian's introduction, was willing to elaborate Seth's sketches. Finally there resulted a large, highly coloured poster well calculated to

convey to the illiterate the benefits of birth control.
It was in many ways the highest triumph of the new
ministry and Mr. Youkoumian was the hero. Copies
were placarded all over Debra-Dowa; they were sent
down the line to every station latrine, capital and
coast; they were sent into the interior to vice-regal
lodges and headmen's huts, hung up at prisons, barracks, gallows and juju trees, and wherever the
poster was hung there assembled a cluster of inquisi-
tive, entranced Azanians.

It portrayed two contrasted scenes. On one side a
native hut of hideous squalor, overrun with children
of every age, suffering from every physical incapacity—crippled, deformed, blind, spotted and insane;
the father prematurely aged with paternity squatted
by an empty cook-pot; through the door could be
seen his wife, withered and bowed with child bearing, desperately hoeing at their inadequate crop. On
the other side a bright parlour furnished with chairs
and table; the mother, young and beautiful, sat at
her ease eating a huge slice of raw meat; her husband smoked a long Arab hubble-bubble (still a
caste mark of leisure throughout the land), while a
single, healthy child sat between them reading a
newspaper. Inset between the two pictures was a
detailed drawing of some up-to-date contraceptive
apparatus and the words in Sakuyu: *WHICH
HOME DO YOU CHOOSE?*

Interest in the pictures was unbounded; all over the island woolly heads were nodding, black hands pointing, tongues clicking against filed teeth in unsyntactical dialects. Nowhere was there any doubt about the meaning of the beautiful new pictures.

See: on right hand: there is rich man: smoke pipe like big chief: but his wife she no good: sit eating meat: and rich man no good: he only one son.

See: on left hand: poor man: not much to eat: but his wife she very good, work hard in field: man he good too: eleven children: one very mad, very holy. And in the middle: Emperor's juju. Make you like that good man with eleven children.

And as a result, despite admonitions from squire and vicar, the peasantry began pouring into town for the gala, eagerly awaiting initiation to the fine new magic of virility and fecundity.

Once more wrote Basil Seal, in a leading article in the *"Courier," the people of the Empire have overridden the opposition of a prejudiced and interested minority, and with no uncertain voice have followed the Emperor's lead in the cause of Progress and the New Age.*

So brisk was the demand for the Emperor's juju that some time before the day of the carnival Mr. Youkoumian was frantically cabling to Cairo for fresh supplies.

Meanwhile the Nestorian Patriarch became a very frequent guest at the French Legation.

"We have the army, we have the Church," said M. Ballon. "All we need now is a new candidate for the throne."

"If you ask me," said Basil, one morning soon after the distribution of the poster, "loyalty to the throne is one of the hardest parts of our job."

"Oh, gosh, Mr. Seal, don't you ever say a thing like that. I seen gentlemen poisoned dead for less. What's e done now?"

"Only this." He handed Mr. Youkoumian a chit which had just arrived from the Palace:

For your information and necessary action; I have decided to abolish the following:
   Death penalty.
   Marriage.
   The Sakuyu language and all native dialects.
   Infant mortality.
   Totemism.
   Inhumane butchery.
   Mortgages.
   Emigration.
   Please see to this. Also organise system of reservoirs for city's water supply and draft syllabus for competitive examination for public services. Suggest compulsory Esperanto. Seth.

"E's been reading books again, Mr. Seal, that's what it is. You won't get no peace from im not till you fix im with a woman. Why can't e drink or something?"

In fact the Ministry's triumph in the matter of birth control was having highly embarrassing consequences. If before, Basil and Mr. Youkoumian had cause to lament their master's tenacity and single-ness of purpose, they were now harassed from the opposite extreme of temperament. It was as though Seth's imagination like a volcanic lake had in the moment of success become suddenly swollen by the irruption of unsuspected, subterranean streams until it darkened and seethed and overflowed its margins in a thousand turbulent cascades. The earnest and rather puzzled young man became suddenly capricious and volatile; ideas bubbled up within him, bearing to the surface a confused sediment of phrase and theory, scraps of learning half understood and fantastically translated.

"It's going to be awkward for us if the Emperor goes off his rocker."

"Oh, my, Mr. Seal, you do say the most damned dangerous things."

That afternoon Basil called at the Palace to discuss the new proposals, only to find that since his lunch-eon the Emperor's interests had veered suddenly towards archæology.

"Yes, yes, the abolitions. I sent you a list this morning, I think. It is a mere matter of routine. I leave the details to the Ministry. Only you must be quick please . . . it is not that which I want to discuss with you now. It is our Museum."

"Museum?"

"Yes, of course we must have a Museum. I have made a few notes to guide you. The only serious difficulty is accommodation. You see it must be inaugurated before the arrival of the Cruelty to Animals Commission at the beginning of next month. There is hardly time to build a house for it. The best thing will be to confiscate one of the town palaces. Ngumo's or Boaz's would do after some slight adjustments. But that is a matter for the Ministry to decide. On the ground floor will be the natural history section. You will collect examples of all the flora and fauna of the Empire, lions, butterflies, birds' eggs, specimens of woods, everything. That should easily fill the ground floor. I have been reading," he added earnestly, "about ventilation. That is very important. The air in the cases must be continually renewed—a cubic metre an hour is about the right draught—otherwise the specimens suffer. You will make a careful note of that. Then on the first floor will be the anthropological and historical section—examples of native craft, Portuguese and Arab work, a small library. Then in the Central

Hall, the relics of the Royal House. I have some of the medals of Amurath upstairs under one of the beds in a box—photographs of myself, some of my uniforms, the cap and gown I wore at Oxford, the model of the Eiffel Tower which I brought back from Paris. I will lend some pages of manuscript in my own hand to be exhibited. It will be most interesting."

For some days Mr. Youkoumian busied himself with the collection of specimens. Word went round that there was a market for objects of interest at the Ministry of Modernisation and the work of the office was completely paralysed by the hawkers of all races who assembled in and around it, peddling brass pots and necklaces of carved nut, snakes in baskets and monkeys in cages, cloth of beaten bark and Japanese cotton, sacramental vessels pouched by Nestorian deacons, iron-wood clubs, homely household deities, tanned human scalps, cauls and navel strings and wonder-working fragments of meteorite, amulets to ward off the evil eye from camels, M. Ballon's masonic apron purloined by the legation butler, and a vast monolithic phallus borne by three oxen from a shrine in the interior. Mr. Youkoumian bargained briskly and bought almost everything he was offered, reselling them later to the Ministry of Fine Arts of which Basil had created him the director. But when, at a subsequent interview, Basil mentioned their progress to the Emperor he merely nodded a listless approval and even while he unscrewed the cap of his fountain pen to sign the order evicting the Earl of Ngumo from his town house, began to speak of the wonders of astronomy.

"Do you realise the magnitude of the fixed stars? They are immense. I have read a book which says that the mind boggles at their distances. I did not know that word, boggles. I am immediately founding an Institute for Astronomical Research. I must have Professors. Cable for them to Europe. Get me tip-top professors, the best procurable "

But next day he was absorbed in ectogenesis. "I have read here," he said, tapping a volume of speculative biology, "that there is to be no more birth. The ovum is fertilised in the laboratory and then the fœtus is matured in bottles. It is a splendid idea. Get me some of those bottles . . . and no boggling."

Even while discussing the topic that immediately interested him, he would often break off in the middle of a sentence, with an irrelevant question. "How much are autogyros?" or "Tell me exactly, please, what is Surréalism" or "Are you convinced of Dreyfus' innocence?" and then, without pausing for the reply would resume his adumbrations of the New Age.

The days passed rapturously for Mr. Youkoumian

who had found in the stocking of the Museum work for which early training and all his natural instincts richly equipped him; he negotiated endlessly between the Earl of Ngumo and Viscount Boaz, armed with orders for the dispossession of the lowest bidder; he bought and resold, haggled, flattered and depreciated, and ate and slept in a clutter of dubious antiques. But on Basil the strain of modernity began to leave its traces. Brief rides with Prudence through the tinder-dry countryside, assignations furtively kept and interrupted at a moment's notice by some peremptory, crazy summons to the Palace, alone broke the unquiet routine of his day.

"I believe that odious Emperor is slowly poisoning you. It's a thing he does do," said Prudence. "And I never saw any one look so ill."

"You know it sounds absurd but I miss Connolly. It's rather a business living all the time between Seth and Youkoumian."

"Of course you wouldn't remember that there's me too, would you," said Prudence. "Not just to cheer me up you wouldn't?"

"You're a grand girl, Prudence. What Seth calls tip-top. But I'm so tired I could die."

And a short distance away the legation syce moodily flicked with his whip at a train of ants while the ponies shifted restlessly among the stones and shelving earth of a dry water-course.

Two mornings later the Ministry of Modernisation received its sharpest blow. Work was going on as usual. Mr. Youkoumian was interviewing a coast Arab who claimed to possess some "very old, very genuine" Portuguese manuscripts; Basil, pipe in his mouth, was considering how best to deal with the Emperor's latest memorandum, *Kindly insist straw hats and gloves compulsory peerage,* when he received an unexpected and disturbing call from Mr. Jagger, the contractor in charge of the demolition of the Anglican Cathedral; a stocky, good-hearted little Britisher who after a succession of quite honourable bankruptcies in Cape Town, Mombasa, Dar-es-salaam and Aden had found his way to Debra-Dowa where he had remained ever since, occupied with minor operations in the harbour and along the railway line. He threaded his way through the antiquities which had lately begun to encroach on Basil's office, removed a seedy-looking caged vulture from the chair and sat down; his manner was uncertain and defiant.

"It's not playing the game, Mr. Seal," he said. "I tell you that fair and square and I don't mind who knows it, not if it's the Emperor himself."

"Mr. Jagger," said Basil impressively, "you should have been long enough in this country to know that that is a very rash thing to say. Men have been poisoned for less. What is your trouble?"

"This here's my trouble," said Mr. Jagger, producing a piece of paper from a pocket full of pencils and foot rules and laying it on the table next to the mosaic portrait of the late Empress recently acquired by the Director of Fine Arts. "What is it, eh, that's what I want to know."

"What indeed?" said Basil. He picked it up and examined it closely.

In size, shape and texture it resembled an English five-pound note and was printed on both sides with intricate engraved devices of green and red. There was an Azanian eagle, a map of the Empire, a soldier in the uniform of the Imperial Guard, an aeroplane, and a classical figure bearing a cornucopia but the most prominent place was taken by a large, medallion portrait of Seth in top hat and European tail coat. The words *FIVE POUNDS* lay in flourished script across the middle; above them *THE IMPERIAL BANK OF AZANIA* and below them a facsimile of Seth's signature.

The normal currency of the capital and the railway was in Indian rupees, although East African shillings, French and Belgian colonial francs and Marie Therese thalers circulated with equal freedom; in the interior the mediums of exchange were rock-salt and cartridges.

"This is a new one on me," said Basil. "I wonder

if the Treasury knows anything about it. Mr. You-koumian, come in here a minute, will you?"

The Director of Fine Arts and First Lord of the Treasury trotted through the partition door in his black cotton socks; he carried a model dhow he had just acquired.

"No, Mr. Seal," he pronounced, "I ain't never seen a thing like that before. Where did the gentleman get it?"

"The Emperor's just given me a whole packet of them for the week's wages bill. What is the Imperial Bank of Azania anyway. I never see such a thing all the time I been in the country. There's something here that's not on the square. You must understand Mr. Seal that it's not any one's job breaking up that Cathedral. Solid granite shipped all the way from Aberdeen. Why Lord love you the pulpit alone weighs seven and a half ton. I had two boys hurt only this morning through the font swinging loose as they were hoisting it into a lorry. Smashed up double one of them was. The Emperor ain't got no right to try putting that phoney stuff across me."

"You may be quite confident," said Basil with dignity, "that in all your dealings with His Majesty you will encounter nothing but the highest generosity and integrity. However I will institute inquiries on your behalf."

"No offence meant, I'm sure," said **Mr. Jagger**.

Basil watched him across the yard and then snatched up his topee from a fossilised tree-fern. "What's that black lunatic been up to this time?" he asked, starting off towards the Palace.

"Oh, Mr. Seal, you'll get into trouble one day with the things you say."

The Emperor rose to greet him with the utmost cordiality.

"Come in, come in. I'm very glad you've come. I'm in some perplexity about *Nacktkultur*. Here have I spent four weeks trying to enforce the edict prescribing trousers for the official classes, and now I read that it is more modern not to wear any at all."

"Seth, what's the Imperial Bank of Azania?"

The Emperor looked embarrassed.

"I thought you might ask. . . . Well, actually it is not quite a bank at all. It is a little thing I did myself. I will show you."

He led Basil to a high cupboard which occupied half the wall on one side of the library, and opening it showed him a dozen or so shelves stacked with what might have been packets of writing paper.

"What is that?"

"Just under three million pounds," said the Emperor proudly. "A little surprise. I had them done in Europe."

"But you can't possibly do this."

"Oh, yes, I assure you. It was easy. All these on this shelf are for a thousand pounds each. And now that the plates have been made, it is quite inexpensive to print as many more as we require. You see there were a great many things which needed doing and I had not a great many rupees. Don't look angry, Seal. Look, I'll give you some." He pressed a bundle of fivers into Basil's hand. "And take some for Mr. Youkoumian, too. Pretty fine picture of me, eh? I wondered about the hat. You will see that in the fifty pound notes I wear a crown."

For some minutes Basil attempted to remonstrate; then quite suddenly he abandoned the argument.

"I knew you would understand," said the Emperor. "It is so simple. As soon as these are used up we will send for some more. And to-morrow you will explain to me about *Nacktkultur,* eh?"

Basil returned to his office very tired.

"There's only one thing to hope for now. That's a fire in the Palace to get rid of the whole lot."

"We must change these quick," said Mr. Youkoumian. "I know a damn fool Chinaman might do it. Anyway the Ministry of Fine Arts can take one at par for the historical section."

It was on that afternoon that Basil at last lost his confidence in the permanence of the One Year Plan.

SIX

From Dame Mildred Porch to her husband.
S.S. Le President Carnot.
Matodi.
March 8th.

*M*Y DEAR STANLEY,
    *I am writing this before disembarking.
    It will be posted at Marseilles and should
reach you as nearly as I can calculate on 17th of the
month. As I wrote to you from Durban, Sarah and I
decided to break our return journey in Azania. The
English boat did not stop here. So we had to change
at Aden into this outward bound French ship. Very
dirty and* unseamanlike. *I have heard very disagreeable accounts of the hunting here. Apparently the
natives dig deep pits into which the poor animals
fall; they are often left in these traps for several days
without food or water (imagine what that means in
the heat of the jungle) and are then mercilessly
butchered in cold blood. Of course the poor ignorant
people know no better. But the young Emperor is by
all accounts a comparatively enlightened and well
educated person and I am sure he will do all he can
to introduce more humane methods, if it is really
necessary to kill these fine beasts at all—as I very*

much doubt. I expect to resume our journey in about a fortnight. I enclose cheque for another month's household expenses. The coal bill seemed surprisingly heavy in your last accounts. I hope that you are not letting the servants become extravagant in my absence. There is no need for the dining-room fire to be lit before luncheon at this time of year.

Yours affec.

Mildred.

Dame Mildred Porch's Diary.

March 8th.

Disembarked Matodi 12.45. Quaint and smelly. Condition of mules and dogs appalling, also children. In spite of radio message British consul was not there to meet us. Quite civil native led us to his office. Tip five annas. Seemed satisfied. Consul not English at all. Some sort of Greek. Very unhelpful (probably drinks). Unable or unwilling to say when train starts for Debra-Dowa, whether possible engage sleeper. Wired legation. Went to Amurath Hotel. Positive pot-house. Men sitting about drinking all over terrace. Complained. Large bedroom overlooking harbour apparently clean. Sarah one of her headaches. Complained of her room over street. Told her very decent little room.

BLACK MISCHIEF

March 9th.

No news of train. Sarah disagreeable about her room. Saw Roman Missionary. Unhelpful. Typical dago attitude towards animals. Later saw American Baptists. Middle class and unhelpful because unable talk native languages. No answer legation. Wired again.

March 10th.

No news train. Wired legation again. Unhelpful answer. Fed doggies in market place. Children tried to take food from doggies. Greedy little wretches. Sarah still headache.

March 11th.

Hotel manager suddenly announced train due to leave at noon. Apparently has been here all the time. Sarah very slow packing. Outrageous bill. Road to station blocked broken motor lorry. Natives living in it. Also two goats. Seemed well but cannot be healthy for them so near natives. Had to walk last quarter mile. Afraid would miss train. Arrived with five minutes to spare. Got tickets no sleepers. Just in time. V. hot and exhausted. Train did not start until three o'clock. Arrived dinner time Lumo station where apparently we have to spend night. Shower bath and changed underclothes. Bed v. doubtful. Luckily remembered Keatings Durban.

Interesting talk French hotel manager about local conditions. Apparently there was quite civil war last summer. How little the papers tell us. New Emperor v. go-ahead. English advisor named Seal. Any relation Cynthia Seal? Hotel man seemed to doubt government's financial stability. Says natives are complete savages *but no white slave traffic—or so he says.*

March 12th.
Awful night. Bitten all over. Bill outrageous. Thought manager decent person too. Explained provisions hard to get. Humbug. Train left at seven in morning. Sarah nearly missed it. Two natives in carriage. I must say quite civil but v. uncomfortable as no corridor and had left so early. Tiring journey. Country seemed dry. Due in Debra-Dowa some time this afternoon. Must say shall be thankful.

Dame Mildred Porch and Miss Sarah Tin were in no way related to each other but constant companionship and a similarity of interests had so characterised them that a stranger might easily have taken them to be sisters as they stepped from the train onto the platform at Debra-Dowa. Dame Mildred was rather stout and Miss Tin rather spare. Each wore a khaki sun-hat in an oilcloth cover, each wore a serviceable, washable frock, and thick shoes and stockings, each had smoked spectacles and a firm mouth. Each carried an attaché case containing her most inalienable possessions—washing things and writing things, disinfectant and insecticide, books, passport, letters of credit—and held firmly to her burden in defiance of an eager succession of porters who attempted in turn to wrest it from her.

William pushed his way forward and greeted them amiably. "Dame Mildred Porch? Miss Tin? How are you? So glad you got here all right. I'm from the Legation. The Minister couldn't come himself. He's very busy just now, but he asked me to come along and see if you were all right. Any luggage? I've got a car outside and can run you up to the Hotel."

"Hotel? But I thought we should be expected at the Legation. I wired from Durban."

"Yes, the Minister asked me to explain. You see we're some way out of the town. No proper road. Awful business getting in and out. The Minister thought you'd be much more comfortable in the town itself. Nearer the animals and everything. But he particularly said he hoped you'd come over to tea one day if you ever have the time."

Dame Mildred and Miss Tin exchanged that look of slighted citizenship which William had seen in the eyes of every visitor he had ever greeted at Debra-Dowa. "I tell you what," he said. "I'll go and look for the luggage. I daresay it's got stolen on the way. Often is, you know. And I'll get our mail out at the same time. No King's Messengers or anything here. If there's no European travelling it's put in charge of the guard. We thought of wiring to you to look after it and then we thought probably you had the devil of a lot of luggage yourselves."

By the time that the two-seater car had been loaded with the legation bags and the two ladies there was very little room left for their luggage. "I say, d'you mind awfully," said William. "I'm afraid we'll have to leave this trunk behind. The hotel'll fetch it up for you in no time."

"Young man, did you come to meet us or your own mail?"

"Now, you know," said William, "that simply isn't a fair question. Off we go." And the overladen little car began jolting up the broad avenue into the town.

"Is *this* where we are to stay?" asked Miss Tin as they drew up opposite the *Grand Café et Hotel Restaurant de l'Empereur Seth.*

"It doesn't look terribly smart," admitted William, "but you'll find it a mine of solid comfort."

He led them into the murky interior, dispersing a turkey and her brood from the Reception Hall. "Any one in?" There was a bell on the counter which he rang.

"Ullo," said a voice from upstairs. "One minute," and presently Mr. Youkoumian descended, buttoning up his trousers. "Why, it's Mr. Bland. Ullo, sir, ow are you? I ad the Minister's letter about the road this afternoon and the answer I am afraid is 'nothing doing.' Very occupied, the Emperor . . ."

"I've brought you two guests. They are English ladies of great importance. You are to make them comfortable."

"I fix them O.K.," said Mr. Youkoumian.

"I'm sure you'll find everything comfortable here," said William. "And I hope we shall see you soon at the Legation."

"One minute, young man, there are a number of things I want to know."

"I fix you O.K.," said Mr. Youkoumian again.

"Yes, you ask Mr. Youkoumian here. He'll tell you everything far better than I could. Can't keep them waiting for the mail, you know."

"Impudent young puppy," said Dame Mildred as the car drove away. "I'll report him to the Foreign Office as soon as I get home. Stanley shall ask a question about him in the House."

Mail day at the British Legation. Sir Samson and Lady Courteney, Prudence and William, Mr. Legge and Mrs. Legge, Mr. and Mrs. Anstruther, sitting round the fireplace opening the bags. Bills, provisions, family news, official despatches, gramophone records, newspapers scattered on the carpet. Presently William said, "I say, d'you know who I ran into on the platform? Those two cruelty-to-animals women who kept telegraphing."

"How very annoying. What *have* you done with them?"

"I shot them into Youkoumian's. They wanted to come and stay here."

"Heaven forbid. I do hope they won't stay long. Ought we to ask them to tea or anything?"

"Well, I *did* say that perhaps you'd like to see them sometime."

"Hang it, William, that's a bit thick."

"Oh, I don't suppose they thought I meant it."

"I sincerely hope not."

March 12th (continued).
Arrived Debra-Dowa late in afternoon. Discourteous cub from Legation met us and left Sarah's trunk at station. Brought us to frightful *hotel. But Armenian proprietor v. obliging. Saved me visit to bank by changing money for us into local currency. Quaint bank notes with portrait of Emperor in European evening dress. Mr. Seal came in after dinner. He is Cynthia's son. V. young and ill-looking. Off hand manner. V. tired, going to bed early.*

That evening M. Ballon's report included the entry: *Two British ladies arrived, suspects. Met at station by Mr. Bland. Proceeded Youkoumian's.*

"They are being watched?"

"Without respite."

"Their luggage?"

"A trunk was left at the station. It has been searched but nothing incriminating was found. Their papers are in two small bags which never leave their hands."

"Ah, they are old stagers. Sir Samson is calling out his last reserves."

March 13th. Sunday.

No news Sarah's trunk. Went to Anglican Cathedral but found it was being pulled down. Service in Bishop's drawing-room. Poor congregation. V. silly sermon. Spoke to Bishop later about cruelty to animals. Unhelpful. Old Humbug. Later went to write name in book at Palace. Sarah in bed. Town very crowded, apparently preparing for some local feast or carnival. Asked Bishop about it but he could not tell me. Seemed unaccountably embarrassed. Asked Mr. Youkoumian. Either he cannot have understood my question or I cannot have understood what I thought him to say. Did not press point. He did not speak English at all well but is an obliging man.

March 14th.
Hideous night. Mosquito in net and v. large
brown bugs in bed. Up and dressed at dawn and
went for long walk in hills. Met quaint caravan—
drums, spears, etc. No news Sarah's trunk.

Other people besides Dame Mildred were interested in the little cavalcade which had slipped un-
obtrusively out of the city at dawn that day. Un-
obtrusively, in this connection, is a relative term.
A dozen running slaves had preceded the procession,
followed by a train of pack mules; then ten couples
of mounted spearmen, a platoon of uniformed Imperial Guardsmen and a mounted band, blowing
down reed flutes eight feet long and beating hand
drums of hide and wood. In the centre on a mule
loaded with silver and velvet trappings, had ridden
a stout figure, heavily muffled in silk shawls. It was
the Earl of Ngumo travelling incognito on a mission
of great delicacy.

"Ngumo left town to-day. I wonder what he's
after."

"I think the Earl's pretty fed up, Mr. Seal. I
take his 'ouse Saturday for the Museum. 'E's gone
back to 'is estates I expect."

"Estates, nothing. He's left five hundred men in
camp behind him. Besides, he left on the Popo road.
That's not his way home."

"Oh, gosh, Mr. Seal, I 'ope there ain't going to be no bust up."

Only three people in Debra-Dowa knew the reason for the Earl's departure. They were M. Ballon, General Connolly, and the Nestorian Patriarch. They had dined together on Saturday night at the French Legation, and after dinner, when Mme. Ballon and Black Bitch had withdrawn to the salon to discuss their hats and physical disorders, and the sweet champagne frothed in the shallow glasses, the Patriarch had with considerable solemnity revealed his carefully guarded secret of State.

"It happened in the time of Gorgias, my predecessor, of evil memory," said his Beatitude, "and the intelligence was delivered to me on my assumption of office, under a seal so holy that only extreme personal vexation induces me to break it. It concerns poor little Achon. I say 'poor little' although he must now, if he survives at all, be a man at least ninety years of age, greatly my own senior. He as you know was the son of the Great Amurath and it is popularly supposed that a lioness devoured him while hunting with his sister's husband, Seyid, in the Ngumo mountains. My Lords, nothing of the kind happened. By order of his sister and the Patriarch Gorgias the wretched boy was taken while under the influence of liquor to the monastery of St. Mark the Evangelist and incarcerated there."

"But this is a matter of vital importance," cried M. Ballon. "Is the man still alive?"

"Who can say? To tell you the truth I have not visited the Monastery of St. Mark the Evangelist. The Abbot is inclined to the lamentable heresy that the souls in hell marry and beget hobgoblins. He is pertinacious in error. I sent the Bishop of Popo there to reason with him and they drove the good man out with stones."

"Would they accept an order of release over your signature?"

"It is painful to me to admit it, but I am afraid they would not. It will be a question of hard cash or nothing."

"The Abbot may name his own price. I must have Achon here in the capital. Then we shall be ready to strike."

The bottle circulated and before they left for the drawing-room M. Ballon reminded them of the gravity of the occasion. "Gentlemen. This is an important evening in the history of East Africa. The future of the country and perhaps our own lives depend on the maintenance of absolute secrecy in regard to the Earl of Ngumo's expedition on Monday. All inside this room are sworn to inviolable silence."

As soon as his guests were gone he assembled his subordinates and explained the latest developments;

before dawn the news was in Paris. On the way home in the car Connolly told Black Bitch about it. "But it's supposed to be secret for a little, so keep your silly mouth shut, see."

March 14th (continued).
As Keatings obviously deteriorated went to store attached hotel to buy some more. Met native Duchess who spoke English. V. helpful re bugs. Went with her to her home where she gave me insecticide of her own preparation. Gave me tea and biscuits. V. interesting conversation. She told me that it has just been discovered that Emperor is not real heir to the throne. Elderly uncle in prison. They have gone to get him out. Most romantic, but hope new Emperor equally enlightened re animals.

March 15th.
Better night. Native Duchess' insecticide v. helpful though nasty smell. Received invitation dine Palace to-night. Short notice but thought it best accept for us both. Sarah says nothing to wear unless trunk turns up.

It was the first time since Seth's accession that European visitors had been entertained at the Palace. The Ministry of Modernisation was called in early that morning to supervise the invitations and the menu.

"It shall be an entirely Azanian party. I want the English ladies to see how refined we are. I was doubtful about asking Viscount Boaz. What do you think? Will he be sober? . . . and there is the question of food. I have been reading that now it is called Vitamins. I am having the menu printed like this. It is a good, modern, European dinner, eh?"

Basil looked at the card. A month ago he might have suggested emendations. To-day he was tired.

"That's fine, Seth; go ahead like that."

"You see," said the Emperor proudly, "already we Azanians can do much for ourselves. Soon we shall not need a Minister of Modernisation. No, I do not mean that, Basil. Always you are my friend and advisor."

So the menu for Seth's first dinner party went to the *Courier* office to be printed and came back a packet of handsome gilt edged cards, laced with silk ribbons in the Azanian colours and embossed with a gold crown.

March 15th.

*IMPERIAL BANQUET FOR WELCOMING
THE ENGLISH
CRUELTY TO ANIMALS*

Menu of Foods.

Vitamin A
Tin Sardines

Vitamin B
Roasted Beef

Vitamin C
Small Roasted Suckling Porks

Vitamin D
Hot Sheep and Onions

Vitamin E
Spiced Turkey

Vitamin F
Sweet Puddings

Vitamin G
Coffee

Vitamin H
Jam

"It is so English," explained Seth. "From cour-
tesy to your great Empire."

At eight o'clock that evening Dame Mildred and Miss Tin arrived at the Palace for the banquet. The electric light plant was working that evening and a string of coloured bulbs shone with Christmas welcome over the main doorway. A strip of bright linoleum had been spread on the steps and as the taxi drew up a dozen or so servants ran down to conduct the guests into the hall. They were in mixed attire; some in uniforms of a kind, tunics frogged with gold braid discarded or purloined in the past from the wardrobes of visiting diplomats; some in native costume of striped silk. As the two ladies stepped from the car a platoon of guards lounging on the Terrace alarmed them with a ragged volley of welcome.

There was slight delay as the driver of the taxi refused to accept the new pound note which Dame Mildred tendered him in payment, but the captain of the guard, hurrying up with a jingle of spurs curtailed further discussion by putting the man under arrest and signified in a few graphic gestures his sorrow for the interruption and his intention of hanging the troublesome fellow without delay.

The chief saloon was brilliantly lighted and already well filled with the flower of Azanian native society. One of the first acts of the new reign had been an ordnance commanding the use of European evening dress. This evening was the first occasion for it to be worn and all round the room stood sombre but important figures completely fitted up by Mr. Youkoumian with tail coats, white gloves, starched linen and enamelled studs; only in a few cases were shoes and socks lacking; the unaccustomed attire lent a certain dignified rigidity to their deportment. The ladies had for the most part allowed their choice to fix upon frocks of rather startling colour; aniline greens and violets with elaborations of ostrich feather and sequin. Viscountess Boaz wore a backless frock newly arrived from Cairo combined with the full weight of her ancestral jewellery; the Duchess of Mhomala carried on her woolly head a three pound tiara of gold and garnets; Baroness Batulle exposed shoulders and back magnificently tattooed and cicatrised with arabesques.

Beside all this finery the guests of honour looked definitely dowdy as the Lord Chamberlain conducted them round the room and performed the introductions in French scarcely more comfortable than Dame Mildred's own.

Two slaves circulated among them carrying trays of brandy. The English ladies refused. The Lord Chamberlain expressed his concern. Would they have preferred whiskey; no doubt some could be produced? Or beer?

"Mon bon homme," said Dame Mildred severely,

"il vous faut comprendre que nous ne buvons rien de tout, jamais"; an announcement which considerably raised their prestige among the company; they were not much to look at, certainly, but at least they knew a thing or two which the Azanians did not. A useful sort of woman to take on a journey, reflected the Lord Chamberlain, and inquired with polite interest whether the horses and camels in their country were as conveniently endowed.

Further conversation was silenced by the arrival of the Emperor, who at this moment entered the hall from the far end and took his seat on the raised throne which had stood conspicuously on the dais throughout the preliminary presentations. Court etiquette was still in a formative stage. There was a moment of indecision during which the company stood in embarrassed silence waiting for a lead. Seth said something to his equerry, who now advanced down the room and led forward the guests of honour. They curtseyed and stood on one side, while the other guests filed past in strict precedence. Most of them bowed low in the Oriental manner, raising the hand to forehead and breast. The curtsey however had been closely observed and found several imitators among both sexes. One elderly peer, a stickler for old-world manners, prostrated himself fully and went through the mimic action of covering his head with dust. When all had saluted him in

their various ways, Seth led the party in to dinner;
fresh confusion over the places and some ill-natured
elbowing; Dame Mildred and Miss Tin sat on either
side of the Emperor; soon every one was eating and
drinking at a great pace.

> *March 15th (continued).*
> *Dinner at Palace. Food v. nasty. Course after*
> *course different kinds of meat, overseasoned and*
> *swimming in grease. Tried to manage some of it*
> *from politeness. Sarah ate nothing. Emperor asked*
> *great number of questions some of which I was un-*
> *able to answer. How many suits of clothes had the*
> *King of England? Did he take his bath before or*
> *after his breakfast? Which was the more civilised?*
> *What was the best shop to buy an artesian well? etc.*
> *Sara v. silent. Told Emperor about co-education and*
> *'free-discipline.' Showed great interest.*

Dame Mildred's neighbour on her other side was
the punctilious man who had prostrated himself in
the drawing-room; he seemed engrossed in his eating. In point of fact he was rehearsing in his mind
and steeling his nerve to enunciate some English conversation in which he had painfully schooled himself during that day: at last it came up suddenly.

"Ow many ox ave you?" he demanded, lifting
up sideways from his plate a great bearded face.

"ow many sons? ow many daughters? ow many brothers? ow many sisters? My father is dead fighting."

Dame Mildred turned to him a somewhat startled scrutiny. There were crumbs and scraps of food in various parts of his beard. "I beg your pardon?" she said.

But the old gentleman had shot his bolt; he felt that he had said all and more than all that good breeding required, and to tell the truth was more than a little taken aback by his own fluency. He gave her a nervous smile and resumed his dinner without again venturing to address her.

"Which of the white ladies would you like to have?"

"The fat one. But both are ugly."

"Yes. It must be very sad for the English gentlemen to marry English ladies."

Presently when the last vitamin had been guzzled. Viscount Boaz rose to propose the health of the guests of honour. His speech was greeted by loud applause and was then done into English by the Court Interpreter:

"Your Majesty, Lords and Ladies. It is my privilege and delight this evening to welcome with open arms of brotherly love to our city Dame Mildred

Porch and Miss Tin, two ladies renowned throughout the famous country of Europe for their great
cruelty to animals. We Azanians are a proud and
ancient nation but we have much to learn from the
white people of the West and North. We too, in our
small way, are cruel to our animals"—and here the
Minister for the Interior digressed at some length to
recount with hideous detail what he had himself
once done with a woodman's axe to a wild boar—
"but it is to the great nations of the West and North,
and specially to their worthy representatives that are
with us to-night, that we look as our natural leaders
on the road of progress. Ladies and gentlemen we
must be Modern, we must be refined in our Cruelty
to Animals. That is the message of the New Age
brought to us by our guests this evening. May I, in
conclusion, raise my glass and ask you to join with
me in wishing them old age and prolonged fecundity."

The toast was drunk and the company sat down.
Boaz's neighbours congratulated him on his speech.
There seemed no need for a reply and indeed Dame
Mildred, rarely at a loss for telling phrases, would on
this occasion have been hard put to it to acknowl-
edge the welcome in suitable terms. Seth appeared
not to have heard either version of the speech. He
sat inattentive, his mind occupied with remote spec-

ulation. Dame Mildred attempted two or three conversations.

"A very kindly meant speech, but he seems to misunderstand our mission. . . . It is so interesting to see your people in their own milieu. Do tell me who is who . . . Have they entirely abandoned native costume? . . ."

But she received only abstracted answers.

Finally she said, "I was so interested to learn about your uncle Achon." The Emperor nodded. "I do hope they get him out of the monastery. Such a useless life, I always think, and so selfish. It makes people introspective to think all the time about their own souls, don't you think? So sensible of that Earl of wherever it is to go and look for him."

But Seth had not heard a word.

March 16th.

Could not sleep late after party. Attempted to telephone legation. No reply. Attempted to see Mr. Seal. Said he was too busy. No sign of Sarah's trunk. She keeps borrowing my things. Tried to pin down Emperor last night, no result. Went for walk in town. V. crowded, no one working. Apparently some trouble about currency. Saw man strike camel, would have reported him but no policeman about. Begin to feel I am wasting my time here.

BLACK MISCHIEF

The Monastery of St. Mark the Evangelist, though infected of late with the taint of heresy, was the centre of Azanian spiritual life. Here in remote times Nestorian missionaries from Mesopotamia had set up a church and here when the great Amurath proclaimed Christianity the official creed of the Empire, the old foundations had been unearthed and a native community installed. A well substantiated tradition affirmed that the little river watering the estate was in fact the brook Kedron conveyed there subterraneously; its waters were in continual requisition for the relief of skin diseases and stubborn boils. Here too were preserved among other relics of less certain authenticity, David's stone prised out of the forehead of Goliath (a boulder of astonishing dimensions), a leaf from the Barren Fig Tree, the rib from which Eve had been created, and a wooden cross which had fallen from heaven quite unexpectedly during Good Friday luncheon some years back. Architecturally, however, there was nothing very remarkable; no cloister or ambulatory, library, gallery, chapter house or groined refectory; a cluster of mud huts around a larger hut; a single stone building, the church dedicated to St. Mark by Amurath the Great. It could be descried from miles round, perched on a site of supreme beauty, a shelf of the great escarpment that overlooked the Wanda lowlands, and through it the brook Kedron, narrowed at this season to a single thread of silver, broke into innumerable iridescent cascades as it fell to join the sluggish Izol five thousand feet below. Great rocks of volcanic origin littered the fields. The hillside was full of unexplored caverns whence hyenas sallied out at night to exhume the corpses which it was a pious practice to transport from all over the Empire to await the last trump on that holy ground.

The Earl of Ngumo had made good time. The road lay through the Sakuyu cattle country, high plains, covered with brown and slippery grass. At first the way led along the caravan route to the royal cities of the north; a clearly defined track well frequented. They exchanged greetings with mule trains coming in to market and unusual bands of travellers, loping along on foot, drawn to the capital by the name of the great Gala and the magnetic excitement which all the last weeks had travelled on the ether, radiating in thrilling waves to bazaar, farm and jungle, gossiped about over camp fires, tapped out on hollow tree trunks in the swamplands, sniffed, as it were, on the breeze, sensed by sub-human faculties, that something was afoot.

Later they diverged into open country; only the heaps of stones bridging the water courses and an occasional wooden culvert told them they were still on the right road. On the first night they camped among shepherds. The simple men recognised a great nobleman and brought him their children to touch.

"We hear of changes in the great city."

"There are changes."

On the second night they reached a little town. The headman had been forwarned of their approach. He came out to meet them, prostrating himself and covering his head with dust.

"Peace be upon your house."

"You come from the great city of changes. What is your purpose among my people?"

"I wish well to your people. It is not suitable for the low to babble of what the high ones do."

They slept in and around the headman's hut; in the morning he brought them honey and eggs, a trussed chicken, dark beer in a jug and a basket of flat bread: they gave him salt in bars, and continued their journey.

The third night they slept in the open; there was a picket of royal guards somewhere in that country. Late on the fourth day they reached the Monastery of St. Mark the Evangelist.

A monk watching on the hill top sighted them and fired a single musket shot into the still air; a troop of baboons scattered frightened into the rocks. In the church below the great bell was rung to summon the community. The Abbot under his yellow sunshade stood in the enclosure to greet them; he wore steel rimmed spectacles. A little deacon beside him plied a horse-hair fly whisk.

Obeisance and benediction. The Earl presented the Patriarch's letter of commendation, which was slipped unopened into the folds of the Abbot's bosom, for it is not etiquette to show any immediate curiosity about such documents. Official reception, in the twilit hut; the Earl seated on a chair hastily covered with carpet. The chief men of the monastery stood round the wall with folded hands. The Abbot opened the letter of introduction, spat and read it aloud amid grunts of approval; it was all preamble and titles of honour; no word of business. A visit to the shrine of the Barren Fig Tree; the Earl kissed the lintel of the door three times, laid his forehead against the steps of the sanctuary and made a present of a small bag of silver. Dinner in the Abbot's lodging; it was one of the numerous fast days of the Nestorian Church; vegetable mashes in wooden bowls, one of bananas, one of beans; earthenware jugs and brown vessels of rough beer. Ponderous leave takings for the night. The Earl's tent meanwhile had been pitched in the open space within the enclosure; his men squatted on guard; they had made a fire; two or three monks joined them; soon they began singing, wholly secular words in a monotonous cadence. Inside the tent a single small lamp with floating wick. The Earl squatted among his rugs, waiting for the Abbot who, he knew, would come that night. Presently through the flap of the tent appeared the bulky white turban and straggling beard of the prelate. The two great men squatted opposite each other, on either side of the little lamp; outside the guards singing at the camp fire; beyond the stockade the hyenas and a hundred hunting sounds among the rocks. Grave courtesies: "Our little convent resounds with the fame of the great Earl . . . his prowess in battle and in bed . . . the thousand enemies slain by his hand . . . the lions he has speared . . . his countless progeny . . ."

"All my life I have counted the days wasted until I saluted the Abbot . . . his learning and sanctity . . . his dauntless fidelity to the faith, his chastity . . . the austerities of his spiritual practices . . ."

Slowly by a multitude of delicately graded steps the conversation was led to a more practical level. Was there any particular object in the Earl's visit, other than the infinite joy afforded to all by his presence?

What object could be more compelling than the universal ambition to pay respect to the Abbot and the glorious shrine of the Barren Fig Leaf? But there was, as it so happened, a little matter, a thing scarcely worth a thought, which since he was there, the Earl might mention if it would not be tedious to his host.

Every word of the Earl's was a jewel, valued beyond human computation; what was this little matter?

It was an old story . . . in the days of His Beatitude Gorgias of evil memory . . . a prisoner, brought to the convent; now an old man . . . One of whom only high ones might speak . . . supposing that this man were alive . . .

"Oh, Earl, you speak of that towards which my lips and ears are sealed. There are things which are not suitable."

"Abbot, once there comes a time for everything when it must be spoken of."

"What should a simple monk know of these high affairs. But I have indeed heard it said that in the times of His Beatitude Gorgias of evil memory, there was such a prisoner."

"Does he still live?"

"The monks of St. Mark the Evangelist guard their treasures well."

After this all important admission they sat for some time in silence; then the Abbot rose and with ample formalities left his guest to sleep. Both parties felt that the discussion had progressed almost too quickly. There were decencies to be observed.

Negotiations were resumed after Mass next morning and occupied most of the day; before they parted for the night Earl and Abbot had reduced their differences to a monetary basis. Next morning the price was decided and Achon, son of Amurath, legitimate Emperor of Azania, Chief of the Chiefs of Sakuyu, Lord of Wanda and Tyrant of the Seas, was set at liberty.

The event took place without ceremony. After a heavy breakfast of boiled goatsmeat, cheese, olives, smoked mutton, goose and mead—it was one of the numerous feast days of the Nestorian Church—the Earl and the Abbot set out for the hillside unaccompanied except by a handful of slaves. A short climb from the compound brought them to the mouth of a small cave.

"We will wait here. The air is not good."

Instead they sent in a boy with lantern and hammer. From the depths they heard a few muffled words and then a series of blows as a staple was splintered from the rock. Within five minutes the slave had returned leading Achon by a chain attached to his ankle. The prince was completely naked, bowed and shrivelled, stained white hair hung down his shoulders, a stained white beard over his chest; he was blind, toothless and able to walk only with the utmost uncertainty.

The Earl had considered a few words of homage and congratulation. Instead he turned to the Abbot. "He won't be able to ride."

"That was hardly to be expected."

Another night's delay while a litter was constructed; then on the fifth morning the caravan set out again for Debra-Dowa. Achon swung between the shoulders of four slaves, heavily curtained from curious eyes. Part of the time he slept; at others he crooned quietly to himself, now and then breaking into little moans of alarm at the sudden jolts and lurches in his passage. On the eighth day, under cover of darkness, the little procession slipped by side roads and unfrequented lanes into the city and having delivered his charge to the Patriarch, the Earl hurried out to the French Legation to report to M. Ballon the successful performance of his mission.

Meanwhile Dame Mildred was not enjoying herself at all. Every one seemed to conspire to be unhelpful and disobliging. First there was the intolerable impudence of that wretched boy at the Legation. She had attempted to ring them up every morning and afternoon; at last, when she had almost despaired of effecting connection Mme. Youkoumian had announced that she was through. But it had been a most unsatisfactory conversation. After some minutes with an obtuse native butler ('probably drinks' Dame Mildred had decided) the voice had changed to a pleasant, slightly languid English tone.

"I am Dame Mildred Porch. I wish to speak to the Minister."

"Oh, I don't suppose you can do that, you know. Can *I* do anything for you?"

"Who are you?"

"I'm William."

"Well I wish to speak to you in particular—it's about Miss Tin's trunk."

"Drunk?"

"Miss Sarah Tin, the organising secretary of the overseas department of the League of Dumb Chums. She has lost her trunk."

"Ah."

There was a long pause. Dame Mildred could hear a gramophone being played at the other end of the line.

"Hullo . . . Hullo. . . . Are you there?"

Then William's gentle drawl said: "You know the trouble about the local telephone is that one's always getting cut off."

There had been a click and the dance music suddenly ceased. "Hullo . . . Hullo." She rattled the machine but there was no answer. "I'm convinced he did it on purpose," she told Miss Tin. "If we could only prove it."

Then there was trouble about her money. The twenty or so pounds which she had changed into Bank of Azania currency on her first afternoon

235

seemed to be quite worthless. Even Mr. Youkoumian, from whom she had first received them, was
unable to help, remarking that it was a question of
politics; he could not accept the notes himself in
settlement of the weekly hotel bill or in payment for
the numerous articles of clothing which Miss Tin
was obliged to purchase from day to day at his store.

Then there was the Emperor's prolonged neglect
of the cause of animals. The banquet so far from
being the prelude to more practical association,
seemed to be regarded as the end of her visit. Her
daily attempts to obtain an audience were met with
consistent refusal. At times she fell into a fever of
frustration; there, all over the country, were dumb
chums being mercilessly snared and speared, and
here was she, impotent to help them; throughout
those restless Azanian nights Dame Mildred was
continually haunted by the appealing reproachful
eyes, limpid as spaniel puppies', of murdered lions,
and the pathetic patient whinnying of trapped
baboons. Consciousness of guilt subdued her usually
confident manner; who was she to complain—be-
trayer that she was of mandril, hyena, and wild pig,
wart hog and porcupine—if Mr. Youkoumian over-
charged her bill or mislaid her laundry?

"Mildred, I don't think you're looking at all
well. I don't believe this place agrees with you."

"No, Sarah, I'm not sure that it does. Oh, do let's

236

go away. I don't like the people or the way they look or anything and we aren't doing any good."

"Basil, Mum wants me to go home—back to England, I mean."

"I shan't like that."

"Do you mean it? Oh, lovely Basil, I don't want to go a bit."

"We may all have to go soon. Things seem breaking up here . . . only I'm not so sure about going to England. . . . Can't we go somewhere else?"

"Darling, what's the good of talking . . . we'll see each other again, whatever happens. You do promise that, don't you?"

"You're a grand girl, Prudence, and I'd like to eat you."

"So you shall, my sweet . . . anything you want."

Strips of sunlight through the shutters; below in the yard a native boy hammering at the engine of a broken motor car.

"I am sending Mme. Ballon and the other ladies of the legation down to the coast. I do not anticipate serious trouble. The whole thing will pass off without a shot being fired. Still it is safer so. Monsieur Floreau will accompany them. He will have the delicate work of destroying the Lumo bridge. That is necessary because Seth has three regiments at Matodi who might prove loyal. The train leaves on the day before the gala. I suggest that we advise Mr. and Mrs. Schonbaum a few hours before it starts. It would compromise the coup d'etat if there were an international incident. The British must fend for themselves."

"What is the feeling in the army, General?"

"I called a meeting of the Staff to-day and told them of Prince Achon's arrival in Debra-Dowa. They know what is expected of them. Yesterday their salaries were paid in the new notes."

"And the Prince, your Beatitude?"

"He is no worse."

"But content?"

"Who can say? He has been sleeping most of the day. He does not speak. He is all the time searching for something on the floor, near his foot. I think he misses his chain. He eats well."

"Mr. Seal, I think I go down to Matodi day after to-morrow. Got things to fix there, see? How about you come too?"

"No good this week, Youkoumian. I shall have to wait and see poor Seth's gala."

"Mr. Seal, you take my tip and come to Matodi. I hear things. You don't want to get into no bust-up."

"I've been hearing things too. I want to stay and see the racket."

"Damn foolishness."

It was not often that the Oriental Secretary called on the Minister. He came that evening after dinner. They were playing animal-snap.

"Come in, Walsh. Nice to see you. You can settle a dispute for us. Prudence insists that a giraffe neighs like a horse. Now does it?"

Later he got the Minister alone.

"Look here, sir, I don't know how closely you've followed local affairs, but I thought I ought to come and tell you. There's likely to be trouble on Tuesday on the day of this birth control gala."

"Trouble? I should think so. I think the whole thing perfectly disgusting. None of us are going."

"Well, I don't exactly know what sort of trouble. But there's *something* up. I've just heard this evening that the French and Americans are going down to the coast en bloc by the Monday train. I thought you ought to know."

"Pooh, another of these native disturbances. I remember that last civil war was just the same. Ballon thought he was going to be attacked the whole time. I'd sooner risk being bombed up here than bitten by mosquitoes at the coast. Still, jolly nice of you to tell me."

"You wouldn't mind, sir, if my wife and myself went down on the train."

"Not a bit, not a bit. Jolly glad. You can take charge of the bags. Can't say I envy you but I hope you have a jolly trip."

On the morning preceding the gala, Basil went as usual to his office. He found Mr. Youkoumian busily packing a canvas grip with the few portable objects of value that had been collected for the museum. "I better take care of these in case anything appens," he explained. "Catching train eleven o'clock. Very much crowded train. I think many wise men will be aboard. You better come too, Mr. Seal. I fix it O.K."

"What *is* going to happen?"

"I don't know nothing, Mr. Seal. I don't ask no questions. All I think that if there is a bust up I will better be at the coast. They were preaching in all the churches Sunday against the Emperor's birth control. Madame Youkoumian told me, which is a very pious and churchgoing woman. But I think there is more than that going to happen. I think General Connolly knows something. You better come to the coast, Mr. Seal. No?"

There was nothing to do that morning; no letters to answer; no chits from the palace; the work of the Ministry seemed suddenly over. Basil locked his office door, pocketed the key and strode across the yard to see Seth. Two officers at the gate-house hushed their conversation as Basil passed them.

He found Seth, in an elegant grey suit and pale coloured shoes, moodily pouring over the map of the new city.

"They have stopped work on the Boulevard Seth. Jagger has dismissed his men. Why is this?"

"He hadn't been paid for three weeks. He didn't like the new bank notes."

"Traitor. I will have him shot. I sent for Connolly an hour ago. Where is he?"

"A great number of Europeans left for the coast by this morning's train—but I don't think Connolly was with them."

"Europeans leaving? What do I care? The city is full of my people. I have watched them from the tower with my field glasses. All day they come streaming in by the four roads. . . . But the work must go on. The Anglican Cathedral, for example; it should be down by now. I'll have it down if I have to work with my own hands. You see it is right in the way of the great Northern thoroughfare. Look at it on the plan—so straight . . ."

"Seth, there's a lot of talk going about. They say there may be trouble to-morrow."

"God, have I not had trouble to-day and yesterday? Why should I worry about to-morrow?"

That evening Dame Mildred and Miss Tin saw a very curious sight. They had been to tea with the Bishop and leaving him, made a slight detour, in order to take advantage of the singular sweetness of the evening air. As they passed the Anglican Cathedral they noticed a young man working alone. He wore light grey and parti-coloured shoes and he was engaged in battering at the granite archway at the West End with an energy very rare among Azanian navvies.

"How like the Emperor."

"Don't be absurd, Sarah."

They left the grey figure chipping diligently in the twilight, and returned to their hotel where the Youkoumians' departure had utterly disorganised the service.

"Just when we had begun to make them understand how we liked things . . ." complained Dame Mildred.

Next morning the ladies were up early. They had been awaked before dawn by the traffic under their windows, mules and ponies, chatter and scuffling, cars hooting for passage. Dame Mildred opened the shutters and looked down into the crowded street. Miss Tin joined her.

"I've been ringing for twenty minutes. There doesn't seem to be a soul in the hotel."

Nor was there; the servants had gone out last night after dinner and had not returned. Fortunately Dame Mildred had the spirit stove without which she never ventured abroad, some biscuits and cubes of bouillon. They breakfasted in this way upstairs while the crowd outside grew every moment in volume and variety, as the sun, brilliant and piercing as on other less notable mornings, mounted over the city. Dust rose from the crowded street and hung sparkling in the air.

"So nice for the Emperor to have a good day for his Pageant. Not at all like any of the pageants I can remember in England. Do you remember the Girl Guides' rally when there was that terrible hail storm —in August, too? *How* the Brownies cried."

The route of the procession lay past the Hotel de l'Empereur Seth. Shop fronts had been boarded up and several of the householders had erected stands and temporary balconies outside their windows. Some weeks earlier, when the Pageant had first been announced, Mr. Youkoumian had advertised accommodation of this kind and sold a number of tickets to prospective sightseers. In the subsequent uncertainty he had abandoned this among other of his projects. Now however two or three Indians, a Greek and four or five Azanians in gala clothes presented themselves at the hotel to claim their seats in the stand. They explored the deserted vestibule and dining-room, climbed the stairs and finally reached the bedrooms of the English ladies. Hardened by long exposure to rebuffs and injustice, the Indians paid no attention to Dame Mildred's protests. Instead they pulled up the bed across the window, seated themselves in positions of excellent advantage and then producing small bags of betel nuts from their pockets settled down to wait, patiently chewing and spitting. Encouraged by this example the other intruders took possession of the other windows. The Greek politely offered Miss Tin a place in their midst and accepted her refusal with somewhat puzzled concern. The two ladies of the Azanian party wandered round the room picking up and examining the articles on the washstand and dressing table, and chattering with simple pleasure over the contents of the chest of drawers.

"This is an intolerable outrage. But I don't see what we can do about it at the moment. Sir Samson will have to lodge a complaint."

"We can't possibly remain here. We can't possibly go out into the street. There is only one place for us—the roof."

This position was easily accessible by means of a ladder and trap door. Hastily equipping themselves with rugs, pillows, sunshades, two light novels, cameras and the remains of the biscuits, the resolute ladies climbed up into the blazing sunlight. Dame

Mildred handed up their provisions to Miss Tin, then followed her. The trap door could not be bolted from above but fortunately the tin roof was weighted in many places by rock boulders, placed there to strengthen it in times of high wind. One of these they rolled into place, then sliding down the hot corrugations to the low cement parapet, they made their nest in a mood of temporary tranquillity.

"We shall see very well from here, Sarah. There will be plenty of time to have those natives punished to-morrow."

Indeed from where they sat the whole city lay very conveniently exposed to their view. They could see the irregular roofs of the Palace buildings in their grove of sapling blue gums and before them the still unfinished royal box from which the Emperor proposed to review the procession; small black figures could be observed working on it, tacking up coloured flags, spreading carpets and bobbing up the path with pots of palm and fern. They could see the main street of the city diverge, to the barracks on one side and the Christian quarter on the other. They could see the several domes and spires of the Catholic, Orthodox, Armenian, Anglican, Nestorian, American Baptist and Mormon places of worship; the minaret of the mosque, the Synagogue, and the flat white roof of the Hindu snake temple. Miss Tin took a series of snapshots.

"Don't use all the films, Sarah, there are bound to be some interesting things later."

The sun rose high in the heavens; the corrugated iron radiated a fierce heat. Propped on their pillows under green parasols the two ladies became drowsy and inattentive to the passage of time.

The procession was due to start at eleven but it must have been past noon before Dame Mildred, coming to with a jerk and snort, said, "Sarah, I think something is beginning to happen."

A little dizzily, for the heat was now scarcely bearable, the ladies leant over the parapet. The crowd was holloing loudly and the women gave out their peculiar throbbing whistle; there seemed to be a general stir towards the royal box, quarter of a mile down the road.

"That must be the Emperor arriving."

A dozen lancers were cantering down the street forcing the crowds back into the side alleys and courtyards, only to surge out again behind them.

"The procession will come up from the direction of the railway station. Look, here they are."

Fresh swelling and tumult in the crowded street. But it was only the lancers returning towards the Palace.

Presently Miss Tin said, "You know, this may take all day. How hungry we shall be."

"I've been thinking of that for some time. I am going to go down and forage."

"Mildred, you can't. *Anything* might happen to you."

"Nonsense, we can't live on this roof all day with four petit-beurre biscuits."

She rolled back the stone and carefully, rung by rung, descended the ladder. The bedroom doors were open and as she passed she saw that quite a large party was now assembled at the windows. She reached the ground floor, crossed the dining-room and opened the door at the far end where she had been informed by many penetrating smells during the past weeks, lay the kitchen quarters. Countless flies rose with humming alarm as she opened the larder door. Uncovered plates of horrible substances lay on the shelves; she drew back instinctively; then faced them again. There were some black olives in an earthenware basin and half a yard of brick-dry bread. Armed with these and breathing heavily she again climbed to the trap door.

"Sarah, open it at once." The rock was withdrawn. "How could you be so selfish as to shut it? Supposing I had been pursued."

"I'm sorry, Mildred. Indeed I am, but you were so long and I grew nervous. And, my dear, you have been missing such a lot. All kinds of things have been happening."

"What things?"

"Well, I don't know exactly, but look."

Indeed, below the crowds seemed to be in a state of extreme agitation, jostling and swaying without apparent direction around a wedge-shaped phalanx of police who were forcing a way with long bamboo staves; in their centre was an elderly man under arrest.

"Surely, those are the clothes of the native priests? What can the old man have been up to?"

"Almost anything. I have never had any belief in the clergy after that curate we liked so much who was Chaplain of the Dumb Chums and spoke so feelingly and then . . ."

"Look, here *is* the procession."

Rising strains of the Azanian anthem; the brass band of the Imperial Guards swung into sight drowning the sounds of conflict. The Azanians loved a band and their Patriarch's arrest was immediately forgotten. Behind the soldiers drove Viscount and Viscountess Boaz, who had eventually consented to act as patrons. Then marching four abreast in brand new pinafores came the girls of the Amurath Memorial High School, an institution founded by the old Empress to care for the orphans of murdered officials. They bore, somewhat unsteadily, a banner whose construction had occupied the embroidery and dressmaking class for several weeks. It was emblazoned in letters of appliquéd silk with the motto: *"WOMEN OF TO-MORROW DEMAND AN EMPTY CRADLE."* Slowly the mites filed by, singing sturdily.

"Very sensible and pretty," said Miss Tin. "Dear, Mildred, what very stale bread you have brought."

"The olives are excellent."

"I never liked olives. Good gracious, look at this."

The first of the triumphal cars had come into sight. At first an attempt had been made to induce ladies of rank to take part in the tableaux; a few had wavered, but Azanian society still retained certain standards; the peerage were not going to have their wives and daughters exhibiting themselves in aid of charity; the idea had to be dropped and the actresses recruited less ambitiously from the demimonde. This first car, drawn by oxen, represented the place of women in the modern world. Enthroned under a canopy of coloured cotton, sat Mlle. 'Fifi' Fatim Bey; in one hand a hunting crop to symbolise sport, in the other a newspaper to symbolise learning; round her were grouped a court of Azanian beauties with typewriters, tennis rackets, motor bicycling goggles, telephones, hitch-hiking outfits and other patents of modernity inspired by the European illustrated papers. An orange and green appliquéd standard bore the challenging motto *THROUGH STERILITY TO CULTURE.*

Enthusiastic applause greeted this pretty inven-
tion. Another car came into sight down the road,
bobbing decoratively above the black pates; other
banners.

Suddenly there was a check in the progress and
a new note in the voice of the crowd.

"Has there been an accident? I do hope none of
the poor oxen are hurt."

The trouble seemed to be coming from the front
of the procession, where bodies of men had pushed
through from the side streets and were endeavour-
ing to head the procession back. The brass band
stopped, faltered and broke off, scattering before
the assault and feebly defending their heads with
trombones and kettle drums.

"Quick, Sarah, your camera. I don't know what
in the world is happening but I must get a snap of
it. Of course the sun *would* be in the wrong place."

"Try with the very small stop."

"I do pray they come out; I had such bad luck
with those very interesting films of Cape Town that
the wretched man ruined on the boat. You know it
looks like quite a serious riot. Where are the police?"

The attackers having swept the band out of the
road and underfoot, were making easy work of the
High School Orphans; they were serious young men
armed with clubs, the athletic group, as the ladies

learned later, of Nestorian Catholic Action, muscu-
lar Christians who for many weeks now had been
impatiently biding their time to have a whack at
the modernists and Jews who were behind the new
movement.

Down went the embroidered banner as the girls
in their pinafores ran for safety between the legs of
the onlookers.

The main focus of the assault was now the triumphal car immediately in front of the Hotel de
l'Empereur Seth. At the first sign of disturbance
the members of the tableau had abandoned their
poses and huddled together in alarm; now without
hesitation they forsook their properties and bundled
out of the waggon into the street. The Christian
party swarmed onto it and one of them began ad-
dressing the crowd. Dame Mildred snapped him
happily as he turned in their direction, arms spread,
mouth wide open, in all the fervour of democratic
leadership.

Hitherto except for a few jabs with trumpets and
drumsticks, the attackers had met with no opposition. Now however the crowd began to take sides;
individual scuffles broke out among them and a
party of tribesmen from up country, happily welcoming this new diversion in a crowded day, began
a concerted charge to the triumphal car round which
there was soon raging a contest of I'm-king-of-the-

castle game. The Nestorian orator was thrown overboard and a fine savage in lion skins began doing a jig in his place. The patient oxen stood unmoved by the tumult.

"Quick, Sarah, another roll of films. What *can* the police be thinking of?"

Then authority asserted itself.

From the direction of the royal box flashed out a ragged volley of rifle shots. A bullet struck the parapet with a burst of splintered concrete and ricochetted, droning, over the ladies' heads. Another volley and something slapped on to the iron roof a few yards from where they sat. Half comprehending, Dame Mildred picked up and examined the irregular disc of hot lead. Shrill wails of terror rose from the street below and then a clattering of horses and oxen. Without a word spoken Dame Mildred and Miss Tin rolled to cover.

The parapet was a low one and the ladies were obliged to lie full length in positions of extreme discomfort. Dame Mildred slid out her arm for a cushion and hastily withdrew it as a third burst of firing broke out as though on purpose to frustrate her action. Presently silence fell, more frightening than the tumult. Dame Mildred spoke in an awed whisper.

"Sarah, that was a *bullet*."

"I know. Do be quiet or they'll start again."

For twenty minutes by Miss Tin's wrist watch the two ladies lay in the gutter, their faces almost touching the hot, tarnished iron of the roof. Dame Mildred shifted onto her side.

"Oh, *what is it,* Mildred?"

"Pins and needles in my left leg. I don't care if I am shot."

Dim recollections of some scouting game played peaceably in what different circumstances among Girl Guides in the bracken of Epping, prompted Dame Mildred to remove her topee and, holding it at arm's length, expose it over the edge of their rampart. The silence of the stricken field was unbroken. Slowly, with infinite caution, she raised her head.

"For heaven's sake, take care, Mildred. *Snipers.*"

But everything was quiet. At length she sat up and looked over. From end to end the street was silent and utterly deserted. The strings of flags hung limp in the afternoon heat. The banner of the Amurath High School lay spread across the way, dishevelled and dusty from a thousand footsteps but still flaunting its message bravely to the heavens, *WOMEN OF TO-MORROW DEMAND AN EMPTY CRADLE.* The other banner lay crumpled in the gutter. Only one word was visible in the empty street. *STERILITY* pleaded in orange and green silk to an unseeing people.

"I think it is all over."

The ladies sat up and stretched their cramped legs, dusted themselves a little, straightened their hats and breathed deeply of the fresh air. Dame Mildred retrieved her camera and wound on the film. Miss Tin shook out the pillows and looked for food. The olives were dry and dull skinned, the bread crisp as biscuit and gritted with dust.

"*Now* what are we going to do? I'm thirsty and I think one of my headaches is coming on."

Regular steps of marching troops in the street below.

"Look out. They're coming again."

The two ladies slid back under cover. They heard the grounding of rifle butts, some unintelligible orders, marching steps proceeding down the street. Inch by inch they emerged again.

"Some of them are still there. But I think it's all right."

A picket of Guards squatted round a machine gun on the pavement opposite.

"I'm going down to find something to drink."

They rolled back the stone from the trap door and descended into the silent hotel. The sight-seers had left their bedrooms. There was no one about on either floor.

"I wonder where they keep the Evian."

They went into the bar. Alcohol everywhere, but

no water. In a corner of the kitchen they found a dozen or so bottles bearing the labels of various mineral waters—Evian, St. Galmier, Vichy, Malvern —all empty. It was Mr. Youkoumian's practice to replenish them, when required, from the fœtid well at the back of the house.

"I must get something to drink or I shall die. I'm going out."

"*Mildred.*"

"I don't care, I am."

She strode through the twilit vestibule into the street. The officer in charge of the machine gun section waved her back. She walked on, making pacific gestures. He spoke to her rapidly and loudly, first in Sakuyu, then in Arabic. Dame Mildred replied in English and French.

"Taisez-vous, officier. Je désire de l'eau. Ou peut on trouver ça, s'il vous plaît."

The soldier showed her the hotel, then the machine gun.

"British subject. Me. British subject. No savvy? Oh, don't any of you speak a word of English?"

The soldiers grinned and nodded, pointing her back to the hotel.

"It's no good. They won't let us out. We must wait."

"Mildred, I'm going to drink wine."

"Well, let's take it up to the roof—it seems the only safe place."

Armed with a bottle of Mr. Youkoumian's Koniak they strode back up the ladder.

"Oh, dear, it's very strong."

"I think it may help my headache."

The afternoon wore on. The burning sun dipped towards the edge of the mountains. The ladies sipped raw brandy on the iron roof.

At length there was a fresh movement in the street. An officer on mule back galloped up, shouting an order to the picket. They dismantled their machine gun, hoisted it onto their shoulders, fell in, and marched away towards the palace. Other patrols tramped past the hotel. From their eminence they could see bodies of troops converging from all sides on the palace square.

"They're calling in the guard. It must be all right now. But I feel too sleepy to move."

Presently, as the soldier withdrew, little bodies of civilians emerged from hiding. A marauding band of Christians swung confidently into view.

"I believe they're coming here."

Splintering of glass and drunken, boastful laughter came from the bar below. Another party broke in the shutters of the drapers opposite and decked themselves with lengths of bright stuff. But oblivious of the excursions below them, worn out by the heat and anxiety of the day, and slightly drugged by Mr. Youkoumian's spirits, the two ladies slept.

It was after seven when they awoke. Sun had set and there was a sharp chill in the air. Miss Tin shivered and sneezed.

"My head's splitting. I'm very hungry again," she said, "and thirstier than ever."

The windows were all dark. Blackness encircled them save for a line of light which streamed across the street from the door of the bar and a dull red glow along the roof tops of the South quarter, in which the Indian and Armenian merchants had their warehouses.

"That can't be sunset at this time. Sarah, I believe the town is on fire."

"*What* are we to do? We can't stay here all night."

A sound of tipsy singing rose from below and a small knot of Azanians came into sight, swaying together with arms across each other's shoulders; two or three of them carried torches and lanterns. A party sallied out from the bar below; there was a confused scuffling. One of the lamps was dropped in a burst of yellow flame. The tussle broke up, leaving a little pool of burning oil in the centre of the road.

"We can't possibly go down."

Two hours dragged by; the red glow behind the roof tops died, revived, and died again; once there was a short outbreak of firing some distance away. The beleaguered ladies sat and shuddered in the darkness. Then the lights of a car appeared and stopped outside the hotel. A few topers emerged from the bar and clustered round it. There were some words spoken in Sakuyu and then a clear English drawl rose to them.

"Well, the old girls don't seem to be here. These chaps say they haven't seen any one."

And another answered: "I daresay they've been raped."

"I hope so. Let's try the Mission."

"Stop," shrieked Dame Mildred. "Hi! Stop."

The motor car door clicked to; the engine started up.

"Stop," cried Miss Tin. "We're up here."

Then, in a moment of inspiration, untaught in the Girl Guides, Dame Mildred threw down the half-empty bottle of brandy. William's head popped out of the car window and shouted a few words of easily acquired abuse in Sakuyu; then a pillow followed the bottle onto the roadway.

"I believe there's some one up there. Be an angel and go and see, Percy. I'll stick in here if there's going to be any bottle throwing."

The second secretary advanced with caution and had reached only the foot of the stairs when the two ladies greeted him.

"Thank God, you've come," said Miss Tin.

"Well," he said, a little confused by this sudden cordiality; "jolly nice of you to put it like that. All I mean is we just dropped in to see that you were all right. Minister said we'd better. Not scared or anything, I mean."

"*All right?* We've had the most terrible day of our lives."

"Oh, I say, not as bad as that I hope. We heard at the Legation that there'd been some kind of a disturbance. Well, you'll be right as rain now, you know. Everything pretty quiet except for a few drunks. If there's anything we can do, just let us know."

"Young man, do you intend leaving us here all night?"

"Well . . . I suppose it sounds inhospitable, but there's nothing else for it. Full up at the Legation you know. The Bishop arrived unexpectedly and two or three of the commercial fellows took fright and came over for some reason. Jolly awkward. . . . You see how it is, don't you?"

"Do you realise that the town is on fire?"

"Yes, rare old blaze. We passed quite near it. It looks awfully jolly from the Legation."

"Young man, Miss Tin and myself are coming with you now."

"Oh, look here, I say, you know . . ."

"Sarah, get in the car. I will bring down a few things for the night."

The discussion had brought them to the street. William and Anstruther exchanged glances of despair. Sir Samson's instructions had been: 'Just see that those tiresome old women are safe, but on no account bring them back here. The place is a bear garden already.' (This with a scowl towards the Bishop who was very quietly playing Pegity with Prudence in a corner of the drawing-room.)

Dame Mildred, putting little trust in Miss Tin's ability to restrain the diplomats from starting without her, took few pains with the packing. In less than a minute she was down again with an armful of night clothes and washing materials. At last with a squeeze and a grunt she sank into the back seat.

"Tell me," asked William with some admiration, as he turned the car round. "Do you always throw bottles at people when you want a lift?"

SEVEN

SIR SAMSON COURTENEY arose next morning in a mood of high displeasure, which became the more intense as with every minute of his leisurely toilet he recalled in detail the atrocious disorders of the preceding evening.

"Never known anything like it," he reflected on the way to the bathroom. "These wretched people don't seem to realise that a legation is a place of business. How can I be expected to get through the day's work, with my whole house overrun with uninvited guests?"

First there had been the Bishop, who arrived during tea with two breathless curates and an absurd story about another revolution and shooting in the streets. Well, why not? You couldn't expect the calm of *Barchester Towers* in a place like Azania. Missionary work was known to involve some physical work. Nincompoops. Sir Samson lashed the bath water in his contempt and vexation. Then, when they were half-way through dinner who should turn up but the Bank Manager and a scrubby little chap named Jagger. Never heard of him. More wild talk about murder, loot and fire. Dinner started all over again with the result that the duck was ruined. And then the most damnable treachery of all: his wife, of all people, infected with the general panic, had begun to ask about Dame Mildred and Miss Tin. Had they gone down to the coast when the other English people left? Should not something be done about them? The Minister pooh-poohed the suggestion for some time but at length so far yielded to popular appeal as to allow William and Percy to take the car and go out, just to see that the old women had come to no harm. That was the explicit limit of their instructions. And what did they do but bring *them* along too. Here in fact was the entire English population of Debra-Dowa taking refuge under his roof. "They'll have to clear out today," decided the Minister as he lathered his chin, "every man jack of them. It's an intolerable imposition."

Accommodation in the compound had eventually been found for all the newcomers. The Bishop slept in the Legation, the curates with the Anstruthers, who, in the most sporting manner, moved the children into their own room for the night, Dame Mildred and Miss Tin at the Legges, and the Bank Manager and Mr. Jagger alone in the bungalow vacated by the Walshes. By the time Samson came down to breakfast, however, they were all together again, chattering uproariously on the croquet lawn.

". . . my back quite sore . . . not really accus-

tomed to riding." "Poor Mr. Raith." "The Church
party started it. The priests had been haranguing
them for days against birth control. The police
learned that an attempt would be made to break up
the procession so they arrested the Patriarch just before it was due to start . . ." "Troops cleared the
streets . . . fired over their heads . . . no damage
done . . ." ". . . a bullet within a few inches, literally *inches,* of my head . . ." Seth went back to
the Palace as soon as it was clear the procession
couldn't take place. My word, he looked angry . . ."
"Young Seal with him . . ." ". . . it wasn't so bad
when the beast was going uphill. It was that terrible
sliding feeling . . . "Poor Mr. Raith . . ." "Then
the patrols were all withdrawn and concentrated in
front of the Palace. Jagger and I were quite close
and saw the whole thing. They had the whole army
drawn up in the square and gradually when they
realised the shooting was over the crowd began to
come back, little knots of sixes and sevens creeping
out from the side alleys and then creeping in round
the soldiers. This was about half-past five . . ."
". . . and not having proper breeches my knees got
so *rubbed* . . ." "Poor Mr. Raith . . ." "Every one
thought Seth was going to appear. The royal box
was still there, shoddy sort of affair but it provided
a platform. Every one kept looking in that direction.
Suddenly who should climb up but the Patriarch,

who had been released from prison by the rioters, and after him Connolly and old Ngumo and one or two others of the notables. Well, the crowd cheered like mad for the Patriarch, and Ngumo, and the soldiers cheered for Connolly and started firing off their rifles again into the air and for a quarter of an hour the place was in an uproar . . ." ". . . and two bruises on the lower part of my shin where the stirrups came . . ." "Poor Mr. Raith . . ." "Then came the big surprise of the day. The patriarch made a speech, don't suppose half the people heard it. Announced that Seth had abdicated and that Achon, Amurath's son who's supposed to have been dead for fifty years, was still alive and would be crowned Emperor to-day. The fellows near started cheering and the others took it up—they didn't know why—and soon they had a regular party going. Meanwhile the Christians had been making hay in the Indian and Jewish quarters, breaking up the shops and setting half the place on fire. That's when Jagger and I made our get-away . . ." ". . . very stiff and chafed . . ." ". . . poor, poor Mr. Raith."

"All talking shop as usual," said Sir Samson, as these voices floated in to him through the dining-room windows. "And eating me out of house and home," he added sourly as he noted that there was a shortage of kedgeree that morning.

"But what about Basil Seal?" Prudence asked.

"He went off with Seth, I believe," said the Bank Manager, "wherever that may be."

Lady Courteney appeared among her guests, wearing gum boots and pushing a barrow and spade. Emperors might come and go, but there was heavy digging to be done in the lily pond.

"Good-morning," she said. "I do hope you all slept well after your adventures and found enough breakfast. I'm afraid this is a very topsy-turvy house party. Prudence, child, I want you to help with the mud-puddle this morning. Mr. Raith, I'm sure you're tired after your ride. Take an easy morning like a sensible man. The Bishop will show you the best parts of the garden. Take some deck chairs. You'll find them on the porch. Dame Mildred and Miss Tin, *how* are you both? I hope my maid found you all you needed. Do please all make yourselves at home. Mr. Jagger, perhaps you play croquet."

The Envoy Extraordinary finished his second cup of coffee, filled and lit his pipe, and avoiding the social life of the lawn, pottered round by the back way to the Chancery. Here at least there survived an atmosphere of normal tranquillity. Anstruther, Legge and William were playing cut-throat bridge.

"Sorry to disturb you, fellows. I just wanted to know whether any of you knew anything about this revolution?"

"Not much, I'm afraid. Care to take a hand, sir?"

"No, thanks very much. I think I'll have a talk with the Bishop about his Cathedral. Save writing that letter. Daresay everything'll be all right now that Seth's left—I suppose I shall have to write a report of this business. No one will read it. But one of you might pop down into town sometime and see exactly what's happened, will you?"

"That's going to be a bore," said William, as the Minister left them. "God, what a mean dummy."

An hour later he visited them again.

"I say, I've just got a letter asking me to this coronation. I suppose some one from here ought to go? It means putting on uniform and mine's got so infernally tight. William, be a good fellow and represent me, will you?"

The Nestorian Cathedral, like the whole of the city, was of quite recent construction, but its darkness and stuffiness endowed it with an air of some antiquity. It was an octagonal, domed building, consisting of a concentric ambulatory round an inner sanctuary. The walls were painted in primitive simplicity with saints and angels, battle scenes from the Old Testament history and portraits of Amurath the Great, faintly visible in the murky light of a dozen or so branch candlesticks. Three choirs had been singing since dawn. There was an Office of enormous length to be got through before the coronation Mass—psalms, prophecies, lections, and many minor but prolix rites of purification. Three aged lectors recited Leviticus from manuscript scrolls while a band of deacons played a low rhythm on hand drums and a silver gong. The Church party were in the ascendent at the moment and were not disposed to forego a single liturgical luxury.

Meanwhile chairs and carpets were being arranged in the outer aisle and an awning improvised through which, after the Mass, the new Emperor was to be led to take the final vows in the presence of the populace. All roads to the Cathedral were heavily policed and the square was lined with guardsmen. At eleven M. Ballon arrived and took his place in the seats set aside for the diplomatic corps. The Americans had all left the town so that he was now in the position of doyen. The native nobility had already assembled. The Duke of Ukaka found a place next to the Earl of Ngumo.

"Where's Achon now?"

"Inside with the priests."

"How is he?"

"He passed a good night. I think he finds the robes uncomfortable."

Presently the Office ended and the Mass began, said behind closed doors by the Patriarch himself, with all the complex ritual of his church. An occasional silver tinkle from inside informed the worshippers of the progress of the ceremony, while a choir of deacons maintained a solemn chant somewhere out of sight in the gloom. M. Ballon stirred uneasily, moved by tiny, uncontrollable shudders of shocked atheism. Presently William arrived, carrying cocked hat, white gloves, very elegant in gold braid. He smiled pleasantly at M. Ballon and sat beside him.

"I say, have they started?"

M. Ballon nodded but did not reply.

A long time passed and the diplomat shifted from buttock to buttock in his gilt chair. It was no longer a matter of anti-clericalism but of acute physical discomfort.

William twiddled his gloves and dropped his hat and gaped miserably at the frescoed ceiling. Once absent-mindedly he took out his cigarette case, tapped a cigarette on the toe of his shoe and was about to light it when he caught a glance from M. Ballon which caused him hastily to return it to his pocket.

But eventually an end came. The doors of the inner sanctuary were thrown open; the trumpeters on the Cathedral steps sounded a fanfare; the band in the square recognised their signal and struck up the Azanian Anthem. The procession emerged into the open. First came the choir of deacons, the priests,

Bishops and the Patriarch. Then a canopy of bro-
cade supported on poles at each corner by the four
premier peers of the Empire. Under it shuffled the
new monarch in the robes of state. It was not clear
from his manner that he understood the nature of
the proceedings. He wriggled his shoulders irritably
under the unaccustomed burden of silk and jewellery, scratched his ribs and kept feeling disconsolately towards his right foot and shaking it sideways
as he walked, worried at missing his familiar chain.
Some drops of the holy oil with which he had been
recently anointed trickled over the bridge of his
nose and, drop by drop, down his white beard.
Now and then he faltered and halted in his pace
and was only moved on by a respectful dig in the
ribs from one of his attendant peers. M. Ballon,
William and the native nobility fell in behind him
and with slow steps proceeded to the dais for the
final ceremonies.

A great shout rose from the concourse as the imperial party mounted the steps and Achon was led to
the throne prepared for him. Here, one by one, he
was invested with the royal regalia. First, holding
the sword of state, the Patriarch addressed him:

"Achon, I give you this sword of the Empire of
Azania. Do you swear to fight in the cause of Justice
and Faith, for the protection of your people and
the glory of your race?"

The Emperor grunted and the ornate weapon was laid across his lap and one of his listless hands placed upon its hilt while cannonades of applause rose from his assembled subjects.

Then the gold spur.

"Achon, I give you this spur. Do you swear to ride in the cause of Justice and Faith for the protection of your people and the glory of your race?"

The Emperor gave a low whimper and turned away his face; the Earl of Ngumo buckled the spur about the foot that had so lately borne a graver weight. Huzzas and holloing in the crowded square.

Finally the crown.

"Achon, I give you this crown. Do you swear to use it in the cause of Justice and Faith for the protection of your people and the glory of your race?"

The Emperor remained silent and the Patriarch advanced towards him with the massive gold tiara of Amaruth the Great. With great gentleness he placed it over the wrinkled brow and straggle of white hairs; but Achon's head lolled forward under its weight and the bauble was pitched back into the Patriarch's hands.

Nobles and prelates clustered about the old man and then dismay spread among them and a babble of scared undertones. The people, seeing that something was amiss, broke off short in their cheering and huddled forward towards the dais.

"Tcha!" exclaimed M. Ballon. "This is something infinitely vexatious. It was not to be foreseen."

For Achon was dead.

"Well," said Sir Samson, when, rather late for luncheon, William brought back news of the coronation, "I can't for the life of me see how they think they're any better off. They'll have to get Seth back now I suppose and we've all been disturbed for nothing. It'll look infernally silly when we send in a report of this to the F.O. Not sure we hadn't better keep quiet about the whole business."

"By the way," said William. "I heard something else in the town. The bridge is down at Lumo, so there'll be no more trains to the coast for weeks."

"One thing after another."

They were all there, cramped at the elbows, round the dining-room table, Bishop and curates, Bank Manager and Mr. Jagger, Dame Mildred and Miss Tin, and they all began asking William questions about the state of the town. Was the fire completely put out? Was there looting in the shops? Did the life of the place seem to be going on normally? Were there troops patrolling the streets? Where was Seth? Where was Seal? Where was Boaz?

"I don't think it at all fair to tease William," said Prudence, "particularly when he looks so nice in his uniform."

"But if, as you say, this bridge is demolished," demanded Dame Mildred, "how can one get to Matodi?"

"There isn't any other way, unless you like to ride down on a camel with one of the caravans."

"D'you mean to say we must stay here until the bridge is rebuilt?"

"Not here," interposed Sir Samson involuntarily, "not here."

"I think the whole thing is *scandalous*," said Miss Tin.

At last, before coffee was served, the Minister left the table.

"Got to get back to work," he said cheerfully, "and I shall be at it all the afternoon so I'd better say good-bye now. I expect you'll all be gone before I get through with it."

And he left in the dining-room seven silent guests whose faces were eloquent of consternation. Later they assembled furtively in a corner of the garden to discuss their circumstances.

"I must admit," said the Bishop, "that it seems to me unreasonable and inconsiderate of the Minister to expect us to return to the town until we have more reassuring information about the conditions."

"As British subjects we have the right to be protected by our flag," said Dame Mildred, "and I for one intend to stay here whether Sir Samson likes it or not."

"That's right," said Mr. Jagger.

And after further mutual reassurances, the Bishop was sent to inform their host of their decision to remain. He found him peacefully dozing in a hammock under the mango trees.

"You put me in a very difficult position," he said when the situation had been explained to him. "I wish that nothing of the sort had occurred at all. I am sure you would all be much more comfortable and equally safe in the town, but since you wish to remain pray consider yourselves my guests for as long as it takes to relieve your apprehensions," and feeling that affairs had got completely outside his control, the Envoy relapsed into sleep.

Later that afternoon, when Lady Courteney had contrived to find occupation for all her guests, some at the bagatelle board, others with Pegity, photograph albums, cards or croquet, the party suffered a further and far from welcome addition; a dusty figure in native costume who propped a rifle against the fireplace before coming forward to shake her hand.

"Oh, dear, oh, dear," she said, "have *you* come to stay with us too?"

"Only for to-night," said Basil. "I've got to be off

first thing to-morrow. Where can I put up my camels?"

"Good gracious, I don't think we've ever had such a thing here before. Have you more than one?"

"Ten. I'm passing as a Sakuyu merchant. They're outside with the boys. I daresay they'll find a place for them. They're vicious beasts though. D'you think I could have some whiskey?"

"Yes, no doubt the butler can find you some, and would you like William to lend you some clothes?"

"No, I'll stay in these, thanks. Got to get used to moving about in them. It's the only way I can hope to get through. They had two shots at bumping me off yesterday."

The company forsook their pastimes and crowded round the newcomer.

"How are things in the city?"

"As bad as can be. The army feel they've been sold a pup and won't leave barracks. Connolly's gone off with most of his staff to try and find Seth. The Patriarch's in hiding somewhere in the town. Ngumo's men have had a big dust up with the police and are pretty well on top at the moment. They've got into the liquor saloons which Connolly closed yesterday. As soon as it's dark they'll start looting again."

"*There*," said Dame Mildred, "and the Minister expected us to leave to-day."

"Oh, I shouldn't count on being too safe here. There's a gang breaking up the American Legation now. Ballon's ordered an aeroplane from the mainland. I expect you'll get a raid to-night or to-morrow. Your sowars don't look up to much serious work."

"And where are you going?"

"After Seth and Boaz. We've a rendezvous five days' ride out of town at a farm of Boaz's on the edge of the Wanda country. There's just a chance of getting the boy back if he plays his cards properly. But there's bound to be serious fighting whatever happens."

Shivers of half-pleasant alarm went through his listeners.

"Mr. Seal," Lady Courteney benignly interposed at last. "I think it's very mischievous of you saying all this. I'm sure that things are not nearly as bad as you make out. You're just *talking*. Now go and get yourself some whiskey and talk to Prudence and I think you might put that dirty gun outside in the lobby."

"Oh, Basil, what *is* going to happen? I can't bear your going off like this and everything being so messy."

"Don't you worry, Prudence, everything'll be all right. We'll meet again. I promise you."

"But you said it was dangerous."

"I was just piling it on to scare the old women."

"Basil, I don't believe you were."

"I should think they'll take you off by air from Khormaksar. You've got Walsh down at Matodi. He's a sound enough fellow. As soon as he learns what's happened he'll get through to Aden and arrange everything. You'll be all right, just you see."

"But it's you I'm worrying about."

"Don't you do that, Prudence. It's one of the things there's no sense in at all. People are always doing it and it doesn't get them anywhere."

"Anyway, you look lovely in those clothes."

Basil talked a great deal at dinner; the same large party was assembled but he kept them all silent with tales of Sakuyu savagery, partly invented, partly remembered from the days of Connolly's confidence. ". . . shaved all the hair off her head and covered it with butter. White ants ate straight through into her skull . . . you still find blind old Europeans working with the slaves on some of the farms in the interior; they're prisoners of war that were conveniently forgotten about when peace was made . . . the Arab word for Sakuyu means Man-without-mercy . . . when they get drink in them they go completely insane. They can stay like that for days at a time, utterly unconscious of fatigue. They'd think nothing of the road out here if they thought they'd find alcohol when they got here. May I have another glass of whiskey? . . ."

When the men were left together at the table, the Minister said, "My boy, I don't know how much truth there is in all you've been saying but I think you might not have talked like that before the ladies. If there *is* any danger, and I for one don't for a moment believe there is, the ladies should be kept in ignorance of the fact."

"Oh, I like to see them scared," said Basil. "Pass the decanter, will you, Jagger, and now, sir, what arrangements are we making for defence?"

"Arrangements for defence?"

"Yes, of course, you can't possibly have every one separated in the different bungalows. They could all have their throats cut one at a time and none of us any the wiser. The compound is far too big to form a defensible unit. You'd better get every one up here, arrange for shifts of guard and put a picket of your sowars with horses half a mile down the road to the town to bring the alarm if a raiding party comes into sight. You run in and talk to the women. I'll arrange it all for you."

And the Envoy Extraordinary could find nothing to say. The day had been too much for him. Every one was stark crazy and damned bad-mannered too.

They could do what they liked. He was going to smoke a cigar, alone, in his study.

Basil took command. In half an hour the Legges and the Anstruthers bearing children wrapped in blankets and their meagre supply of firearms, arrived in the drawing-room.

"I suppose that this is necessary," said Lady Courteney, "but I'm afraid that you'll none of you be at all comfortable."

An attempt to deceive the children that nothing unusual was afoot proved unsuccessful; it was not long before they were found in a corner of the hall enacting with tremendous gusto the death agonies of the Italian lady whose scalp was eaten by termites.

"The gentleman in the funny clothes told us," they explained. "Coo, mummy, it must have hurt."

The grown-ups moved restlessly about.

"Anything we can do to help?"

"Yes, count the cartridges out into equal piles . . . it might be a good thing to prepare some bandages too . . . Legge, the hinges of this shutter aren't too good. See if you can find a screw driver."

It was about ten o'clock when it was discovered that the native servants who had been massed in the legation kitchens from the surrounding households, had silently taken their leave. Only Basil's camel boys remained in possession. They had compounded for themselves a vast stew of incongruous elements and were sodden with eating.

"Other boys going home. No want cutting off heads. They much no good boys. We like it fine living here."

News of the desertion made havoc among the nerves in the drawing-room. Sir Samson merely voiced the feelings of all his guests when, turning petulantly from the table, he remarked: "It's no good. My heart is *not* in halma this evening."

But the night passed and no assault was made. The men of the party watched, three hours on, three hours off, at the various vulnerable points. Each slept with a weapon beside him, revolver, rook rifle, shot-gun or meat chopper. Continuous low chattering in the rooms upstairs, rustle of dressing gowns, patter of slippers and frequent shrill cries from the youngest Anstruther child in nightmare, told that the ladies were sleeping little. At dawn they assembled again with pale faces and strained eyes. Lady Courteney's English maid and the Goan butler went to the kitchen and, circumventing with difficulty the recumbent camel boys, made hot coffee. Spirits rose a little; they abandoned the undertones which had become habitual during the last ten hours and spoke in normal voices; they began to yawn. Basil said, "One night over. Of course your real danger will come when supplies begin running short in the town."

That discouraged them from any genuine cheerfulness.

They went out onto the lawn. Smoke lay low over the town.

"Something still burning."

Presently Anstruther said, "I say, though, look over there. Aren't those clouds?"

"It's a week early for the rains."

"Still, you never know."

"That's rain all right," said Basil. "I was counting on it to-day or to-morrow. They got it last week in Kenya. It'll delay the repairs on the Lumo bridge pretty considerably."

"Then I must get those bulbs in this morning," said Lady Courteney. "It'll be a relief to have something sensible to do after tearing up sheets for bandages and sewing sandbags. You might have told me before, Mr. Seal."

"If I were you," said Basil, "I should start checking your stores and making out a scheme of rations. I should think my boys must have eaten a good week's provisions last night."

The party split up and attempted to occupy themselves in useful jobs about the house; soon, however, there came a sound which brought them out helter-skelter, all together again, chattering on the lawn; the drone of an approaching aeroplane.

"That'll be Ballon," said Basil, "making his get-away."

But as the machine came into sight it became clear that it was making for the Legation; it flew low, circling over the compound and driving the ponies to frenzy in their stables. They could see the pilot's head looking at them over the side. A weighted flag fluttered from it to the ground, then the machine mounted again and soared off in the direction of the coast. The Anstruther children ran, crowing with delight, to retrieve the message from the rose garden and bring it to the Minister. It was a brief pencil note, signed by the squadron-leader at Aden. *Am bringing two troop carriers, three bombers. Be prepared to evacuate whole British population from Legation in one hour from receiving this. Can carry official archives and bare personal necessities only.*

"That's Walsh's doing. Clever chap, always said so. But I say, though, what a rush."

For the next hour the Legation was in a ferment as a growing pile of luggage assembled on the lawn.

"*Official archives,* indeed. There may be some papers about somewhere, William. See if any of them seem at all interesting."

"We'll have to put the ponies out to grass and hope for the best."

"Lock all doors and take the keys away. Not that it's likely to make any difference."

"Envoy, you can't bring *all* the pictures."

"How about passports?"

The visitors from the town, having nothing to pack, did what they could to help the others.

"I've never been up before. I'm told it often makes people unwell."

"Poor Mr. Raith."

Basil, suddenly reduced to unimportance, stood by and watched the preparations, a solitary figure in his white Sakuyu robes leaning over his rifle like a sentinel.

Prudence joined him and they walked together to the edge of the compound, out of sight behind some rhododendrons. She was wearing a red béret jauntily on one side of her head.

"Basil, give up this absurd Emperor, darling, and come with us."

"Can't do that."

"Please."

"No, Prudence, everything's going to be all right. Don't you worry. We'll meet again somewhere."

Rain clouds on the horizon grew and spread across the bright sky.

"It seems so much *more* going away when it's in an aeroplane, if you see what I mean."

"I see what you mean."

"Prudence, Prudence," from Lady Courteney beyond the rhododendrons. "You really can't take so many boxes."

In Basil's arms Prudence said, "But the clothes smell odd."

"I got them second-hand from a Sakuyu. He'd just stolen an evening suit from an Indian."

"Prudence!"

"All right, mum, *coming* . . . sweet Basil, I can't really bear it."

And she ran back to help eliminate her less serviceable hats.

Quite soon, before any one was ready for them, the five aeroplanes came into sight, roaring over the hills in strictly maintained formation. They landed and came to rest in the compound. Air Force officers trotted forward and saluted, treating Sir Samson with a respect which somewhat surprised his household.

"We ought to start as soon as we can, sir. There's a storm coming up."

With very little confusion the party embarked. The Indian troopers and the Goan butler in one troop carrier, the children, clergy and senior members in the other. Mr. Jagger, William and Prudence

took their places in the cockpits of the three bombers. Just as they were about to start, Prudence remembered something and clambered down. She
raced back to the Legation, a swift, gay figure under
her red beret, and returned panting with a loose
sheaf of papers.

"Nearly left the *Panorama of Life* behind," she
explained.

The engines started up with immense din; the
machines taxied forward and took off, mounted
steadily, circled about in a neat arrow head, dwin-
dled and disappeared. Silence fell on the compound.
It had all taken less than twenty minutes.

Basil turned back alone to look for his camels.

Prudence crouched in the cockpit, clutching her
beret to her head. The air shrieked past her ears
while the landscape rolled away below in a leisurely
fashion; the straggling city, half shrouded in smoke,
disappeared behind them; open pasture dotted with
cattle and little clusters of huts; presently the green
lowlands and jungle country. She knew without
particular regret that she was leaving Debra-Dowa
for good.

"Anyway," she reflected, "I ought to get some
new ideas for the *Panorama*," and already she
seemed to be emerging into the new life which her
mother had planned for her, and spoken of not long
ago seated on Prudence's bed as she came to wish

her good-night. Aunt Harriet's house in Belgrave Place; girls' luncheons, dances and young men, week-ends in country houses, tennis and hunting; all the easy circumstances of English life which she had read about often but never experienced. She would resume the acquaintance of friends she had known at school, "and shan't I be able to show off to them. They'll all seem so young and innocent . . ." English cold and fog and rain, grey twilight among isolated, bare trees and dripping coverts; London streets when the shops were closing and the pavements crowded with people going to Tube stations with evening papers; empty streets, late at night after dances, revealing unsuspected slopes, sluiced by men in almost mediæval overalls . . . an English girl returning to claim her natural heritage . . .

The aeroplane dipped suddenly, recalling her to the affairs of the moment. The pilot shouted back to her something which was lost on the wind. They were the extremity of one of the arms of the V. A goggled face from the machine in front looked back and down at them as they dropped below him but her pilot signalled him on. Green undergrowth swam up towards them; the machine tilted a little and circled about, looking for a place to land.

"Hold tight and don't worry," was borne back to her on the wind. An open space appeared among the trees and bush. They circled again and dropped precisely into place, lurched for a moment as though about to overturn, righted themselves and stopped dead within a few feet of danger.

"Wizard show that," remarked the pilot.

"Has anything awful happened?"

"Nothing to worry about. Engine trouble. I can put it right in two shakes. Stay where you are. We'll catch them up before they reach Aden."

Rain broke late that afternoon with torrential tropic force. The smouldering warehouses of the city sizzled and steamed and the fire ended in thin black mud. Great pools collected in the streets; water eddied in the gutters, clogging the few drains with its burden of refuse. The tin roofs rang with the falling drops. Sodden rioters waded down the lanes to shelter; troops left their posts and returned to barracks huddled under cover in a stench of wet cloth. The surviving decorations from the pageant of birth control clung limply round the posts or, grown suddenly too heavy, snapped their strings and splashed into the mud below. Darkness descended upon a subdued city.

For six confused days Basil floundered on towards the lowlands. For nine hours out of the twenty-four the rain fell regularly and unremittingly so that it usurped the sun's place as the measure of time and the caravan drove on through the darkness striving hopelessly to recover the hours wasted under cover during the daylight.

On their second day's journey Basil's boys brought a runner to him, who was carrying a sodden letter in the end of a cleft staff.

"A great chief will not suffer his messengers to be robbed."

"There is a time," said Basil, "when all things must be suffered."

They took the message. It read:

From Viscount Boaz, Minister of the Interior of the Azanian Empire, to the Earl of Ngumo, Greeting. May this reach you. Peace be upon your house. Salute in my name and in the name of my family, Achon whom some style Emperor of Azania, Chief of the Chiefs of Sakuyu, Lord of Wanda and Tyrant of the Seas. May his days be many and his progeny uncounted. I, Boaz, no mean man in the Empire, am now at Gulu on the Wanda marches; with me is Seth whom some style Emperor. I tell you this so that Achon may know me for what I am, a loyal subject of the crown. I fear for Seth's health and await word from your Lordship as to how best he may be relieved of what troubles him. Boaz.

"Go on in front of us," Basil ordered the man, "and tell Lord Boaz that Achon is dead."

"How can I return to my Lord, having lost the letter he gave me. Is my life a small thing?"

"Go back to your Lord. Your life is a small thing beside the life of the Emperor."

Later two beasts lost their footing in the bed of a swollen watercourse and were washed down and tumbled among the boulders; during the third night's march five of the hindermost deserted their leaders. The boys mutinied, first for more money; later they refused every inducement to proceed. For two days Basil rode on alone, swaying and slipping towards his rendezvous.

Confusion dominated the soggy lanes of Matodi. Major Walsh, the French secretaries and Mr. Schonbaum daily despatched conflicting messages by wireless and cable. First that Seth was dead and that Achon was Emperor, then that Achon was dead and Seth was Emperor.

"Doubtless Mme. Ballon could tell us where General Connolly is to be found."

"Alas, M. Jean, she will not speak."

"Do you suspect she knows more?"

"M. Ballon's wife should be above suspicion."

The officials and soldiers loafed in the dry intervals about barracks and offices; they had no instructions and no money; no news from the capital. Destroyers of four nations lurked in the bay standing by to defend their nationals. The town governor made secret preparations for an early escape to the mainland. Mr. Youkoumian, behind the bar at the Amurath Hotel, nervously decocted his fierce spirits.

"There ain't no sense in aving bust-ups. Ere we are, no Emperor, no railway, and those low niggers making ell with my property at Debra-Dowa. And just you see, in less than no time the civilised nations will start a bombardment. *Gosh.*"

In the dingy calm of the Arab club the six senior members munched their khat in peace and spoke gravely of a very old error of litigation.

Amidst mud and liquid ash at Debra-Dowa a leaderless people abandoned their normal avocations and squatted at home, occupying themselves with domestic bickerings; some of the rural immigrants drifted back to their villages, others found temporary accommodation in the saloons of the deserted palace, expecting something to happen.

Among the dry clinkers of Aden, Sir Samson and Lady Courteney waited for news of the missing aeroplane. They were staying at the Residency where everything was done that hospitality and tact could do, to relieve the strain of their anxiety; newspaper agents and sympathetic compatriots were kept from them. Dame Mildred and Miss Tin were shipped to Southampton by the first P. & O. Mr.

Jagger made preparations to leave a settlement he had little reason to like. Sir Samson and Lady Courteney walked alone on the cliff paths, waiting for news. Air patrols crossed to Azania, flying low over the impenetrable country where Prudence's machine was last observed, returned to refuel, set out again and at the end of the week had seen nothing to report. The military authorities discussed and despaired of the practicability of landing a search party.

In the dry spell between noon and sunset, Basil reached Seth's encampment at Gulu. His men had taken possession of a small village. A dozen or so of them, in ragged uniforms, sat on their haunches in the clearing, silently polishing their teeth with pieces of stick.

His camel lurched down onto its knees and Basil dismounted. None of the guardsmen rose to salute him; no sign of greeting from inside the mud huts. The squatting men looked into the steaming forest beyond him.

He asked: "Where is the Emperor?" But no one answered.

"Where is Boaz?"

"In the great house. He is resting."

They indicated the headman's hut which stood on the far side of the compound, distinguished from the others by its superior size and a narrow verandah, floored with beaten mud and shaded by thatch.

"Why is the Emperor not in the great house?"

They did not answer. Instead they scoured their teeth and gazed abstractedly into the forest, where a few monkeys swung in the steaming air, shaking the water from bough to bough.

Basil crossed through them to the headman's hut. It was windowless and for a short time his eyes could distinguish nothing in the gloom. Only his ears were aware of a heavily breathing figure somewhere not far distant in the dark interior. Then he gradually descried a jumble of household furniture, camp equipment and the remains of a meal; and Boaz asleep. The great dandy lay on his back in a heap of rugs and sacking; his head pitched forward into his blue-black curly beard. There was a rifle across his middle. He wore a pair of mud-splashed riding breeches, too tight to button to the top, which Basil recognised as the Emperor's. A Wanda girl sat at his head. She explained: "The Lord has been asleep for some time. For the last days it has been like this. He wakes only to drink from the square bottle. Then he is asleep again."

"Bring me word when he wakes."

Basil approached the oafish fellows in the clearing.

"Show me a house where I can sleep."

They pointed one out to him without rising to

accompany him to its door. Water still dripped through its leaky thatch, there was a large puddle of thin mud made during the rain. Basil lay down on the dry side and waited for Boaz to wake.

They called him an hour after sunset. The men had lit a fire, but only a small one because they knew that at midnight the rain would begin again and dowse it. There was a light in the headman's hut— a fine brass lamp with wick and chimney. Boaz had put out two glasses and two bottles of whiskey. Basil's first words were, "Where is Seth?"

"He is not here. He has gone away."

"Where?"

"How shall I know? Look, I have filled your glass."

"I sent a messenger to him, with the news that Achon was dead."

"Seth had already gone when the messenger came."

"And where is the messenger?"

"He brought bad tidings. He is dead. Turn the light higher. It is bad to sit in the dark."

He gulped down a glass of spirit and refilled his glass. They sat in silence.

Presently Boaz said, "Seth is dead."

"I knew. How?"

"The sickness of the jungle. His legs and his arms

swelled. He turned up his eyes and died. I have seen others die in just that way."

Later he said, "So now there is no Emperor. It is a pity that your messenger did not come a day sooner. I hanged him because he was late."

"Boaz, the sickness of the jungle does not wait on good or bad news."

"That is true. Seth died in another way. By his own hand. With a gun raised to his mouth and his great toe crooked round the trigger. That is how Seth died."

"It is not what I should have expected."

"Men die that way. I have heard of it often. His body lies outside. The men will not bury it. They say it must be taken down to Moshu to the Wanda people to be burned in their own fashion. Seth was their chief."

"We will do that to-morrow."

Outside round the fire, inevitably, they had started singing. The drums pulsed. In the sodden depths of the forest the wild beasts hunted, shunning the light.

"I will go and see Seth's body."

"The women are sewing him up. They made a bag for him out of pieces of skin. It is the custom when the chief dies. They put grain in with him and several spices. Only the women know what. If they can get it they put a lion's paw, I have been told."

"We will go and look at him."

"It is not the custom of the people."

"I will carry the lamp."

"You must not leave me in the dark. I will come with you."

Past the camp fire and the singing guardsmen to another hut: here by the light of a little lamp four or five women were at work stitching. Seth's body lay on the floor half covered by a blanket. Boaz leant tipsily in the doorway while Basil went forward, lamp in hand. The eldest of the women tried to bar his entrance, but he pushed her aside and approached the dead Emperor.

His head lay inclined to one side, the lips agape, the eyes open and dull. He wore his guards tunic, buttoned tight at the throat; the epaulettes awry and bedraggled. There was no wound visible. Basil drew the blanket higher and rejoined the Minister.

"The Emperor did not shoot himself."

"No."

"There is no wound to be seen."

"Did I say he was shot? That is a mistake. He took poison. That is how it happened . . . it has happened before in that way to other great men. It was a draught given him by a wise man in these parts. When he despaired he took some of it . . . a large cupful and drank it . . . there in the hut. I was with him. He made a wry face and said that

294

the draught was bitter. Then he stood still a little until his knees gave. On the floor he rolled up and down several times. He could not breathe. Then his legs shot straight out and he arched his back. That is how he lay until yesterday when the body became limp again. That was how he died. . . . The messenger was late in coming."

They left the women to their work. Boaz stumbled several times as he returned to the headman's hut and his bottle of whiskey. Basil left him with the lamp and returned in the fire-lit night to his hut.

A man was waiting for him in the shadows. "Boaz is still drunk."

"Yes. Who are you?"

"Major Joab of the Imperial Infantry at your service."

"Well, major?"

"It has been like this since the Emperor's death."

"Boaz?"

"Yes."

"Did you see the Emperor die?"

"I am a soldier. It is not for me to meddle with high politics. I am a soldier without a master."

"There is duty due to a master, even when he is dead."

"Do I understand you?"

"To-morrow we take down the body of Seth to be burned at Moshu among his people. He should

295

rejoin the great Amurath and the spirits of his father like a king and a fine man. Can he meet them unashamed if his servants forget their duty while his body is still with them?"

"I understand you."

After midnight the rain fell. The men round the fire carried a burning brand into one of the huts and lit a fire there. Great drops sizzled and spat among the deserted embers; they changed from yellow to red and then to black.

Heavy patter of rain on the thatched roofs, quickening to an even blurr of sound.

A piercing, womanish cry, that mounted, soared shivering, quavered and merged in the splash and gurgle of the water.

"Major Joab of the Imperial Infantry at your service. Boaz is dead."

"Peace be on your house."

Next day they carried the body of the Emperor to Moshu. Basil rode at the head of the procession. The others followed on foot. The body, sewn in skins, was strapped to a pole and carried on the shoulders of two guardsmen. Twice during the journey they slipped and their burden fell in the soft mud of the jungle path. Basil sent on a runner to the Chief saying: "Assemble your people, kill your best meat and prepare a feast in the manner of your people. I am bringing a great chief among you."

But the news preceded him and tribesmen came out to greet them on the way and conduct them with music to Moshu. The wise men of the surrounding villages danced in the mud in front of Basil's camel, wearing livery of the highest solemnity, leopards' feet and snake-skins, necklets of lions' teeth, shrivelled bodies of toads and bats, and towering masks of painted leather and wood. The women daubed their hair with ochre and clay in the fashion of the people.

Moshu was a royal city; the chief market and government centre of the Wanda country. It was ditched round and enclosed by high ramparts. Arab slavers had settled there a century ago and built streets of two-storied, lightless houses; square, with flat roofs on rubble walls washed over with lime and red earth. Among them stood circular Wanda huts of mud and thatched grass. A permanent artisan population lived there, blacksmiths, jewellers, leather workers, ministering to the needs of the scattered jungle people. There were several merchants in a good way of business with barns storing grain, oil, spices and salt, and a few Indians trading in hardware and coloured cottons, products of the looms of Europe and Japan.

A pyre had been heaped up, of dry logs and

straw, six-foot high, in the market place. A large crowd was already assembled there and in another quarter a communal kitchen had been improvised where great cook pots rested over crackling sticks. Earthenware jars of fermented cocoanut sap stood ready to be broached when the proper moment arrived.

The feast began late in the afternoon. Basil and Joab sat among the chiefs and headmen. The wise men danced round the pyre, shaking their strings of charms and amulets, wagging their tufted rumps and uttering cries of ecstasy. They carried little knives and cut themselves as they capered round. Meanwhile Seth's body was bundled on to the faggots and a tin of oil sluiced over it.

"It is usual for the highest man present to speak some praise of the dead."

Basil nodded and in the circle of fuzzy heads rose to declaim Seth's funeral oration. It was no more candid than most royal obituaries. It was what was required. "Chiefs and tribesmen of the Wanda," he said, speaking with confident fluency in the Wanda tongue of which he had acquired a fair knowledge during his stay in Azania. "Peace be among you. I bring the body of the Great Chief, who has gone to rejoin Amurath and the spirits of his glorious ancestors. It is right for us to remember Seth. He was a great Emperor and all the peoples of the world vied with each other to do him homage. In his own island, among the peoples of Sakuyu and the Arabs, across the great waters to the mainland, far beyond in the cold lands of the North, Seth's name was a name of terror. Seyid rose against him and is no more. Achon also. They are gone before him to prepare suitable lodging among the fields of his ancestors. Thousands fell by his right hand. The words of his mouth were like thunder in the hills. Weep, women of Azania, for your royal lover is torn from your arms. His virility was inexhaustible, his progeny numerous beyond human computation. His staff was a grown palm tree. Weep, warriors of Azania. When he led you to battle there was no re- treating. In council the most guileful, in justice the most terrible, Seth the magnificent is dead."

The bards caught phrases from the lament and sang them. The wise men ran whooping among the spectators carrying torches. Soon the pyre was en- veloped in towering flames. The people took up the song and swayed on their haunches, chanting. The bundle on the crest bubbled and spluttered like fresh pine until the skin cerements burst open and revealed briefly in the heart of the furnace the in- candescent corpse of the Emperor. Then there was a subsidence among the timbers and it disappeared from view.

Soon after sunset the flames declined and it was

necessary to refuel them. Many of the tribesmen had joined the dance of the witches. With hands on each other's hips they made a chain round the pyre, shuffling their feet and heaving their shoulders, spasmodically throwing back their heads and baying like wild beasts.

The chiefs gave the sign for the feast to begin.

The company split up into groups, each round a cook pot. Basil and Joab sat with the chiefs. They ate flat bread and meat, stewed to pulp among peppers and aromatic roots. Each dipped into the pot in rotation, plunging with his hands for the best scraps. A bowl of toddy circulated from lap to lap and great drops of sweat broke out on the brows of the mourners.

Dancing was resumed, faster this time and more clearly oblivious of fatigue. In emulation of the witch doctors, the tribesmen began slashing themselves on chest and arms with their hunting knives; blood and sweat mingled in shining rivulets over their dark skins. Now and then one of them would pitch forward onto his face and lie panting or roll stiff in a nervous seizure. Women joined in the dance, making another chain, circling in the reverse way to the men. They were dazed with drink, stamping themselves into ecstasy. The two chains jostled and combined. They shuffled together interlocked.

Basil drew back a little from the heat of the fire,

his senses dazed by the crude spirit and the insistence of the music. In the shadows, in the extremities of the market place, black figures sprawled and grunted, alone and in couples. Near him an elderly woman stamped and shuffled; suddenly she threw up her arms and fell to the ground in ecstasy. The hand drums throbbed and pulsed; the flames leapt and showered the night with sparks.

The headman of Moshu sat where they had dined, nursing the bowl of toddy. He wore an Azanian white robe, splashed with gravy and spirit. His scalp was closely shaven; he nodded it down to the lip of the bowl and drank. Then he clumsily offered it to Basil. Basil refused; he gaped and offered it again. Then took another draught himself. Then he nodded again and drew something from his bosom and put it on his head. "Look," he said. "Pretty."

It was a beret of pillar-box red. Through the stupor that was slowly mounting and encompassing his mind Basil recognised it. Prudence had worn it jauntily on the side of her head, running across the Legation lawn with the *Panorama of Life* under her arm. He shook the old fellow roughly by the shoulder.

"Where did you get that?"

"Pretty."

"Where did you get it?"

"Pretty hat. It came in the great bird. The white

woman wore it. On her head like this." He giggled weakly and pulled it askew over his glistening pate.

"But the white woman. Where is she?"

But the headman was lapsing into coma. He said "Pretty" again and turned up sightless eyes.

Basil shook him violently. "Speak, you old fool. Where is the white woman?"

The headman grunted and stirred; then a flicker of consciousness revived in him. He raised his head. "The white woman? Why, here," he patted his distended paunch. "You and I and the big chiefs—we have just eaten her."

Then he fell forward into a sound sleep.

Round and round circled the dancers, ochre and blood and sweat glistening in the firelight; the wise men's headgear swayed high above them, leopards' feet and snake skins, amulets and necklaces, lions' teeth and the shrivelled bodies of bats and toads, jigging and spinning. Tireless hands drumming out the rhythm; glistening backs heaving and shivering in the shadows.

Later, a little after midnight, it began to rain.

EIGHT

WHEN the telephone bell rang Alastair said: "You answer it. I don't think I can stand up," so Sonia crossed to the window where it stood and said: "Yes, who is it? . . . *Basil* . . . well, who'd have thought of that? Where *can* you be?"

"I'm at Barbara's. I thought of coming round to see you and Alastair."

"Darling, do . . . how did you know where we lived?"

"It was in the telephone book. Is it nice?"

"Lousy. You'll see when you come. Alastair thought it would be cheaper, but it isn't really. You'll never find the door. It's painted red and it's next to a pretty shady sort of chemist."

"I'll be along."

Ten minutes later he was there. Sonia opened the door. "We haven't any servants. We got very poor suddenly. How long have you been back?"

"Landed last night. What's been happening?"

"Almost nothing. Every one's got very poor and it makes them duller. It's more than a year since we saw you. How are things at Barbara's?"

"Well, Freddy doesn't know I'm here yet. That's

why I'm dining out. Barbara's going to tell him gently. I gather my mamma is sore with me about something. How's Angela?"

"Just the same. She's the only one who doesn't seem to have lost money. Margot's shut up her house and is spending the winter in America. There was a general election and a crisis—something about gold standard."

"I know. It's amusing to be back."

"We've missed you. As I say, people have gone serious lately, while you've just been loafing about the tropics. Alastair found something about Azania in the papers once. I forget what. Some revolution and a minister's daughter who disappeared. I suppose you were in on all that."

"Yes."

"Can't think what you see in revolutions. They said there was going to be one here, only nothing came of it. I suppose you ran the whole country."

"As a matter of fact, I did."

"And fell madly in love."

"Yes."

"And intrigued and had a court official's throat cut."

"Yes."

"And went to a cannibal banquet. Darling, I just don't want to hear about it, d'you mind? I'm sure it's all very fine and grand but it doesn't make much sense to a stay-at-home like me."

"That's the way to deal with him," said Alastair from his arm chair. "Keep a stopper on the far-flung stuff."

"Or write a book about it, sweety. Then we can buy it and leave it about where you'll see and then you'll think we know. . . . What are you going to do now you're back?"

"No plans. I think I've had enough of barbarism for a bit. I might stay in London or Berlin or somewhere like that."

"That'll be nice. Make it London. We'll have some parties like the old ones."

"D'you know I'm not sure I shouldn't find them a bit flat after the real thing. I went to a party at a place called Moshu . . ."

"*Basil.* Once and for all, we don't want to hear travel experiences. Do try and remember."

So they played happy families till ten, when Alastair said, "Have we had dinner?" and Sonia said, "No. Let's." Then they went out to a new cocktail club which Alastair had heard was cheap, and had lager beer and liver sandwiches; they proved to be very expensive.

Later Basil went round to see Angela Lyne, and Sonia as she undressed said to Alastair, "D'you

know, deep down in my heart I've got a tiny fear
that Basil is going to turn serious on us too."

Evening in Matodi. Two Arab gentlemen, hand
in hand, sauntered by the sea wall.

Among the dhows and nondescript craft in the
harbour lay two smart launches manned by British
and French sailors, for Azania had lately been man-
dated by the League of Nations as a joint protectorate.

"They are always at work polishing the brass."

"It must be very expensive. And they are building a new customs house."

"And a police station and a fever hospital, a
European club."

"There are many new bungalows on the hills."

"They are making a big field to play games in."

"Every week they wash the streets with water.
They take the children in the schools and scratch
their arms to rub in poison. It makes them very ill."

"They put a man in prison for overburdening his
camel."

"There is a Frenchman in charge at the post office. He is always hot and in a great hurry."

"They are building a black road through the hills
to Debra-Dowa. The railway is to be removed."

"Mr. Youkoumian has bought the rails and what

was left of the engines. He hopes to sell them in Eritrea."

"Things were better in the time of Seth. It is no longer a gentleman's country."

The muezzin in the tower turned north towards Mekka and called azan over the city. The Arabs paused reverently and stood in silence . . . God is great . . . There is no God but God. . . . Mahomet is the apostle of God. . . .

A two-seater car whizzed by, driven by Mr. Reppington, the district magistrate. Mrs. Reppington sat beside him.

"The little bus took that nicely."

Angelus from the mission church . . . gratia plena: dominus tecum; Benedicta tu in mulieribus . . .

The car left the town and mounted towards the hills.

"Phew. It's a relief to get out into the fresh air."

"Awful road. It ought to be finished by now. I get quite afraid for her back axle."

"I said we'd drop into the Brethertons for a sundowner."

"Right you are. Only we can't stay long. We're dining with the Lepperidges."

A mile above the town they stopped at the second of six identical bungalows. Each had a verandah and a garden path; a slotted box on the gate-post for

calling cards. The Brethertons were on the verandah.

"Cheerio, Mrs. Reppington. Cocktail?"

"Please."

"And you, Reppington?"

"Chota peg."

Bretherton was sanitary inspector and conse-
quently of slightly inferior station to Reppington,
but that year he would sit for his Arabic exam; if
he brought it off it would make them level on the
salary list.

"What sort of day?"

"Oh, the usual. Just tooled round condemning
native houses. How are things at the Fort?"

"Not so dusty. We settled that case I told you
about. You know, the one of the natives who built
a house in a broken lorry in the middle of the road."

"Oh, ah. Who won it?"

"Oh, we gave it to the chap in possession on both
counts. The Arab who originally owned the car was
suing him. So were the Works Department—wanted
to evict him because he blocked the traffic. They'll
have to make a new road round him now. They're
pretty fed up, I can tell you. So are the Frenchies."

"Good show."

"Yes, give the natives respect for British justice.
Can't make your Frenchy see that . . . Why, it's
later than I thought. We must be pushing along,

old girl. You're not dining with the Lepperidges by any chance?"

"No."

The Brethertons were not on dining terms with the Lepperidges. He was O.C. of the native levy, seconded from India and a very considerable man in Matodi. He always referred to Bretherton as the "latrine wallah."

So the Reppingtons went to dress in their bungalow (fifth of the row), she in black lace, he in white mess jacket. Punctually at 8.15 they stepped across to the Lepperidges. There were five courses at dinner, mostly from tins, and a glass dish in the centre of the table held floating flower heads. Mr. and Mrs. Grainger were there; Mr. Grainger was immigration officer. He said: "We've had rather a shari this afternoon about that fellow Connolly. You see, strictly speaking he can claim Azanian nationality. He seems to have been quite a big bug under the Emperor. Ran the army for him. Got made a Duke or something. Last sort of fellow one wants hanging about."

"Quite."

"Jungly Wallah. They say in the old days he had an affair with the wife of the French minister. That made the Frenchies anxious to get rid of him."

"Quite. It helps if one can oblige them now and then in small things."

"Besides, you know, he's married to a wog. Well,
I mean to say . . ."

"Quite."

"But I think we're going to get rid of him all
right. Deport him D.B.S. He lost all his money in
the revolution."

"And the woman in the case?"

"Well, that's no business of ours once we clear
him out of here. They seem struck on each other all
right. He'll find it pretty awkward. Aren't many
places would have him. Abyssinia might. It was different when this place was independent."

"Quite."

"Jolly good tinned fruit salad, if you don't mind
my saying so, Mrs. Lepperidge."

"So glad you like it. I got it from Youkoumian's."

"Useful little fellow, Youkoumian. I use him a
lot. He's getting me boots for the levy. Came to me
himself with the idea. Said they pick up hookworm
through going barefoot."

"Good show."

"Quite."

Night over Matodi. English and French police
patrolling the water-front. Gilbert and Sullivan
played by gramophone in the Portuguese Fort.

Three little maids from school are we,
Pert as a schoolgirl well can be

BLACK MISCHIEF

Filled to the brim with girlish glee—
Three little maids from school.

The melody and the clear voices floated out over the harbour and the water lapping very gently on the sea-wall. Two British policemen marched abreast through the involved ways of the native quarter. The dogs had long ago been rounded up and painlessly put away. The streets were empty save for an occasional muffled figure, slipping by them silently with a lantern. The blank walls of the Arab tenements gave no sign of life.

On a tree by a river a little tomtit
Sang, 'Willow, tit-willow, tit-willow!'
And I said to him, 'Dicky bird, why do you sit
Singing: "Willow, tit-willow, tit-willow?" '

Mr. Youkoumian tactfully ejected his last customer and fastened the shutters of the café. "Very sorry," he said. "New regulation. No drinking after ten-thirty. I don't want no bust-ups."

'Is it weakness of intellect, birdie?' I cried,
'Or a rather tough worm in your little inside?'
With a shake of his poor little head, he replied,
'Oh, willow, tit-willow, tit-willow!'

The song rang clear over the dark city and the soft, barely perceptible lapping of the water along the sea-wall.

STONYHURST-CHAGFORD-MADRESFIELD.
Sept., 1931—*May*, 1932.